I0569713

DAYLING

Gabriel Madison

Whimsical Publications, LLC

Florida

Dayling is a work of fiction. Names, characters, and incidents are the products of the author's imagination and are either fictitious or are used fictitiously. Any resemblance to actual events or persons, living or dead, is entirely coincidental.

If you purchased this book without a cover, you should be aware that this book may have been stolen property and reported as "unsold and destroyed" to the publisher. In such case, neither the publisher nor the author has received payment for this "stripped book."

To purchase the authorized electronic edition of *Dayling,* visit
www.whimsicalpublications.com

Cover art by Traci Markou
Editing by John McAllister

Published in the United States by
Whimsical Publications, LLC
Florida

ISBN-13: 978-1-936167-15-9

Printed in the United States of America

"Yo, haven't seen you around here before," he slurred out as he gazed at Sophia.

Her black eyes gleamed as she stared at the inebriated jock. A playful half smile slowly crept across her smooth, innocent ooking face. I'd seen that look before. It had gotten us into as much trouble as it had gotten us out of. But, it never failed in achieving whatever task Sophia conjured it up for.

"We've lived up the block for a little over two years. Never made the time to make the rounds. Making the time now." Sophia moved her long black hair behind her ears. She allowed her seductive gaze to fully light up her beautiful Spanish face. "You're Eliot right? The man of the house?" She spoke with a slow rhythm.

Eliot almost fell over with excitement. His eyes became glazed with longing. His entire body stiffened. He had no idea the game being played on him. Nigel knew, which is why he quietly laughed at the enthralled football jock. Personally, I just wanted to get this over with so I could go home.

Stumbling again, Eliot quickly re-gathered himself. "Yeah I'm the man of the house. And you and your friends are invited to my party." He moved out of the way for us to enter; never once taking his eyes from Sophia's as he closed the door behind us.

Teenage kids grinding against each other filled the first floor of the house. I'd never gone to a teenage party before. I'd only read about them and seen them on TV or in movies. I thought Hollywood exaggerated what went on at these events, I had no idea how tamed the Hollywood versions were compared to the real thing.

A few kids were scattered around making out. I saw an area where belly shots were taking place. And of course, no party would be complete without the triple-kiss being performed in front of a crowd of cheering onlookers. I'd learned about the triple-kiss from Angela, who swore she'd never participated in one, but saw them on MTV Spring Break.

"Okay, I'm ready to leave now. I came, I saw," I quickly shook my body, "I danced. See you guys back home."

Sophia stepped in front of me. The flashing lights bounced off her face, giving her skin a slightly unnatural porcelain glow. She locked her shimmering black eyes onto mine. Unlike Eliot, she wasn't trying to seduce me. Instead, she tried to intimidate me. And as much as I hated to admit it, it worked. "You're going to stay here with us, mingle, and have some fun. In a few weeks, Haven, you'll be like me. But for now, you're more like them. So enjoy it while you can *chica*"

I stared back into Sophia's eyes, trying not to show the fear building inside me. "I'm nothing like them. And I'm never going to be like you, Sophia."

"Three weeks until your eighteenth b-day. Looks like someone has already started Crossing Over. Are we getting a little feisty there Haven?" Nigel said with a lopsided smile.

I turned from Sophia to face him. His skin also had a slightly porcelain glow to it. His frosty blond hair sat perfectly on top of his head. His light blue eyes gleamed with playfulness. He seemed as relaxed as always. I gave him a frown before I turned back to Sophia.

"Why am I here anyway? I thought this was supposed to be about Angela?"

She placed her left arm around her kid sister's shoulder, pulling her in closer to her body. If hadn't known any better, the embrace would have seemed comforting, almost loving. However, the malice in Sophia's eyes always gave her true nature away. "It *is* about me, mamacita. And she wants you to stay. Isn't that right Angela?"

I looked at Angela hoping for her to say the words to excuse me from this torment. Instead, I got the top of her head as she stared at the floor, her telltale sign when she's about to say something you don't want to hear.

"It's true. I'd feel better if you were here with me, Haven." Angela mumbled. Sophia kissed Angela on the jaw before she released her.

Sophia stalked up to me, only stopping inches from my face. I could feel her slightly cool breath, and taste her unnatural sent as a chill gradually entered my body, leaving me frozen in place. "While Nigel and I check out this place for some after party fun, I want you to take Angela around for some introductions." As she spoke, Sophia slowly leaned towards me, bearing her perfect white teeth while gazing longingly at my exposed neck. I tried to move. The fear flooding inside of me left me petrified in place. Sophia giggled before kissing me on the jaw, and then disappearing into the swarm of dancing teenagers with Nigel.

PREFACE

The door to my cell closed, leaving nothing except the intoxicating smell of blood. My newly formed fangs ached as the aroma suffocated the room. The thirst pulsated in my head, drowning out every rational thought, becoming the only thing that existed to me.

I could hear him talking, pleading with me in his familiar tone. But all I could concentrate on was my hunger. My throat hurt, my insides burned, my skin felt tight and awkward. I needed to feed, to consume every drop of the strawberry-scented blood flooding my imprisonment.

And then, all of a sudden I found myself free from the chains.

ONE

Blood!

Thick. Red. Filled with living cells and disease fighting substances. Also, absolutely disgusting.

I pushed the glass of blood towards my cousin Angela, as we lay on top of my family's mansion located in the middle of the lavish neighborhood of Summerbrooke. We've lived in Tallahassee for a little over two years now, but I very rarely left the mansion, choosing to spend my time alone, like I've done for the last seventeen years of my life.

Angela moved away from the blood with a frown on her beautiful face. "Eww, gross. Is that, um, human blood?"

I couldn't help my normal sarcasm from sneaking out. "Yep, I found some drunken college kid stumbling around and thought, hey, why not kill him and pour his blood in a glass for my cousin."

For a second, she looked at me with horror, until finally Angela remembered who she was talking to, and lay back down after putting her shades back over her eyes.

The heat over Tallahassee could literally cook and egg. Angela had talked me into following her to the top of the mansion for some sunbathing. She lay on the roof, in her two-piece-bikini, showing off her smooth perfectly toned body. I, on the other hand, lay beside her in a white t-shirt and shorts.

Two weeks and counting, I thought. Two more weeks before I wouldn't be able to do something like this ever again. Not like I did it a lot before.

I looked over to Angela as she rolled over on her stomach

to work on her back. Angela had decided to attend Lexington High School for her junior year, instead of being home schooled like me. I'm a year older than her, and I had no intentions of spending my senior year trapped inside of an old grungy desk, surrounded by strangers. So I'd declined my father's offer to matriculate at Lexington with Angela. She would be on her own with that adventure.

My mind began to question Angela's sanity. With everything we knew about high school, why on Earth would anyone choose to go to one? I had enough drama with the people living in the mansion with us, than to add more drama with high school kids.

My body relaxed a little as the sun slowly caressed me. I had put on a whole bottle of sunscreen, protecting myself from sunburn as I enjoyed the last rays shinning down on us. Night was slowly coming, and I could almost feel it as time ticked away. Soon, *very* soon, night would be all my body craved; night and the disgusting blood that was starting to smell beside us.

Angela frowned again as she raised her head and pushed the blood away. She lay back down with a slight smile on her face, enjoying her victory over the smell.

The thought of my upcoming birthday wouldn't leave my mind. I placed my arms behind my head as I closed my eyes and focused on pleasant memories. Most of them were of me alone with a good book, but a few were of being around family and friends. None had to do with being around people outside of my world. Being on my families estate, only dealing with the people closest to me, would be all I needed after my eighteenth birthday.

I must have dozed off for a moment, because *she* was standing over me when I opened my eyes, and the moon reflected behind her. Angela still lay beside me on her back, obviously asleep. But *she* didn't seem to care about her kid sister at the moment; instead, she stared directly at me. "Time to wake up, pequeña princesa. You need to get ready for a party."

Slowly I sat up on my elbows. "I know you're insane Sophia, but are you also delusional?"

She kneeled down beside me. "Since my little sister is starting real school soon, Nigel and I are going to take her to this party we heard about. Give her and opportunity to check out the locals at play." Sophia leaned in closer to me, causing my entire body to shiver uncontrollably as she whispered, "You don't have a choice in this chica." She reached over and shook Angela awake while continually staring at me. I hated Sophia thinking she scared me, even though she did scare the crap out of me, but it was a major blow to my pride how much she knew she scared me. Angela looked over to her sister. Finally, Sophia turned to face Angela. "Time to go party with your soon to be class mates. Get up, take a quick shower, get dressed in something slutty, and let's go introduce the students of Lexington High School to their future queen." She smiled at both of us, before she stood up and walked away.

Angela groggily looked over to me. "What?"

The fear finally left my body. A frown covered my face as I looked in the direction Sophia had walked away in. "Hell! She is dragging us to hell!" Angela gave me a confused look. "We're going to a high school party." Why couldn't I have simply died from a heat stroke while I slept? Because I'm Haven Vigano, and my luck doesn't work like that.

A few hours later, we were making our way up a long driveway towards the party, and I was thinking about making a run for it. I was fast enough, not to mention the only real light source came from a half moon looming above us in a starless night sky. On top of that, Sophia wore her favorite high heels; the ones that formed a thin spike at the end, and made it seem as if she walked on her tiptoes. I felt that those god-forsaken shoes gave me a good chance of getting away before she caught me, and I would have taken that chance, if my other cousin Nigel, hadn't kept glancing back at me every time I thought about dashing towards our estate.

We stopped at the front door of Eliot Little's two-days-until-back-to-school-party. I could hear music pulsating out of the den, a type of techno hip-hop blend. Glimpses of blue and red lights flashed out of a window. My body tensed. Every cell inside of me screamed for an escape route. I couldn't believe the jock had disco lights for his house party.

Sophia knocked on the door; a moment later the door opened with a short, muscular guy standing in the entrance.

The jock stumbled a little as he tried to gather himself. His eyes were barely open, and he reeked of alcohol. His

short, black hair hung disheveled over his forehead. He held
a beer can in one hand, while using the other to gain balance
on the side of the doorframe.

"Yo, haven't seen you around here before," he slurred out
as he gazed at Sophia. Her black eyes gleamed as she stared
at the inebriated jock. A playful half smile slowly crept across
her smooth, innocent ooking face. I'd seen that look before.
It had gotten us into as much trouble as it had gotten us out
of. But, it never failed in achieving whatever task Sophia
conjured it up for.

"We've lived up the block for a little over two years.
Never made the time to make the rounds. Making the time
now." Sophia moved her long black hair behind her ears. She
allowed her seductive gaze to fully light up her beautiful
Spanish face. "You're Eliot right? The man of the house?" She
spoke with a slow rhythm.

Eliot almost fell over with excitement. His eyes became
glazed with longing. His entire body stiffened. He had no idea
the game being played on him. Nigel knew, which is why he
quietly laughed at the enthralled football jock. Personally, I
just wanted to get this over with so I could go home.

Stumbling again, Eliot quickly re-gathered himself. "Yeah
I'm the man of the house. And you and your friends are invited to my party." He moved out of the way for us to enter;
never once taking his eyes from Sophia's as he closed the
door behind us.

Teenage kids grinding against each other filled the first
floor of the house. I'd never gone to a teenage party before.
I'd only read about them and seen them on TV or in movies.
I thought Hollywood exaggerated what went on at these
events, I had no idea how tamed the Hollywood versions
were compared to the real thing.

A few kids were scattered around making out. I saw an
area where belly shots were taking place. And, of course, no
party would be complete without the triple-kiss being performed in front of a crowd of cheering onlookers. I'd learned
about the triple-kiss from Angela, who swore she'd never
participated in one, but saw them on MTV Spring Break.

"Okay, I'm ready to leave now. I came, I saw," I quickly
shook my body, "I danced. See you guys back home."

Sophia stepped in front of me. The flashing lights
bounced off her face, giving her skin a slightly unnatural por-

celain glow. She locked her shimmering black eyes onto mine. Unlike Eliot, she wasn't trying to seduce me. Instead, she tried to intimidate me. And as much as I hated to admit it, it worked. "You're going to stay here with us, mingle, and have some fun. In a few weeks, Haven, you'll be like me. But for now, you're more like them. So enjoy it while you can *chica*"

I stared back into Sophia's eyes, trying not to show the fear building inside me. "I'm nothing like them. And I'm never going to be like you, Sophia."

"Three weeks until your eighteenth b-day. Looks like someone has already started Crossing Over. Are we getting a little feisty there Haven?" Nigel said with a lopsided smile.

I turned from Sophia to face him. His skin also had a slightly porcelain glow to it. His frosty blond hair sat perfectly on top of his head. His light blue eyes gleamed with playfulness. He seemed as relaxed as always. I gave him a frown before I turned back to Sophia.

"Why am I here anyway? I thought this was supposed to be about Angela?"

She placed her left arm around her kid sister's shoulder, pulling her in closer to her body. If hadn't known any better, the embrace would have seemed comforting, almost loving. However, the malice in Sophia's eyes always gave her true nature away. "It *is* about me, mamacita. And she wants you to stay. Isn't that right Angela?"

I looked at Angela hoping for her to say the words to excuse me from this torment. Instead, I got the top of her head as she stared at the floor, her telltale sign when she's about to say something you don't want to hear.

"It's true. I'd feel better if you were here with me, Haven." Angela mumbled. Sophia kissed Angela on the jaw before she released her.

Sophia stalked up to me, only stopping inches from my face. I could feel her slightly cool breath, and taste her unnatural sent as a chill gradually entered my body, leaving me frozen in place. "While Nigel and I check out this place for some after party fun, I want you to take Angela around for some introductions." As she spoke, Sophia slowly leaned towards me, bearing her perfect white teeth while gazing longingly at my exposed neck. I tried to move. The fear flooding inside of me left me petrified in place. Sophia giggled before kissing me on the jaw, and then disappearing into the swarm of dancing teenagers with Nigel.

I released a long deep breath before turning around to face Angela, who continued to look at the floor. "Thanks a lot." I turned from her heading through the crowd. Angela hurried behind me.

It felt strange, the scent coming from the kids dancing around me. The swaying of their bodies triggered a sensation that had nothing to do with hormones. A craving I didn't know I had. I could feel it, slowly building beneath my skin as I walked. They all looked so... appealing. And again, not in a 'bow chicka wow wow' way, but in a way I couldn't comprehend. I only knew I had to get the hell out of there.

When I made it to the backdoor, I could hear Angela calling after me. "Haven. Wait up Haven."

I placed my hand on the doorknob, before sighing and quickly turning around to face my cousin. "What?"

Angela stopped in front of me. She looked around the room with panic in her dark eyes. The flashing lights illuminated the nervousness encompassing her face. "You can't just leave me here. Please Haven, stay for a little while." She lowered her voice. "And Sophia isn't going to like it if you leave."

"I don't care what Sophia likes or doesn't like. What is she going to do, video tape me singing 'Private Dancer' in my underwear and post it online?" I paused. "Which, now that I think about it, would be a fate worse than death." I took my hand off the doorknob and gently placed it on the side of Angela's shoulder. She tried to defuse my escape plan with her large sad puppy dog brown eyes, but I'd grown immune to their affects after years of practice. "You don't need me here anyway Angela. This isn't my scene. This is where *you* want to be. Not me. I'll see you back home."

I turned from Angela, opened the backdoor, and made my way out of the jock's house before she could respond. The heat radiating in the air suffocated the night. I had been so nervous on the way over I didn't pay attention to the weather. I took off my wool sweater and tied it around my waist. It felt as if Hades had made his way through the city with a gang of his minions tagging along. Even demons from the deepest pits in hell would make their way back to their fiery home to escape the heat infecting the night's air.

Yet I could also feel a slight shiver taking hold of my body as I made my way through the nauseating heat. I'd told Angela I wasn't afraid of Sophia, but deep inside, I've always feared her. And leaving the party after she told me not to would seem like a challenge to her queen bee status. I didn't want to be queen bee. I just wanted to be left alone. But, knowing Sophia, she would find a way to put me in my place in front of the others.

I decided to stop thinking about Sophia as I made my way out of the back gate of the jock's yard, finding myself in a long dark alley. Trashcans and a few scattered streetlights were located on each side of the dirt road. Each house had massive gates to create the narrow alley.

After taking a few steps, the muffled sound of someone trying to speak came from ahead of me. A part of me was ready to turn around and head the opposite way. That was the smart part of me, the part I rarely listened to.

I made my way to the sound, my heart rate and breath quickening as I went. The sound became louder with each step I took, as Itried to ready myself for anything.

A flickering streetlight stood over to the right of me. Beneath it stood five guys who all looked about my age. I figured they must have been at Eliot's party before heading to the alley to handle whatever disagreement they were having. When I say disagreement, I mean by four of them beating the crap out of the fifth.

The guy being beaten had his head hung down. I could see, as well as smell, the blood and sweat dripping from his face to his red letterman jacket. His clothes were completely soiled with bodily fluids, and his legs wobbled perilously as the two guys standing beside him held him upright. Te guy giving the beating laughed each time he punched his victim in the stomach.

The lookout hadn't seen me yet. I had time to leave. My heart continued to pound as I watched the beat down. My muscles tightened, and my flight or fight instinct was working overtime.

Everything inside of me screamed for me to walk away. And that's exactly what I should've done, but that would mean listening to the smart part of my brain. Seeing as I never did before, no need to start at the expense of the guy getting the hell kicked out of him.

I walked towards Mr. Lookout. A few more steps and the idiot would have to see me. And then, there would be no turning back.

As soon as Mr. Lookout eyes focused on me, he slowly backed away towards the guy giving the beating. I could make out the smirk on his face. The sight of a seventeen-year-old girl walking through a dark alley obviously didn't frighten him. He actually looked pleased, as if my presence would cause a new game for him and his friends to play.

I stepped to the edge of the flickering light as everyone turned towards me. The guy administering the beating smirked at me. He had long, blond hair and he looked to be about 6'3 with the frame of a basketball player. The blue letterman's jacket sporting a large W insignia seemed to support that idea.

The other three guys involved with the beating were as tall as Mr. Blonde. They all wore the same type of letterman jacket, and the same smirk.

My eyes focused on the guy getting the beating for a moment. He had spiky, dark hair, exotic black eyes and a beautiful, slightly feminine, face – even though it had become a little swollen and covered with blood, I couldn't stop thinking how beautiful this guy looked. I hadn't known what my plan was when I first decided to walk towards the guy getting his ass kicked, but after seeing him, I knew the guys doing the ass kicking had to pay. No one should be able to get away with disfiguring such a gorgeous creature.

"Keep moving if you know what's good for you." Mr. Blonde said with a frown at me.

I took a step into the flickering light; my long, curly hair hung all the way down my back – more a byproduct of my Italian father than my London-born mother. To be truthful, I take more after my Italian ancestors than my English, except of course for my emerald-green eyes.

My eyes still focused on the beautiful—slightly swollen—face of the guy who had taken the beating. I could still feel my heart pounding as I stared at him; could feel my blood boiling furiously through my veins. My flight or fight needle pointed completely towards fight.

"Don't you understand English bitch? We said keep moving." Mr. Lookout said as he took a step toward me.

I fixed my gaze upon M. Lookout. "I don't know when

that word became okay to use, but I'm from the old school; where bitch normally came before a fist. Either by the person saying it or the person it was said to." I said, taking a step closer. "So the next time you call me a bitch, be ready to swing."

The four guys started to laugh. My beautifully swollen spiky-haired prince—yeah, that's what he became in my mind... a prince—tried to say something, but couldn't force the words out.

Mr. Lookout took another step towards me. He stretched his arms out to the side in a taunting manner. "Okay then, I'm ready to swing... bitch."

Without warning, I lunged at Mr. Lookout, knocking him clean across the temple, causing him to hit the ground like a sack of bricks. The other three guys were stunned by what I'd done. That gave me the opening I needed to finish this quickly.

I wasn't much of a fighter. I could hold my own when necessary, but I never found myself in situations where I needed to. Getting into fights with four guys in dark alleys wasn't normally my thing. Then again, neither was going to house parties, so I guess there was a first time for everything.

I made it to Mr. Blonde next; his eyes were still wide fromwhat I did to Mr. Lookout. I used the adrenaline rushing through my body to place my fist as hard as I could into his chest. I felt his ribs caving in as I landed my punch, and I heard his breath leaving his body as he went airborne. He flew a good twenty feet before he came crashing down behind my spiky-haired prince and the two jocks holding him up.

I turned on the two guys just as they released my prince. He dropped to his knees still unable to talk. His dark eyes never left my face.

A type of energy ran through me. I felt supercharged from the fighting. I couldn't believe it, but I enjoyed the damage I caused. I'd heard the closer you get to Crossing Over, the wilder you become. I was three weeks away from the change, but I could feel the monster growing inside of me. It craved destruction.

My heart had actually slowed a little as I ducked the punch of one of the guys that held my prince. I came up with blinding speed to catch him square across the jaw, and heard it shatter as my fist smashed home. The guy dropped to the ground with blood spilling out of his mouth. This new scent of the blood and fear fueled the monster inside of me.

The last guy paused for a half a second; all the time I needed to grab him by his shirt and toss him to the other side of the alley. I heard a few of his bones snapping as he came crashing down.

Without knowing it, I let out a low, menacing growl, which echoed through the alley. Iglanced down at the whimpering fools rolling around on the ground in pain. I loved it, the beast inside wanted more to come out of the shadows for me to punish.

The sound of my spiky-haired prince moaning in pain on the ground pulled me out of my battle mode. Everything calmed down. My heart completely slowed to a steady pace. The rage left my body, and was quickly replaced by concern.

I leaned beside him; gently helping him to his feet. He felt light to me, but his body felt hard as a rock.

"Are you okay," I whispered to him as I held him up.

His mesmerizing, dark eyes gazed into mine. "What... the... hell... are... you?" He mumbled before he passed out in my arms.

TWO

I hate hospitals, almost as much as I hate high school parties. The bland monotonous walls always gave me the creeps. Nothing about them felt warm or comforting. I never understood why the people designing them didn't try to liven them up a bit. Throw some lighter colors around the rooms; maybe put a few paintings of something other than gardens on the walls. Just once I would love to walk into a hospital and see nurses wearing something more playful. Not slutty or sexy, just playful, like a Catholic School Girl uniform... okay, that might be a tad bit slutty. Instead, every single one of them I have ever been in has been exactly the same... bland.

The one I took my sleeping, spiky-haired prince to was no different. I took him to the emergency room and watched as the nurses frantically tried to wake him. He wasn't dead as I'd feared, but he lay unconscious from the massive blood loss. The nurses asked me a few questions when I laid him down in front of them. Like, what happened? Who is he? Who am I to him? I told them I didn't know what happened or who he was. I told them I was walking home and found him unconscious on the ground. I told them I'd decided to be a Good Samaritan and bring him to the hospital.

The nurses listened to my story as they rushed him to the back. An orderly stopped me as I followed behind them. He advised me to have a seat in the waiting room and he would send someone with word when he could.

Taking the hint, I turned and went to the waiting area like every other worried family member or friend, even though I was neither to this guy. I sat there, as my fingers frantically tapped on the side of a hard chair, trying to understand why the hell I didn't leave. I should have left as soon as I had the chance. I got him to the hospital, that alone was more than anyone could ask of me. I'd done my good deed for the year. When he awakes, I should be long gone. He would have questions I couldn't answer. But I couldn't force myself to leave; that would mean listening to the smart part of my brain.

I sat in the waiting room for a little over two hours watching all the people around me. A slender woman with long blond hair sat beside me coughing uncontrollably. To the other side of me, a large elderly man sat frozen in place. I'd heard a few of his family members talking about his extremely ill wife. I occasionally glanced over to him. His round face was pale, and his skin sagged a little as he stared off into nothing. He didn't move, only the slow rhythmic expansion of his chest revealed he was alive. My heart ached for him. I couldn't imagine, nor did I want to imagine, what went on inside of him. The coughing woman on the other hand, I was planning on taking a swing at if she coughed on me one more time.

Sagging a little in my seat, I wondered again why I didn't do the smart thing and leave, just when a nurse came to get me. I couldn't look at the old man as the nurse led me to my spiky-haired prince.

They'd given him a private room, with a single bed in the middle. It also had a recliner beside the bed, a TV hanging from the ceiling, and bland curtains over the window. Just like every other hospital room I've ever been in.

I sat beside the bed in the recliner, watching my sleeping spiky-haired prince as the questions of what the hell I was doing continued to attack my mind. Staying would be stupid! Every part of me knew I should leave before he awoke.

Besides, my sleeping prince was the least of my problems. If my family found out what I had done, what I continued to do, I would be dead meat. I wouldn't have to stress about Sophia getting revenge on me. My father would take care of that for her.

I stood from the recliner, deciding to pace around the room. Somewhere during the middle of my pacing, a short nurse walked in catching me a little off-guard. She said a few words about everything being okay, and that he would be fine. Obviously, she thought the stress etched across my face had to do with the cute unconscious high school boy lying in the bed. Little did she know it was because of the very temperamental father I had waiting for me back home. Keeping things from my family could be difficult to say the least. I would have to do some major lying to get myself out of this.

After the nurse left, I sat back in the recliner. I didn't know how long I would wait for my sleeping prince to wake up, nor did I have a clue what I would say to him once he did. I only knew I had to talk with him.

Every half hour I looked up at the clock hoping for time to slow down. Each minute my prince slept, meant a minute I would have to explain to my family. I would have killed for Hiro's power. Blink my eyes and then bam... everything freezes. No such luck in the real world. Speaking of families, my prince's wallet had been missing, along with any identification. The hospital staff said they would keep an eye out for any missing person report fitting his description. Nothing could be done except to wait for him to come to.

At one in the morning, he slowly opened his eyes. It felt odd, the sensations rushing through my body as his beautiful dark eyes focused on me. I could see the confusion racing through them. Surprisingly, I didn't see what I was looking for... fear.

I tried to think of something witty to say to break the ice, but "hey," was all I could come up with.

"Hey back," he said as he smiled at me.

I couldn't help but smile back. For the first time in my life, I felt like one of those love-smitten teenage girls I hated. I leaned forward in the recliner. "How do you feel?"

"Head hurts. Guess that comes from being repeatedly punched on it."

"Or having it sat on by an elephant. Saw a guy do that once at the circus. It didn't go as planned. It was pretty messy. So how did you piss those guys off that bad?"

He grunted as he sat up a little in the bed. His slender face still looked swollen from the beating. "What can a guy do to make another guy want to pound on him?"

I sat back in the recliner. "Was she worth it?"

"Sadly, no. She wasn't that great of a kisser."

We both laughed at the same time. He grunted again as

a wave of pain encompassed his face. "It would probably hurt less if you stop moving."

He looked around the hospital room before focusing his dark, sexy eyes on me again. "How did I get here?"

I ran my hand through my long curly hair. "How do you think?"

"Right, so are we going to talk about how you took out four athletes in a blink of an eye, or are we going to exchange names first?"

As I met his gaze, I found it difficult to lie to him. Something in his eyes made me feel safe, which wasn't a terribly good thing considering what telling him the truth could mean. "My name's Haven."

He slowly reached out his hand for me to take it. "Philip. And please, don't call me Phil. I hate it when people call me Phil."

"Nice to meet you Philip," I said, slowly taking his hand into mine. His skin was warm and soft to the touch

The door to his room burst open just before the short nurse walked in. Reluctantly I released Philip's hand. The nurse smiled as she saw the now fully awakened prince.

"And how are you feeling? You gave us quite a fright." The nurse said as she stood over Philip's bed.

"Head hurts. Ribs hurt. Basically, entire body hurts. Other than that I feel fine." He said with a playful smile.

"You took a pretty good beating. Do you have any idea why someone would want to hurt you like that?" She asked.

"A girl," I answered before Philip could.

The nurse gave him a displeasing look as she slowly shook her head. "Do you have anyone you want us to contact?"

"My mom. When you call the house, ask to speak with Mrs. Flowers." Philip gave her his home number before she gave me a slight smile and walked out of the room. He turned back to me. "Now can we talk about what happened in the alley?"

I sat up in the recliner again. I tried to think up a good lie to tell him. I was a master of thinking up quick lies. At least, I thought I was. "Does it really matter?"

He gave me a sexy half smile. "I need to know if you're the only one that can fight like that, or will I need to hire an army of bodyguards to protect me from your boyfriend."

"Can you really hire an army? Cause if so, there are a few places I would like to invade. Queen Haven of Hawaii. Yeah, I can see that." I paused for a moment as if in deep contemplation. "You don't have to worry about a boyfriend."

"What were you doing walking down an alley at night?"

The thoughts of dancing teenagers came back to me, and I shivered. "Escaping a party."

Philip laughed, his face scrunching in pain as he did so. "Eliot's disco-themed party? Doesn't seem like your scene."

I frowned at him. "It wasn't."

He gave me his half smile. "You didn't like the belly shots? They were my idea."

"Figures."

He stared at my face for a moment in silence. I felt a little self-conscious, until I realized what floated around in his beautiful dark eyes. "Come on, you can't stop a guy from getting his ass kicked by an angry boyfriend and his three steroid using flunkies and not tell him how you did it." Philip lowered his voice. "I've never seen anyone move like that before. I'm just curious is all."

The urge to tell him the truth felt overwhelming. Maybe it had something to do with his beautiful black eyes, or maybe it had something to do with his intoxicating scent. Maybe it had something to do with the lust running through my body for the first time in my life. Either way, I could feel myself on the verge of opening my mouth and ruining both our lives.

I stood from the recliner. "I think I should leave. Give you a chance to get some rest."

He let out a low moan as he tried to roll out of bed. I could see the anguish stretching across his face. It hurt me to see him in pain. I quickly made my way over to him and had my hands gently pushing against his chest to stop him from moving.

In that moment, with my hands touching his hard chest, I felt light-headed and almost lost my balance. *Get a grip Haven; he's just a guy*.

I awkwardly pulled away from him as I stood back from the bed. "You shouldn't move. You're going to hurt yourself more."

Philip gazed up at me with his sexy half smile. "No pain, no gain." He slowly lay back on the bed. My mind drifted on lying beside him, feeling his solid frame against me, gently running my fingers along his... "No way am I letting you leave without finding out who you are."

"Queen Haven of Hawaii," I slowly stood above him. I needed to keep some distance from him to keep my composure. "And how are you planning on stopping me if I decide to leave?"

"I'll keep trying to get out of bed, forcing you to keep me in."

I slowly made my way to the foot of the bed. Again, the logical thought of leaving as quickly as I could re-entered my mind, and again I ignored it.

"I'm a good fighter. My father taught me." Which wasn't a lie; it wasn't the complete truth, but mostly true.

Philip stared at me for a moment. My heart sped up a little as our eyes locked in silence. I *so* had to get away from this guy. He drove me crazy, and there wasn't anything I could do to stop it.

Finally, he broke the silence. "Fine, I get it. You don't trust me. How about we catch a movie, get something to eat, and talk? Get to know each other better."

I laughed. "Are you asking me out on a date? You don't think it's a little strange doing that from your hospital bed?"

"To be truthful, I think I should *always* ask girls out while lying in a hospital bed. I mean think about it, it would take a cold-hearted chick to say 'no' to a man during his time of need." Philip said before he winked at me.

I found myself laughing again like a lovesick little girl. It started to freak me out. The entire night had freaked me out. I don't do love. I don't do crushes or dates or longing. Never have, and never going to start; except the idea of seeing a movie with Philip slowly grew into a happy thought. "Can I get back to you?"

"No. If you plan on walking out of here without telling me how you took out four guys without breaking a sweat, then you'll have to agree to go out on a date with me."

I used the sleeve from my wool sweater to wipe a few drops of sweat from my head. It felt just as hot inside of the hospital as it felt outside. The heat coming from my body didn't help either. "Fine, when you get out of the hospital, I'll go on a date with you."

A large smile spread across his face. I could tell from the gleam in his eyes he felt victorious. The thing about it, I didn't care if I lost.

"So what's your number?" Philip asked.

"Don't worry, I'll find you." I turned to walk out of the room.

"That's not going to work." He called from the bed.

"It'll have to." I said just before I walked out of the hospital room.

I made my way down the hallway as quickly as I could. I felt if I didn't get out of that place I would lose my mind. I couldn't think; I couldn't breathe; I needed to get as far away as I could, or die from my own pathetic crush.

The elevator took forever to reach Philip's floor. Once it did, I jumped in and rode it down to the lobby. As soon as I got to the ground floor, I dashed out into the lobby and out of the building before the elevator door had even closed.

I exited the hospital at around three in the morning, but the heat coming from the pavement made it feel like noon. I could see vapors hovering over the ground like small tentacles from an invisible octopus. The heat felt so intense; each time I took a step felt as if the tentacles were pulling on my feet.

I'd only walked a block or so before I turned around to stare at the window belonging to Philip. I didn't understand why I couldn't get this guy out of my head. I needed to walk around the city while I thought this through.

More importantly, I needed to walk because by this time I was sure the others were more than likely looking for me. Knowing my father the way I did, I could see him going insane from worrying. If he found out I had been out all night with a guy, his worry would change to rage. I couldn't allow them to find me. I needed to avoid them for the night and return home while they're all sleeping.

I said a final goodbye to the night before I turned from the hospital to head to my secret hiding place. Not even Angela knew about it. I'd found out when we first moved to Tallahassee that the others couldn't track me there.

Old City Cemetery had been the oldest public cemetery in Tallahassee. It was established in 1829 by the Territorial Legislative Council and acquired by the city eleven years later. The ground was laid out in its system of squares and lots when a yellow fever epidemic swept the city and regulations were required to assure order and sanitation to protect the public. When the cemetery was created, it was located outside the city boundaries on the far side of a 200-foot-wide clearing that surrounded the town to protect it from Native American attacks. But over the years, Tallahassee had grown around the old cemetery.

I'd kept to the shadows during my journey to the cemetery. It didn't feel as if someone followed me, but I didn't want to take a chance, so I circled around once before actually going inside.

I quickly made it to my secret hiding place. My hideout had belonged to a wealthy man who died in the early 1920s. I'd done my homework on every major lot in the cemetery after I first discovered it. The crypt I chose belonged to a man who moved from New York to Tallahassee in 1900. He lived here for over twenty years before he died of cancer. I picked this one in particular because he was the only one who didn't have any family still alive. No one came to his grave except for maintenance. No one would think to look for a runaway in it.

I closed the rusty metal door of the crypt behind me. I had only a few more hours before sunrise, and then I would be able to go home, which would give me an entire day to come up with something before I would have to face my father. There's a conversation I wasn't eager to have.

I had a few blankets and books stored here just in case. The sarcophagus holding Robert Fletcher, the man whose crypt I borrowed, sat in the middle of the mausoleum.

I thought about putting a few posters on the walls, to liven up the place, but decided that would really be disrespecting the dead.

I made my way to the sarcophagus and sat on top of it. I picked up a book I had been reading, and after only a few moments placed it back down beside me. I couldn't calm my mind long enough to read.

I didn't know what the hell I was doing. I'd just spent all night with a guy I didn't know, only to end up hiding from my family in a crypt of a man that had been dead for over eighty years. I knew my life would get weirder after I Crossed Over, but that was still three weeks away.

I wondered if my longing for Philip had anything to do with my impending birthday, if what I felt for him had been caused by my body getting ready to change. I hoped it would hurry up and give me back some self-control, or at least a moment of peace where I didn't think about how good Philip's chest felt against my hands.

I lay back on the sarcophagus, trying to force my mind to think about something other than Philip. It didn't work. I couldn't get him out of my head. I couldn't get his scent from around me. I couldn't get his voice from my mind. I was going insane. I started to hate Sophia. If she hadn't pulled me to that stupid party, I wouldn't be finding myself trapped thinking about a guy I'd just met.

THREE

I awoke in the crypt as soon as the sun came up, and rolled off the sarcophagus of the poor and long dead Robert Fletcher. I stretched, trying to loosen the tight muscles along my back. Sleeping in a mausoleum isn't as pleasant as they made it seem on Buffy. I had to work out the cramps in my legs before I could even walk towards the exit.

I slowly slipped out of my hideout making sure no one could see me.

The light from the sun stung my eyes. My flesh tingled as sunrays caressed my bare arms. I was getting closer to Crossing Over, and my body knew it. Not to mention, it continued to feel hot as hell all around Tallahassee.

I made my way out of Old City Cemetery to Thomasville Road. I stayed on Thomasville until I got to Bannerman and then continued on to my family's estate in Summerbrooke.

I needed the nice long walk. The heat hadn't subsided, but I needed time to come up with an excuse for staying out all night. It was forbidden. No one in the family was allowed to be away from the safety of our estate alone all night. I'd had this rule pounded into my skull by the man who created it, my father.

By the time I made it to Summerbrooke, my heart raced in my chest. I'd lost a few pounds from sweating in the heat, and my feet were killing me.

The large gates that protect our six acres of land from the outside world, slowly opened after I typed in the code. I walked through the gates before they closed behind me, and proceeded up the long driveway to my family's mansion.

Towering over both sides of the driveway were rows of bluff oak trees. I found myself staring up at the dark green, lustrous leaves as I made it to the front door of my family's three-level mansion.

Just as I reached the door, and placed my fingers on the doorknob, it swung open. I almost jumped back thinking one of the others had opened the door, even though I knew it was impossible for them to be up during the day.

"Where were you Haven?" Angela demanded as she stood in the entrance of the mansion.

I pushed past her as I shrugged and walked into the manor. Being grilled by my father was one thing, but I wasn't going to be handled by Angela.

The familiar sight of our marble floors, dual custom oak staircases and crystal chandeliers greeted me. The cold air in the mansion relaxed by body a little. The refuge from the heat outside made my mind forget about the hell waiting for me when night falls. Then Angela crushed my moment of bliss with the words I didn't want to hear.

"Your dad said for you to see him as soon as you got in. Night or Day." She said with her arms wrapped around her chest. I noticed she wore the same outfit from the night before. She must have stayed up all night waiting for me. Which meant everyone must have stayed up also. Not good.

I walked through the long hall to one of the sitting rooms in the mansion. The room had two velvet chairs sitting in front of a large window to the left, an oak piano sitting on top of a Persian rug in the center, 16th century Oriental vases scattered around the room, and a long velvet couch located to the right. Paintings of ancient Asian villages hung on the walls.

I walked to the velvet couch and flopped on it. My sweaty arms stuck to the material as I tried to get comfortable.

"Didn't you hear me?" Angela said as she followed me to the sitting room. "You better go and see him before he comes looking for you."

I sighed. "He's more than likely asleep right now. I'll see him in a few hours."

"He said as soon..." She started.

I cut her off with a wave of my hand. "Don't you have something better to do than to annoy me?"

Angela flopped on the couch beside me. "You really have

no idea how much trouble you're in do you? Sophia was already planning on killing you for leaving the party, but after you didn't come back to the estate, and your dad tore into her for not knowing where you were, she's now planning a trip to Guantanamo Bay with you."

"There won't be anything left to torture after my dad gets through with me." I said as I turned towards Angela.

Her eyes focused on me for a moment. I could see how worried she felt for me. "Where were you Haven?"

I thought about lying to her, but if I wanted my plan to work, I needed her to know what had happened. "I met a guy."

"What? There were other Daylings at the party? I didn't see any."

I leaned closer to Angela. I knew the others were sleeping, but I still felt the need to whisper. "Not a Dayling, but a human."

Angela jumped from the couch as if an electric current had run through her body. She nervously began pacing in front of me. "You spent all night with a human? What were you thinking?"

"Technically, he was unconscious most of the night. And I was thinking how cute he looked laying in that hospital bed." I said truthfully. I thought about Philip. His dark, mesmerizing eyes staring into mine, his sexy half-smile playfully tempting me to kiss him, his hard chest begging for me to...

"Hello?" Angela screamed bringing me out of my fantasy. I had it bad for this guy. I couldn't deny it. "You spent all night with a human at a hospital? Your father is going to do more than kill you."

"No he isn't. Because he's not going to find out." I said as I held Angela in my gaze. "Why are you talking about humans as if they're beneath you? Aren't you the one dying to go to school with them?"

She stopped in front of me. Her arms were wrapped around her chest again. "All these years you've had to be around humans, you've chosen not to have anything to do with them. Now three weeks before you Cross Over, you spend all night with one. You're insane you know that?"

I didn't have a reply for her insult, simply because she was right. I've lived amongst humans for almost eighteen years, the amount of time it takes for a Dayling to Cross

Over to a Nightling.

Angela, my younger brother Franklin, my niece Dorothy, my two other cousins Raffaele and Margaret, and myself are the only Daylings living in the mansion. The other twelve family members are Nightlings.

When my kind is born, we age just like humans for the first seventeen years of our lives. We can eat food, be out in the day and blend into the human world, but all of that changes on our eighteenth birthday. That's when we Cross Over to the world of Nightlings.

Nightlings can't move during the day without feeling a stabbing pain racing through their bodies. They can't consume solid food, but they can drink any type of liquid they want. They age different than humans; it takes twelve human years to equal one Nightling year, and then they eventually stop aging altogether. They do have reflections, contrary to popular mythos, and they can fly, which is something I'm looking forward to. They also possess the ability to read thoughts. I've learned how to mask my mind when talking with them. And, yes, they have an insatiable lust for human blood, which I'm not looking forward to.

In three weeks, I'm going to have my eighteenth birthday, and the next night I will wake up a creature of the dark, a Nightling, or as humans call us... a vampire.

I've been looking forward to Crossing Over for as long as I could remember. I've never been a fan of the human race. I wasn't looking forward to feeding from them, but I had no desire to spend time with them. Most Daylings spend as much of their lives being as human as they can, before they have to give it all up for eternity, but not me. I hated the human world: the smells, the distrust, the malice, the bad hair trends.

Philip had changed everything I've thought about humans. Three weeks before I have to say good-bye to the human world, I fall in love with one. Life surely does suck.

"So who is he?" Angela asked as she sat back next to me on the couch.

"A guy I saved from getting his ass kicked by four other guys." I whispered.

She moved her long hair out of her face. Her eyes widened as she stared at me. "Does he know what you are?"

"No. But he did see me take out those four jerks before

he passed out." I said as I sunk deeper into the couch.

"What are you going to do?"

"Think of a lie to tell my father. Then pray he believes it." I stood from the couch. "But first I'm going to take a shower."

I walked out of the sitting room towards the stairs that lead to the second floor. All of the Nightlings slept underground in hidden rooms, while us Daylings slept upstairs like normal people. In three weeks, I'll have to start sleeping with the others, if I survived my father's wrath that is.

I made it to my room and locked the door behind me. Not like locking it would keep my father, or Sophia, or any other Nightling out by any means. It just made me feel as if I had a little control.

My room was my personal paradise. My masterpiece. I wanted a contemporary bedroom with lots of blues and greens and a retro feel. A gorgeous, periwinkle blue had been applied to the walls, with a funky chartreuse color accenting the wall space around the dormer window. A white built-in vanity with lots of space for tennis shoes and other supplies sat to the rear of the room. A queen-sized bed, with blue sheets sat to the right of the room. Sitting in the center were two large, half-circular, green leather couches. The couches faced each other, leaving enough room between them to walk through. In-between the couches sat a small table.

I turned on my room's lights, which were five circular halogen bulbs dug into the ceiling. They shed a pure, white light that made the periwinkle on the walls look true blue.

I made my way to the vanity and pulled out a towel and washcloth. I slowly walked to my bathroom and undressed. My clothes were sweaty and sticky from the heat. I jumped in the shower and turned on the faucet. My body screamed from relief when the cold water caressed it. I allowed it to run from my face all the way down my body, enjoying every sensation the cold water caused. My mind began to drift with thoughts of Philip. I couldn't get that damn sexy, half-smile out of my head. *Get a grip dork!*

I finished showering, quickly dried off, and walked to my bed with the wet towel wrapped around my body. A few outfits were laid out on top of it. Okay, I had a few t-shirts and jeans sitting on top of my bed. I picked the black t-shirt with

HIM written in white across the front of it, and jeans that didn't smell, and then quickly got dressed.

When I returned to the sitting room, I found Angela sitting in the same place staring at one of the 16th century Oriental vases. It was red, with pictures of blue symbols all around it. I had no idea what the symbols meant, but they were pretty to look at.

We stared at the vase for what felt like an hour in silence before Angela turned to me. "Are you going to see him again?"

"Yeah," I said without looking at her. I knew seeing Philip would be a huge mistake. I knew involving myself with a human so close to Crossing Over was a huge no-no. I still hadn't learned how to listen to that smart part of my brain yet. "Okay, it's time." I said as I took in a deep breath.

Angela looked up at me. Her dark eyes glazed with worry. "Time for what?"

"To see my father." I said as I walked out of the sitting room.

I walked down the long hallway until I entered a large library with books all around the walls. Most of the books were bound in dirty brown lace. I'd heard some of the books went back to the Dark Ages. I'd never read any of them, because it's forbidden for a Dayling to read them. The bookshelves towered all the way to the ceiling. A painting of a dark-haired man riding a horse, with a bloodied sword in his right hand covered the ceiling. The carpet in the room was light green, with white symbols located all around it – I never knew what those symbols meant either.

I'd always find myself gazing up at the painting. The man's dark eyes seemed as if they were looking through me.

I walked through the library to a door located at the rear. Beside the door sat a keypad. I punched in the code, and then opened the door, revealing a large stairway that led beneath the mansion.

As I walked down the stairs, I tried to calm my nerves. If my father sensed any deception from me, I was done for.

I made my way to a large door at the bottom. Another keypad sat to the right of it. I punched in another code, and then walked through that door. Nightlings were always super-cautious. I couldn't blame them; not being able to move during the day had to make one very paranoid.

The lower level of the mansion was just as plush as the top levels. Ancient furniture and paintings were all around me. A piano sat in the center of the room, and multiple doors were all around. I've always thought of this room like the waiting area of a brothel. Or at least what I thought a brothel's waiting room would look like – dark colors of red and blue surrounded the room. Expensive artwork to show the clients they were in a high class establishment, which meant they were going to have to pay a good amount of money for their moment of pleasure.

Unfortunately, half-naked women weren't waiting behind each door willing to fulfill my fantasies, and to be truthful, if it had been my fantasy, it wouldn't be half-naked women anyway, just a half-naked Philip.

I tried to mask my thoughts as I made my way to my father's door. I froze in front of the 16th century Spanish door, made from the wood of a sunken caravel, and took in deep breaths. *He's my father. He wouldn't actually kill me... would he?*

The sun blazed outside, so he would be lying in bed. He wouldn't be sleeping; no way would I be that lucky. I could picture him lying there, waiting for the sun to go down so he could find me and tear me apart. I couldn't believe I planned on walking into the lion's den like a sickly gazelle with a broken hoof. I was done for. I knew this as soon as I decided to stay with Philip at the hospital. Nothing left to do but hope for a quick death.

I knew my father wouldn't *literally* kill me, but I've always feared him. Everyone did. When my father had been a Dayling, Henry II's army attacked Florence, and my father convinced his father to allow him to fight in the Fifth Italian war against France. He spent some time in Germany training as a Landsknecht, becoming one of the deadliest warriors of our kind. He became a legend among Nightlings, his skilled fighting techniques, along with his lethal temper, made everyone quiver at the thought of pissing him off. Not to mention, he and I never really had a great relationship. I've always thought I had one more major screw up before he simply '*got rid*' of me. Angela would always say I was overly paranoid. I *so* hoped she was right.

I opened my father's door without knocking, stepped in and closed it behind me. I stood in front of the door frozen in place, staring at the king-size bed to the rear of the room. On both sides of the bed sat two, red velvet, French Sitting Chairs. Candles surrounded the room, illuminating most of it, while casting shadows over the rest. An oak dresser sat to the right of the door, but other than that, nothing else occupied the room except the man lying in the king-size bed.

He didn't move as I stood in front of the door fighting back my fear. He wouldn't move, simple because he couldn't. My fear didn't subside from the knowledge of Nightlings inability to move during the day. I've seen my father force his way across rooms during the middle of the afternoon on account of being pushed too far by my uncle Myron.

My father was the head of the family, and it's tradition for every member of the household to take on the last name of the head. Myron and my father had different dads. Myron wanted to keep his dad's last name, and for a very long time defied my father by not changing it to Vigano like everyone else. Finally he gave in, but the damage had been done. The two were on the verge of ripping each other apart every night. Both men were born during the Renaissance, yet they spent last movie night arguing about the artistic value of 'The Hangover'.

"I know you're there." I heard my father's deep, Italian voice say from the king-size bed. "Come closer."

I slowly crept to his bed with my head hung low. My heart tried to jump out of my chest, but I pushed it back down. I stood over the bed. My father lay motionless under red velvet sheets. His smooth, handsome, porcelain face looked as if he was in his late thirties or early forties, with the type of sophistication that comes with a beautifully aged man. And his dark, wavy, long hair lay along his shoulders in the bed. His shimmering, dark brown eyes slowly focused on me. They glowed from the joy and misery hiding behind them. To my surprise, he forced out a slight smile, before his face returned to the motionless mask he wore during the day.

"Sit", he whispered.

I sat in the chair to left of him. I pulled it closer to the bed, so my father wouldn't have to strain for me to hear him.

My father's shimmering eyes glazed over for a moment as he stared up at the ceiling. Another painting of the black haired man, holding a bloodied sword while riding a horse was above his bed. I'd never asked about the man in the painting. I never really cared. I spent most of my time in my own little world, and did my best to stay out of the worlds of humans and Nightlings. Not to mention, the man truly creeped me out.

Slowly my father's eyes moved towards me. The rest of his head stayed still, only his dark, powerful eyes readjusted to focus on mine. "As the sun came, and I found myself un-able to move in the daytime, I felt a type of helplessness I haven't felt in a long time. I didn't know where you were or what had happened to you." He paused for a moment to col-lect his thoughts. Every word that came from his mouth sent a shot of pain through his body.

I wanted to lean over and hug him. I wanted to tell him that I loved him and that I hadn't been in any danger and it would never happen again. I couldn't, partly because I don't do the hugging thing, but mostly because I knew I planned to see Philip again. So, instead I placed my hand on his mo-tionless cold hand, gently giving it a squeeze, feeling the hard flesh in my hand. "I'm sorry dad. I left the party and ran into a group of girls that shared my distaste of hormone-induced teenage parties. We spent the whole night hanging out at one of the girl's place, while talking about high school." My heart almost stopped beating as I waited to see if my father had bought my lie.

"You spent the night with a group of human girls?" He forced out.

I decided to see how far I could take this. "Yeah, they were telling me about high school and all the stuff they are dealing with. It kinda made me feel envious of them."

Despite the pain it must have caused, my father allowed a deep laugh to escape is mouth. "You, envious of humans? I thought you didn't want anything to do with them."

I tried to mask my thoughts. "I didn't. I guess the closer I'm getting to Crossing Over, the more I've become curious of them." Which wasn't exactly a lie, I had definitely become curious about Philip.

My father's dark eyes seemed to deepen in his head. He stared at me as if I was a large, blue lake in the middle of the Sahara. "How curious?"

I had pushed my lie this far, no need to back out now. If my father agreed to what I requested, I would be home free.

If not, then it would mean he knew I hid something. "I was thinking about attending school with Angela."

Shock and pain raced across his porcelain face. It had been the shock of my words that caused the pain. "Three weeks before you Cross Over, you want to live like a human? This because of your conversation with high school girls?"

I leaned in closer. I could smell the scent of decay hovering above him. His pale skin, along with the scent of decay revealed to me that he hadn't fed in a while. If a Nightling feeds, they smell as fresh as humans. Their flesh also looks as human as Nightlings flesh can look. But if they go awhile without feeding, then they begin to resemble and smell like walking death. "How long has it been since you've fed?" I asked as I gently ran my hand over my father's forehead.

A slight smile crept across his face. "*Mio fiore dolce*, we are not talking about me."

"But we should. You don't look well. Is something wrong?"

"Aside from my daughter disappearing," my father glanced back at the painting on the ceiling. "*Lo stesso problema, giorno differente.*" He closed his eyes before he opened them, staring at me. "If you wish to spend your last three weeks as a Dayling in a human school with Angela, then so be it."

My heart skipped in my chest. I could feel all the stress I'd felt for the last twenty-four hours fade away. My father would not kill me, plus I would be able to go to school with Philip. Everything had worked out wonderfully.

"You may leave now *mio fiore dolce*. I must try to rest." My father said as he closed his eyes. I gently kissed him on top of his head before I stood from the velvet chair. I strolled towards the door, and had my hand on the doorknob when I heard my father's voice call to me from behind. "But be waiting in your room when I awake. We must discuss your punishment for disobeying my rule."

FOUR

I didn't look back as I quickly walked out of my father's chambers. I walked through the lower sitting room until I got to the long staircase. I hurried up the stairs and through the library and then up the left, custom-oak staircase. I made it to my room before I realized I hadn't taken a breath. I felt so nervous about seeing my father that the relief of not being killed overwhelmed me a little. My father threatening to punish me after he awoke was an empty threat. I'd broken too many rules, and had been threatened too many times to fear a 'wait until I awake' warning.

My father was the head of the Vigano family. He had a million things to deal with every night. Remembering to punish me would always be one of those things he simply forgot to do. The initial meeting is what had me scared. I thought if he could somehow read my mind during the day, and found out about my night with Philip, the little inconvenience of earth-shattering pain and agony wouldn't stop him from losing his temper, and snatching off my head before he knew what he'd done. No, I'd made it through the hard part. I should be safe!

I opened my door. To my surprise Angela sat in one of my large, half-circular, green, leather couches. She gazed up at me with relief in her eyes when I walked into the room with all my limbs attached. She'd thought the same thing I'd thought... I wouldn't return completely whole.

I walked to the other couch in front of Angela. I sat down unable to hide my joy. A smile the size of the Nile spread across my face.

"So what happened?" Angela asked as she sat up in my leather couch.

"We talked, I lied, he bought it... it's all good." I said as I sat back in my couch feeling victorious. "Look and be envious Angela. I'm the master."

Angela laughed as she sat back in the couch. Her skin glowed in the halogen lights. Everyone considered Sophia to be the prettiest of us all, but I felt Angela had her beat when it came to pure beauty. Sophia had a better body, with her perfect waist; round, bouncy rear end; and perky chest. Sophia oozed sensuality. No man, or woman, was safe from her sensual movements. She mesmerizes everyone she comes in contact with, and then she uses them until she gets all she wants, even if what she wants is their blood.

Nightlings don't have to kill their victims to feed. When their fangs penetrate human flesh, their saliva enters the bloodstream, leaving the victim enraptured, and open for suggestions. They can take as much blood as needed, and then simply send the human on their merry way with visions of passionate kisses dancing around in their blood-deprived heads. The taking of *innocent* human life is one of the un-breakable Nightling rules. It's punishable by death. They can only kill if they have no other choice. My father insists this has been a rule since the beginning, but I swear they got it from Anne Rice. No matter how many times my father tries to deny it, I'm convinced his obsession with red velvet is also because of '*Marius de Romanus*'.

But back to Angela, she didn't have Sophia's body or natural sensuality, although no one had Sophia's body or un-natural sensuality, Angela possessed a face that could only be described as flawless. She was beautiful, from her full lips to her thin cheekbones. She was shy most of the time; she only let loose when Sophia was around. I've always thought if Sophia weren't around, Angela would spend most of her times at sci-fi conventions.

Angela squirmed a little in the couch in front of me. I could tell from the sudden darkness in her eyes something started to bother her.

"What's wrong," I asked.

"Everything is squared away with your father, but what about Sophia? She still has vengeance in her blood from you ditching the party and getting her in trouble."

I'd forgotten about Sophia's impending revenge. I was so relieved my father wasn't going to kill me; I'd forgotten someone else was plotting my death.

I stood from the couch and made my way to my king-size bed. I lay on my back, allowing the cool air flowing from the vent in my ceiling to wash over my face. I had a few hours before nightfall. I planned on enjoying as much of my time as I could before having to deal with Sophia and her vengeance.

The bed sunk in beside me. I looked over to see Angela lying there, allowing the cool air to wash over her also.

I closed my eyes as I pushed all thoughts of Sophia out of my mind. My skin began to tingle as my mind drifted with thoughts of my spiky-haired prince.

I could feel the sun beginning to set. My body had begun to slowly change into what I would spend the rest of my life being, an eternal creature of the dark.

Before I knew it, I'd fallen fast asleep:

I dreamt about spending a day with Philip, relaxing on some tropical island surrounded by dancing monkeys in hula dresses... don't ask. Philip was drinking gin, while I sipped on a margarita. The sun blazed above us, yet a gentle breeze came from the ocean caressing our nude bodies. Which would make it a nudist beach I guess. The warm sunlight, also, wasn't like the claws of hell encompassing Tallahassee. It felt nice, tender to the skin.

Sand covered Philip's slim, but muscular, body. I brushed some of the sand away, grazing my fingers against his hard chest. I've never been comfortable nude before, but I felt at ease while Philip looked me up and down. His spiky hair sat perfectly on top of his head. His dark eyes gazed into mine. It was heaven, lying in the sand, feeling the breeze and smelling the wonderful scent of the ocean.

All of a sudden, the heat from the sun became painful. Philip gave me his playful half-smile as I lay in the sand filled with panic. I tried to move, but my body ached every time I tried. My flesh became cold, despite the heat building beneath my skin.

I had started Crossing Over. Right there on the beach I was becoming a Nightling. Philip didn't seem to notice as he looked around at the dancing monkeys. I tried to scream for help, but nothing would come from my mouth. The pain of my boiling flesh became more intense. The pain from trying to move increased as well. I couldn't do anything but lay in the sand with my spiky-haired prince and wait for the moment when the sun would finish me off.

I couldn't take much more of the pain. Suddenly, I felt lips against mine. I gazed up at Philip leaning over me. His playful half-smile etched across his beautiful face. He leaned closer towards me until I could feel his lips over mine. He kissed me. It felt deep and passionate. All the pain, the agony, the fear had gone from me. Nothing was left except Philip's kiss.

And then I woke up. I lay alone in bed. Angela must have snuck out as soon as I fell asleep. Sweat covered me all over. I didn't know if it was because I'd dreamed of burning alive from the sun, or the passionate kisses from my spiky-haired prince, or the damnable heat wave attacking Tallahassee, Florida.

"Wakey wakey." I heard a voice say.

I didn't have to see the person sitting in one of my green leather couches to know whom the voice belonged to. I knew they would come for me. I didn't think they would come so soon.

I rolled out of bed, walked over to my couches, and then sat in the couch in front of my guest. "I'm guessing this isn't a social call, is it Sophia?"

Sophia leaned back in the green couch. Her shimmering, black eyes beamed in the light. Her beautiful porcelain face became darker as she smiled at me. "You had us all worried last night chica. We thought you could've been laying in a ditch or something."

"Why do people go straight to a *ditch* when someone is missing? Do that many people really get found in ditches?" I tried to joke.

"I don't know. I'll have to look it up." She smiled at me as she tilted her head a little. I knew what she tried to do, and since the sun had set, she would have an easier time getting inside my thoughts. I did everything I could to mask them. She smiled. "Why are you trying to keep whatever's in your head so secretive chica? Eventually it's gonna come out."

I shrugged as I looked away.

Sophia pulled out a pack of cigarettes. She took one out,

and then lit it. She pulled in a deep drag as she continued to stare at me. She knew I hated the smell of cigarettes. She was testing me. She wanted to know if I would challenge her queen bee status.

I didn't say anything about the swirling smoke as I returned my eyes to her. "So what's next?"

She blew out a large cloud of smoke. "Your father is talking with the others. I'm to wait up here with you while they decide what to do." She took in another deep drag from the cigarette. "I know what I'm hoping the punishment will be."

"Having to spend my last three weeks as a Dayling with you?"

Sophia's beautiful porcelain face lit up. A wicked smile slowly crept across it. "Exactly."

I crossed my arms in front of me. I wasn't going to show her my fear. I'd won my father over, that's all I needed. The others would follow whatever he wanted.

An hour later my father stepped inside my room. Sophia and I both stood. We bowed at my father as he made his way over to the couches.

He turned to Sophia. "You may leave us." He said in his deep, Italian accent.

Sophia didn't look at me as she walked out of the room. My father waited for Sophia to close the door behind her before he gestured for me to sit.

I sat back down trying to remain calm. My father didn't have a pleased look on his face. He sat in the other couch as his dark brown, shimmering eyes focused on something behind me. He then stared at me, while trying to force a smile on his face. "*Mio fiore dolce*. Did you sleep well?"

I wondered for a moment if he knew about my dream. I didn't know the limits to his powers. I'd never known him to see my dreams before, but that didn't mean it was impossible. "As well as a convicted felon can, while waiting to be sentenced."

He laughed. It looked genuine, which made me feel a little better. "Yes, as for your sentence... you are to be grounded for a week."

"That's it? No flogging?"

"We have not flogged anyone in centuries." He said, giving me a half-smile. "If you would like a tougher punishment, it can be arranged."

"Nope, a week's grounding sounds about right to me," I said. "So were the others okay with this?"

"The others are okay with whatever I decide." My father sunk a little in the couch. The halogen lights bounced off his porcelain skin, making him resemble a marble statue. I could actually see stress enter him. "We have more important things to deal with besides my daughter's discipline." He said, glaring at me, sending shivers throughout my body. "Never do that again Haven."

"I won't," I forced out. I'd never seen my father so stressed out before. I felt I needed to help. "Do you want to talk about what's going on?"

He slowly shook his head no before he stood up. "In less than three weeks, everything is going to change for you Haven. You need to be ready. Until then, you will attend Lexington High with Angela." My father turned and walked towards my door. As he opened the door, I heard him whisper, "You remind me so much of your mother. You have no idea how much I miss her." Then he walked out, closing the door behind him and leaving me speechless.

My father never talked about my mother. He mentioned her once when I was twelve. I'd gotten into a fight with my cousin Raffaele.

I'm six months older than Raffaele, and a lot nicer. Raffaele was almost as mean as Sophia. I feel sorry for the human race once he Crosses Over and joins forces with her. But until then, Raffaele had decided to take out his malevolence on the Daylings living in our house.

He'd bullied me for about two months before I'd finally had enough and caught him clean across the nose. He stood in front of me with shock in his eyes. Blood ran down his face and the other Daylings were laughing at him. The next thing I knew he was on me. He'd beaten me up pretty good before my aunt Constance pulled him off. She slung him to the other side of the room, and stood between us as he hit the ground, rolled and stood back up. He charged me with murder in his eyes. Constance, being a very powerful Nightling, easily slung him around until he finally gave up his attack.

She picked me up from the ground and took me to my father. He sat in his study reading when Constance carried me in. She laid me on my father's desk, and said I was his responsibility before she disappeared out of the room.

My father didn't lose his famous temper as I lay on the desk bleeding and crying. He slowly stroked my hair while trying to calm me. He whispered in my ear, "do not cry in front of them *mio fiore dolce*. Your mother was stronger than that. And so shall you be."

It was the first, and last, time he'd talked about my mother. But it worked. I sucked it up and stopped crying hoping he would tell me more about her. Instead, he carried me from his desk to a small couch in his study. He laid me in the couch, and then returned to his reading. I lay there wanting him to tell me more about my mother. He never did. To be truthful, everything I knew about her I'd learned from my aunt Constance.

Her name was Lillian Anne Carpenter, and she was born in 1660, London England. She came up during the era of Charles II, or the Merry Monarch, as he was known because of his lifting of Puritan restrictions on entertainment and his own love of pleasure. And my mother was a full-fledged intellect. She also loved the theater and law. Girls weren't privileged to attend schools like boys during those times, but her father had been a reformer. He believed girls should learn just as boys. So he allowed her to study philosophies and read poetry and learn arithmetic.

From all the stories I'd heard about her, she was a bit of a deviant when she was younger as well.

She and my father didn't meet until 1702. He was sitting in a tavern listening to drunken Englishmen arguing about Queen Anne's war with France. The intellectually challenged Anne was a new Queen fighting an inherited war, but my father didn't care about the politics of the time. He doesn't really care about politics these days either.

Anyway, the way the story goes next is, my mother walked into the tavern and sat next to my father without asking his permission. When he looked up, he was hooked. Her skin had been pale, as if drowned in white powder, and her mesmerizing green-eyes stared directly into his.

She got him to leave the tavern, and they walked the streets of London arguing about England and Italy. I had my aunt describe the scene to me completely. She was the only one who my father had opened up to about that night.

She said my mother wore a long black gown, with it's neck line cut to expose the tops of her full pale breast, the sleeves wrapped tightly around her wrist, and the bottom of the gown dragged along the ground concealing her feet. Her long red hair draped to her thin waist. And her movements were slow and calculated like a lioness on the prowl.

My father loved her from that night on. They never left each other's side until the night I was born, and she died.

For the most part, Nightlings are sterile, but there are times when female Nightlings become fertile. The thing is, there isn't a cycle, so we don't know when it will happen, if it will happen, or how often it will happen. It's also different for each female Nightling. The males are always sterile, but once females become fertile (and they are only fertile for twenty-four hours when it happens) their wombs give the male 'swimmers' life, and that's how Nightlings become pregnant. When females become pregnant, they revert to being a Day-ling during the pregnancy. Once they have the child, they cross back over to being a Nightling. Unfortunately, it is also common for a mother to die after childbirth.

I've always felt my father blamed me for my mother's death. He loved her more than anything. I came and messed everything up. He'd never say it of course, but I knew he felt it.

I stood from the couch and made my way downstairs. All of the Nightlings were in the main sitting room having a meeting. All except Sophia and Nigel, they were sitting with Angela, Raffaele, and my younger brother Franklin in the kitchen.

Franklin was twelve years old. My father and Constance had a short-lived fling, which produced hard feelings, an un-fixable rift in the family, and Franklin. The hard feelings and unfixable family rift came because Constance is my Uncle Myron's ex-wife.

Franklin rarely acknowledged me. He kept to his routine as I walked into the kitchen. He sat on the kitchen table, dressed in a black t-shirt and black pants. He had long, black hair like our father, but deep-blue eyes like his mother.

Next to him stood the infamous Raffaele. He was going though a rock faze. His head was shaved bald, with a tattoo on the back of it. He wore a long, black jacket and a chain around his jeans. Unlike Franklin, he acknowledged me, but with disgust. "How did you get away with only a slap on the wrist?" He spat out.

"She's the head of the family's daughter. Little Miss Princess can do whatever she wants, and others will get punished for it." Sophia said as she stared at me.

I walked up to Angela, the only person in the room to smile at me. "So what's going on with the others? Why have they locked themselves in the main sitting room?"

Angela shrugged. "Nobody knows. Something big is going on though."

I turned to Sophia and Nigel. "Aren't you two Nightlings? Shouldn't you be in there with the others? What's wrong, they don't like you either?"

Sophia took a step towards me. She stopped inches from my face. Her eyes gleamed a little as I found myself trapped in her stare. "We're left in charge of you runts. And I'm not gonna let what happened last night happen again."

"Because of you, no one can leave tonight." Raffaele said to me.

"I'm going back to my room," Franklin said as he walked away from everyone.

I didn't know if he would ever grow out of hating me. At the time, I didn't care. I'd planned on trying to find Philip. But if I tried to leave, Sophia and Nigel would love the excuse to put a beating on me.

I turned to Sophia. "So what are we suppose to do?"

"Don't know, don't care... just don't leave." She said before she walked away. Nigel followed behind her as usual. Raffaele frowned at me before walking away as well.

I stood next to Angela. "So what do you want to do?"

"I don't know. We start school tomorrow. I was thinking about getting ready for that."

I looked away from Angela towards the main sitting room. "What do you think is going on in there?"

"Your father and my dad are at it again." Angela said.

"But they're always at it." I said.

"Something is different this time. Something they're trying not to let us know about." She started walking away from the kitchen.

I followed behind her to her room.

Unlike my room, Angela's room was like a typical sixteen-year-old girl's room. Her room was decorated in animal prints, rattan furniture, leather accents and grass cloth on the walls. Her cushion covers, bed sheets, bedcover, and computer cover were in animal print. Okay, so her room looked like a typical sixteen-year-old girl's room that was also an animal lover.

We sat on Angela's couch and stared at her closet. We had to prepare ourselves before we went about picking out our first-day-of-school-ever fashion statements. We were going to start with Angela's look, and then do mine. I had no doubt our task would take us the rest of the night.

FIVE

When the next day came, I found myself sitting on the side of my bed, fully dressed, unable to breath. I was about to do the most frightening thing I'd ever done in my life—I was going to high school for the first time.

A million thoughts raced through my mind as I stared off into darkness. Would the other students realize that I wasn't like them? Would they sense something off about me? I looked like a human, talked like a human, moved like a human, and smelled like a human, but I've never spent enough time around humans to gauge how they responded to my kind during large chunks of time. Could the facade of what I am fade after a week or two of being around me? Would little Dayling traits start popping up? Traits I didn't even know I had. Also, what if they all plain and simply hated me?

How many books and movies I've come across portrayed teenage girls instinctively hating the new girl? Would that be my fate? Shunned by the cool clique while being made fun of as I made my way from class to class? Why was I doing this to myself?

Philip! His half smile crept into my mind as I asked the question. I would brave the madness of high school to be near my spiky-haired prince. I would only have to bear it for three weeks. And then, I would have to say goodbye to the human world, including my prince.

I stood from my bed as Angela peeped through the door. She gave me a nervous smile as I walked towards her. We would share this torturous experience together.

A business partner of the family waited for Angela and I

at the bottom of the stairs. I wore my usual white t-shirt, torn jeans, and tennis shoes. While Angela wore a blue AE Blouson Halter, tight blue jeans, and blue platform wedges.

The partner; a man by the name of Vincent; greeted Angela and I, before leading us out the door and into the back of a black BMW. He was dressed from head to toe in Calvin Klein. He was also wearing Calvin Klein cologne. He had short blond hair that was only long enough to cover his forehead. He was attractive, with deep blue eyes that kept Angela's attention the entire ride to school.

Vincent was one of the few humans that knew we existed. His father's father worked for us, along with his father and now Vincent. He ran our family businesses, he helped to keep us in the lavish lifestyles we lived in, and he'd been a pain in my side for years. One of his jobs included keeping me and the other Daylings in check.

We pulled up to the school just as most of the kids that drove were arriving. Vincent leaned over to us. "I'll take care of getting you both registered."

We all got out of the car. I could feel the heat of the day slowly wrapping itself around me as soon as I left the comfort of the air-conditioned BMW.

We quickly made our way inside the two level building. It resembled every typical high school I'd seen on TV. The entrance led to the second level, where most of the classrooms, the principle's office, and the main office were located. The lower level had a few classrooms, the cafeteria, and the gym. Red and white paint covered the walls. Paintings of an old man, dressed in an American Civil war uniform, holding a musket, were scattered around the school. A banner across one of the walls read, 'Welcome to Lexington High, home of the four time state champions Lexington High Patriots boys' basketball team'.

We walked toward the main office as kids watched us. Most of the guys focused on Angela as usual. I got a few glances here and there, but Angela and her form-fitting clothes captured the attention she had hoped for. She moved through the hall trying to imitate her sister's sultry walk. I could see the lust forming in the eyes of every guy we passed. I could also see the hatred forming in the guys' girlfriends. Great, my fear of being hated seemed to be manifesting in front of me as the girls glared at Angela's twisting hips.

We made it to the main office. Angela and I sat in two seats while Vincent walked to the receptionist. He leaned over the receptionist's desk and began to whisper to the, obviously smitten, middle-aged woman.

I sat in the seat with my head leaned back. I could smell them, walking around in the halls heading towards their classes. The scent of them sent shivers through my body. I wanted them. I wanted to feel them, to consume them, to have them in every way possible.

I shook my head to snap myself back to reality. It was less than three weeks left until my Crossing Over. My lust for human contact was starting to become unbearable. I wanted everything to slow down. I wanted more time to figure out how to deal with my newfound desires. I couldn't imagine how it would be after I'd Cross Over. I didn't want to think about that.

I could hear Angela's breathing increase as she sat next to me. She wore the persona of an alpha female on the outside, but I knew how shy and frightened she was on the inside. It was all a front, her overly confident, sexual guise. I turned to her and gave her a slight smile to comfort her, but to be truthful, I was freaking out on the inside just as bad as she was. I knew why I wanted to attend Lexington High in the beginning, but I wasn't sure it had been the right idea.

Vincent returned to us with two pieces of paper in his hands. He handed one to Angela and then another to me. "These are your schedules. Your transcripts will be sent over later this afternoon. But you can start attending classes now." I took the paper from Vincent just as Angela did. "You both are in different grade levels of course, but I managed to get you both scheduled for lunch at the same time." Vincent placed his hands in his pockets as he smiled at us. He was feeling pretty full of himself for handling everything without a fuss. We were registered to attend school without too many questions being asked. He'd earned his ridicules paycheck. "Two students are being summoned to the main office. They will show you both around your grade levels." Vincent bowed before he walked out of the receptionist area, but not before he glanced back at the middle-aged women with a smile. I saw the woman's entire face blush from the smile.

There had been a time I would have had a wise crack

about the receptionist. I never understood how a simple look from a man could make a woman look like a complete idiot. I couldn't understand until I thought about Philip. He made me feel like one of those girls that wait in long lines just to get a glimpse of their favorite pop star each time he gave me that half-smile in the hospital. I'd become fully aware of all the stupid behavior people did in the presence of attraction.

The door to the office opened. I smelled him before he walked in. This newly developed sense was becoming a very handy tool, except for when it kicked in around someone who didn't smell all that pleasant. Philip, on the other hand, smelled very pleasing as he strolled into the main office.

He wore a simple short-sleeved brown shirt, blue jeans and basketball shoes. A girl walked in behind him, who looked to be Angela's age. She wore a thick, over-sized sweater and brown pants. She looked uncomfortable in her own skin. She had this nervousness oozing from her essence. Her inability to look people in their eyes helped to finish my conclusion that she had to be the shyest girl at school.

Philip and the girl walked to the receptionist desk. My heart stopped in my chest as I watched them standing in front of the receptionist. Philip hadn't seen me sitting in the corner. A part of me thought about sneaking out before he did, running home to my father, and then vowing never to think about public school ever again. But that was the part of my brain I'd never paid attention to.

Philip slowly turned towards Angela and me. His dark eyes began to glow as he recognized me. His half-smile finished the beautiful masterpiece known as his face.

Philip and the shy girl walked over to Angela and I. "Hello ladies, it seems that Rebecca and myself have been chosen to be your escorts."

Rebecca, with her long dark hair, light brown skin, and stoic face continued to stare at the ground. I didn't really care about her though; all I'd been able to think about was Philip. His spiky hair sat perfectly on top of his head – just like it did in all of my fantasies. I stared into his face, noticing slight bruises left over from his encounter in the alley. He was still beautiful, no matter how many battle scars he wore. My insides began to warm as he stared at me. My entire being began to call for him as I stared back.

Angela poked me in the side with a giggle. I couldn't believe how I lost my self-control in front of this guy. The one thing I'd learned about guys over my time avoiding them was that they loved a challenge. I wasn't presenting myself as much of a challenge as I stared into his deep black eyes.

"Rebecca is going to show... Angela right?" Angela shook her head in agreement. "Angela around school, while I show Mara Jade here around." Philip said with his half smile.

Rebecca finally gazed up from the floor towards Angela. "You ready?"

Angela shook her head yes with a smile, before Rebecca looked back down at the floor and then led Angela out of the main office.

Phillip held the door open for me to walk through. I walked out into the empty hallway. A part of me wished for kids to be walking around, while another part of me loved the solitude with Philip.

He walked beside me. "Don't you owe me a date?"

"As long as I owe you, you'll always have something to look forward to." I joked trying to be funny and seductive at the same time. I felt way out of my element. I didn't know if the moves I made with Philip came off charming, or ridiculous.

"I'm more of a live-for-the-moment type guy." Philip said.

"I suppose that had something to do with that ass-whopping you were taking."

He laughed. The sound coming from him sounded sincere. A small part of my chest began to ache after I realized I'd actually made him laugh. Then a bit of nausea entered me as I realized I enjoyed making this guy laugh. Pathetic!

"Why did you call me Mara Jade?" I asked as we made our way down the hallway.

Philip gave me his half-smile. "Sorry, she's a Star Wars character. Guess you're too cool for sci-fi."

"My cousin Angela is into that type stuff. She dragged me to a convention a few months ago."

He stopped in the middle of the hall. His half-smile turned into a full out smile. "You were at Comicfest? You're becoming even more mysterious."

I walked by him continuing to head down the hallway. "Nothing is mysterious about me."

He started back. We walked until we got to room 113. He

opened up the door and moved to the side for me to walk in. I stopped just as I entered. The teacher; a tall somewhat overweight man in his early forties, wearing glasses and having short brown hair; turned to look at the intruders interrupting his lecture.

"May I help you?" The teacher said.

Philip stood in front of me, facing the teacher. "New girl. Principle Gregory asked me to show her around. Put her in all my classes."

I tried to hide the excitement building inside me. I couldn't believe I would spend all day with Philip.

"Okay, why don't you both find a seat?" The teacher said. I started to follow Philip when the teacher stopped me. "I'm sorry miss, but why don't you come to the front of the class first and introduce yourself?"

I froze in place. I wasn't one for public speaking. This was my first time being the center of attention, especially in front of humans. A panic built inside of me, but I pushed it away as I made my way to where the teacher stood.

I looked over the class of students. Philip made it to a seat, and watched me with his intense, dark eyes. I felt trapped in his stare for a moment, and then was pulled back into my nightmare of public speaking when the teacher said, "we're waiting."

I moved my long hair out of my face, looked towards the floor like Rebecca had done in the office and took in a deep breath determined not to allow myself to feel fear in front of a class filled with human teenagers. I was stronger, faster, and smarter than all of them combined.

I glanced back up at the waiting students. "My name is Haven Vigano. My family moved here a little over three years ago. I was home-schooled with my cousins. But now I'm here."

That was as much information I felt comfortable giving to the class. I started to make my way to an empty seat next to Philip when the teacher stopped me. "I'm sure there is more about yourself than that."

I looked at the students sitting in their seats giggling at the new girl. Even if I could tell them more about myself, I wouldn't. The only person in the room I wanted to know more about me was Philip, and I wasn't sure how much more about me I wanted him to know. I looked back at the teacher. "Not really."

"How about telling us something you enjoy? What's your favorite movie or music?"

I really just wanted to make it to my seat without making a fool out of myself, but this guy wasn't making it easy. I tried to think of something that would satisfy him, but not warrant a follow-up question. "I don't have a favorite anything." I then quickly made my way to the empty seat before the teacher could ask me something else.

My plan worked. The teacher looked at me for a moment, and then continued his discussion on The American Revolution.

The class went by quickly. I half-heartedly listened to the teacher talk about the founding fathers and how they defeated the mighty British army. I glanced over to Philip a few times during the lecture. His dark eyes seemed to be somewhere else during class. I didn't see him take out a pen or piece of paper. Either he had a great memory, or he didn't much care about General Washington's military genius.

When the bell rung for the class to be over, everyone quickly jumped from their seats and made a dash for the door. Philip turned to me with his half-smile. "You ready MJ?"

I stood from the chair. "I don't know if I like you calling me that."

"It's a compliment." Philip led me out of the classroom, towards a row of lockers. We stopped at his locker, "they're still working on getting you a locker. Until then, you can use mine."

I placed my history book in his locker. After he closed it, I turned to him with a slight frown. "How did you end up my personal tour guide?"

Philip's half-smile crept across his face. "Heard a new girl was coming, took a chance she might be hot, and volunteered."

I rolled my eyes before turning from him, and started walking up the hall. "So, where to next?"

His hand suddenly wrapped around my arm. His touch sent shivers through my body. As much as I hated it, the guy made me feel warm inside, which wasn't a good thing in the middle of a heat wave. "Not that way. We got math next. It's in the opposite direction."

We made it to the math class just before the late bell

rang. Again, the class went by quickly. Philip stared into nothing as the teacher tried to explain calculus to a class filled with students fighting to stay awake. I wondered if this is what school was all about. If so, I didn't miss anything during my time of being home-schooled. No one really paid attention to the teacher. A few students took notes with sparks of interest in their eyes; while everyone else seemed to be doing everything they could to stay awake. I was bored out of my mind, and I tried to think of something to talk to Philip about. He would look at me occasionally and make some joke about something unimportant. I laughed like the silly schoolgirl in love I felt like. I was starting to make my-self sick with my own puppy-love antics.

The rest of the classes until lunch were just like math class. I couldn't wait until I had an hour of free time to talk with Philip. I couldn't wait until I had an hour of free time to escape the extreme boredom of high school.

Thankfully, I remembered that Angela had the same lunch hour as Philip and me. We met in the cafeteria to grab something to eat. She'd ditched her escort, and was being shown around by a guy on the basketball team with Philip.

All four of us found a spot outside of the school to sit and eat. The guy with Angela name was Billy. Billy was as tall as Philip, but not as gorgeous. He *was* attractive, in his own way, just not *Philip* attractive. Billy had short brown hair that looked sticky on top of his head, and large brown eyes, that kept darting from Angela to me.

"So how you girls liking Lexington High so far?" Billy asked as he took a bite of his sandwich.

"It's just how I imagined." Angela answered with a large smile across her face.

"Yeah, me too," I said sarcastically.

"So why did you decide to join us at Lexington MJ?" Philip asked.

"MJ?" Angela asked as she looked at Philip.

"Yeah, for Mara Jade."

"From Star Wars?" Angela said with a gleam in her eyes.

Philip gave her his half smile. "You keep up with Star Wars?"

"I love science fiction." Angela said. "I think we should both work on converting Haven."

"Deal," Philip said with his smile.

I took out an apple and bit into it. "Never gonna happen." I could see a few girls watching me out the corner of my eyes. They were all bleach blondes, with matching tops, although each top was a different color, and shoes that matched their tops. They were all frowning at me while whispering to each other. "Am I going to have to watch out for your adoring fans?"

Philip stared at me with confusion on his face. I then nudged my head towards the frowning blondes. He laughed. "I hooked up with one of them. Now they all think they own me."

"You hooked up with just one of them? Wow, what restraint."

He winked at me. "I have my code. No one in the same family or in the same crew."

I saw the girls continue to whisper while looking at me. It was my first time in high school, so I had no idea how I was suppose to handle girls hating me because of a boy. Why couldn't the movies and books be wrong for once? "For real Philip. You need to tell them to stop staring at me."

"What's wrong, you scared of 'em? I thought you were supposed to be hardcore." Billy said with a smile.

I looked from Billy to Philip. "What have you been telling people?"

"Nothing," Philip said trying, and failing, to look innocent. "Only that you're a good fighter. And that I saw you take some guys out by yourself in an alley."

I frowned at him. "From this point on, can you keep that to yourself? Or would you like me to tell everyone why I was fighting in the alley?"

He stopped smiling. Billy looked from Philip to me. "What? Why were you fighting those guys in the alley?"

"Oh, someone left out that part did they?" I looked over to Billy. "Where should I start?"

Philip raised his hands in mock surrender. "Okay MJ. You win. No more telling the masses of your secret powers."

Billy laughed. Angela, on the other hand, looked at me nervously. "You want to be all cliché and follow me to the restroom?" I said to her as I stood. She stood beside me. I looked down at the guys. "We'll be back."

Philip gave me his half-smile. "We'll be here."

I waited until we were far enough away from Philip and

Billy before I started talking to Angela. "He has no idea what I am."

"Then what did he mean by secret powers?" She whispered.

"First, why are you whispering? Second, he was only talking about me taking out those four guys in the alley."

Angela wrapped her arms around her stomach. "I don't think he's going to stop wondering how you did that. You need to come up with something quick."

I rolled my eyes. "Tell me something I don't know."

We made it to the girl's restroom. I went in first, and walked to the last stall. Thankfully, it was opened. I have this thing about using the last stall in public restrooms. I can't go if it's the first or any in the middle. It has to be that last stall, or I'd have to wait until I got home.

I placed tissue around the stool before using it. After I finished, I walked out of the stall to find the blonde girls standing in front of the sinks. Great! I really didn't feel like having to take out a group of girls on my first day.

The tallest blonde smiled at me. "My name's Diane. You're Haven, right?"

I stood in front of Diane. Her slim frame struggled to hold up the oversized bag around her shoulder. "Yeah. You must be the one out of your crew that Philip hooked up with." Shock flashed across all the girls' faces. Diane opened her mouth to speak, but I cut her off. "Before you threaten me and things get ugly, let me point something out. It might be more of you than there are of me, but look at what you're wearing compared to what I'm wearing. Now do you really want to stain those expensive tops with blood?"

All the girls looked at each other and their clothes. Diane frowned at me before she turned and stormed out of the restroom. The other girls followed behind her, after frowning at me as well.

I turned around to see Angela creeping out of her stall. "Thanks for the back up."

"What? I was ready to rumble if it came to that. I was finishing up is all." Angela said as she made her way to the sink. "Besides, you're the fighter remember."

I turned around to the sink. "That's the thing Angela, I'm not a fighter. They were drunk and it was dark. I had the advantage."

She wiped her hands clean. "Well, everyone at the school thinks you're a fighter. You have a rep now."

I finished washing my hands and cleaned them with hard brown paper towels. "I guess there is a worse rep to have besides being a fighter."

She opened the restroom door for me. "What's that?"

I walked past her with a smile. "Keep dressing like *that* and you'll see."

We made our way back to the guys. The blondes stared at me as they whispered some more to other students. My rep was growing faster than I wanted, so much for staying under the radar.

We sat back down. Philip gave me his half-smile. I looked at him, and then over at the blondes whispering about me. I spent the rest of the lunch period trying to figure out what the hell I was doing chasing after this guy.

SIX

After lunch, the rest of the school day went by pretty fast, and surprisingly, not all that bad. All of the girls didn't hate me like I thought; actually, most of them were pretty nice. They clued me in on all the gossip roaming around school, mostly about Philip's playboy ways. They joked about the boring teachers and the lame parties. Eliot's disco-themed party had been the main topic of discussion. It seemed I'd been wrong about Eliot's party being a typical teenage soiree. It had been a typical Summerbrooke party. The kids from my neighborhood had a rep for overdoing everything. The girls I'd talked to went to the party to see how ridiculous it would be. They couldn't stop laughing about the disco ball. The girls also advised me on TV shows I should watch, foods I should avoid, and books I should read. I met three girls who had the same obsession with Jane Austen as me.

I also met a few of Philip's friends, not surprisingly, a large amount of them were jocks. I even had another opportunity to look into the empty eyes of Eliot Little. I had to fight back laughter as some of the girls' jokes made their way through my mind. He followed me around asking about Sophia. It seemed that he and Sophia had some 'private time' with each other, Eliot didn't remember much about the encounter, but he felt it was something he wanted to do again. The poor guy didn't know he had been seduced and used as a means for substance by a fifty-year-old Nightling. By the gleam in his eyes, I didn't think he would really care.

And, oh yeah, my rep of being a bad ass had increased

since lunch. There were two different accounts of me taking a swing at Diane in the restroom. One of the rumors had me jumping at the bleached blonde like a mad woman screaming at her to stay away from my man—Philip got a kick out of that one. Another rumor had me calmly walking up to Diane, and then quickly taking a cheap shot at her, only missing because my level-headed cousin pushed Diane out of the way before my fist could connect—Angela got a kick out of that one. By the end of the day, everyone at school thought I was this hardcore chick that didn't fear anything. I wondered how they would handle Sophia.

I stood by the sidewalk with Angela, waiting for Vincent to pick us up after school. Angela fanned herself as sweat began to creep down her face. She took in deep breaths as she patted her feet impatiently. I glared down at the pavement trying to focus on something other than the heat. The sun felt as if it had moved closer to the Earth's atmosphere. I could feel it biting at my changing skin. I could feel it declaring its power over my soon-to-be Nightling body. I wanted to throw up my hands and scream that it had won. But a lot of kids already thought I was crazy, no need to fuel that opinion by screaming at nothing.

Again, I could smell him before I saw him. I was beginning to pick his scent out of every other scent lingering in the air.

I turned around just as Philip stepped behind me. "Damn, I was about to try and catch you off-guard. Should've known I couldn't do that to you."

"Why would you even try? Practicing your future stalker moves?"

He laughed. "I don't need to take what gets thrown at me every few seconds." I didn't know if he was joking or not. I'd already learned about him being every girl's dream guy, the bad boy with the cute smile and killer abs. Not to mention his family being loaded helped a little with all the lusting. "So you want to take a ride?"

I looked over to Angela, who stopped patting her foot as she stared at me intensely, with interest spread across her beautiful face. I turned back to Philip. "I don't think that would be a good idea."

Philip smiled at Angela. "She can come too. I know Billy would be happy."

Angela stepped up to Philip and me. She smiled back at Philip. "Naw, I got to get home." She turned to me. "I can cover for you if you want to go with him."

Great, the decision was mine. I hated Angela for being a good cousin. She knew I wanted to go with him. I only needed a little push to help me decide what to do. "Okay, you know what to tell Vincent?"

Angela smiled. "Don't worry about him. Just be back before nightfall."

I turned to Philip. "Lead the way. I don't have to warn you what would happen if you tried something right?"

He reached his hand out for me to take it. "Are you crazy? I've seen you in action Jedi Master."

I looked down at his hand. I wasn't ready for the hand holding stage yet, so I placed my hands in my pockets. "Lead the way."

He didn't seem to take my leaving his hand empty to heart. He turned and began walking away from Angela. I followed behind him after waving good-bye to my uncomfortably sweaty cousin.

We walked to the other side of the school. There were a few cars parked by each other. Each car looked like something out of those Fast and the Furious movies. They were painted in loud colors, with shiny rims and multiple tailpipes hanging from the rear. They were filled with kids blasting rock music and dancing inside of them.

We walked to a yellow jeep, dropped low to the ground, with red writing on the side of it. I felt so out of my element. I felt over dressed as I glanced at the girl sitting in the back with long blond hair, a tank top and very, *very* short jeans. She looked at me as if I was a large bug in the last freshly made cup of ice tea during a picnic in this Tallahassee heat. I returned the look to her.

Philip turned to the girl. "Lindsay, this is Haven. Haven, this is Lindsay."

The girl gave me a forced smile. I gave her a forced smile back. I was willing to play this game with her for the rest of the day if she wanted.

A guy with short blonde hair sat in the passenger front seat. He wore a tank top, but he wore sweat pants instead of the short shorts Lindsay had on.

Philip motioned for the guy to get in the back of the jeep.

The guy stood up and leapt to the back with Lindsay.

Philip walked over to the passenger side and opened up the door for me to get in. I sat in the seat before he closed the door and walked to the driver's side. When he got in the jeep, he looked back at the guy with the short blonde hair. "Say hi to Haven Brian."

Brian leaned over the seat to place his face beside mine. "Hi Haven."

"Hi back," I said before Brian leaned back and yelled at the other cars in the parking lot. All the cars began honking their horns at the same time. That nauseating feeling in my stomach returned. I could not believe I was about to hang out with a bunch of street-racing teenagers. Breathe Haven... just breathe.

Philip turned on the jeep, and then pulled away with the wheels squealing on the cement. I lay back in the jeep, my hair floated in the wind, and little streams of sweat flowed down my arms as the heat above us intensified. You would think the wind flooding through the jeep would cool my body, but it was too hot for anything to work except blasting the A/C. Everyone else in the jeep seemed to be enjoying the hot wind blowing through their hair. I was the only one suffering. It seemed every second that passed, my flesh became more and more sensitive to the sun.

We drove for about twenty minutes before we ended up at one of Philip's friend's house. Everyone got out of their expensive Fast and the Furious cars and made their way to the front door of the house. I walked behind Philip; not wanting to show the slight disappointment on my face when I realized we were at another party. It seemed odd to attend one of these during the day though. But I remembered what all the girls I'd talk to said about Summerbrooke kids... they took *everything* to extremes.

We walked inside of the house. One of the guys quickly made his way to the stereo and turned on the music. The same hip-hop techno blend I'd heard at Eliot Little's house blasted from the speakers.

I didn't have anything against the music, but I was more of a hardcore rock girl myself. Give me some HIM, or Disturbed, or even some Korn, and I'm happy. This dance music was starting to drive me insane.

Philip reached back to take hold of my hand. I could feel

the heat pulsating from his soft skin to mine flash. I loved the way this guy felt. I couldn't deny it, no matter how much I wanted to.

We walked to the back of the house, and out the back door to the swimming pool. There were speakers outside, so the music from the house could be heard in the pool area.

I stared at the pool. The water looked so cool. It was like looking into heaven, the relief my body would feel from plunging into it sung to me like a Celestial choir.

I didn't have a bathing suit, a problem I noticed everyone faced.

Without warning, the five girls in the group started taking off their clothes while the boys cheered them on. The guys then followed the girls, by taking off all their clothes as well. I found myself surrounded by naked teenagers. I slowly began rethinking the wisdom of following Philip to this party.

Philip looked at me with a smirk. I stared at him with a frown. "You don't really think I'm doing that do you?"

"I was hoping, but naw, I didn't think you would take it all off and join in." He pulled a chair up for me to sit in.

I sat down on the chair and watched as the group flayed around in the pool. I wondered if that's what it meant to be young and human. No responsibilities, no ancient rules controlling your every decision, just plain and simple freedom. I mean the kids from Summerbrooke did go to extremes, while the other kids I'd come across seemed more laid back. Either way, it had been their choice. To hang out at the mall, like I'd been invited to do by a few of the girls I'd befriended, or meet up at another girls' house to have an all girl viewing of some reality show they found addictive, which had been another event I'd been invited to, or go skinny dipping with Philip and his friends. Choices! They felt strange to me. Soon I would have only one choice, control my thirst while doing everything my father demanded for me to do. No matter how I looked, walked, talked, or smelled, I wasn't human. I was a monster in waiting.

Philip pulled up another chair beside me. He didn't say anything as he sat down watching the others playing in the pool.

I turned towards him, the sun beamed down on top of his spiky hair. The heat became even more uncomfortable to me. The blazing Tallahassee heat wave was giving my body a hard time.

We sat in silence for a moment before Philip spoke. "Are you ready to tell me how you took out four guys yet?"

I moved my burning hair out of my face. "Is that why you brought me here? To interrogate me?"

"I brought you here to have fun. Hoping you might want to share some information about yourself while having fun."

I rolled my eyes as I looked back out at my 'classmates' playing in the water. I wished I could be like them for the first time in my life. I'd never cared about the human world. I'd never admired it, or craved it. Maybe my father had been right; I'd become envious of mortals. Being normal would have made everything with Philip so much easer. But I wasn't normal, and I couldn't share with him how un-normal I was.

I looked back over to Philip. "Can I have something to drink?"

He quickly stood from his chair and headed inside the house.

I sat back and watched as the other kids played around in the pool. I wondered if I would be able to allow myself to let loose like that. A part of me *did* envy them, while another part of me despised them; the girls in particular, although the guys were slowly making a special place in my heart. It didn't seem right to me, this idea that girls are to be these supposed free-spirited, sexual vixens while the guys enjoyed every second of it, and the girls getting some type of enjoyment by being the punch line of the guys' future stories to the other boys at school. I was determined never to end up 'true' locker room gossip. I had already learned I'd become apart of the who-did-who-and-when wall of shame in the boy's bathroom. That reminded me, I had to find the dork that placed that lie up and make him pay in ways he couldn't understand. One day in a regular school and I already had to plot someone's demise.

Philip returned with two drinks in his hands. The ice in both drinks had already started evaporating in the heat. I wanted to ditch the pool-watching and head inside, but the idea of Philip and me alone in a house, without adult supervision wasn't something I felt ready for yet.

I took the drink and gave him a half-smile. "So what's next?"

Philip sat back down next to me. "I didn't have a plan past getting you in your underwear and in the pool. I thought things would progress from there."

"You thought I was that easy?" I said before I took a deep drink of the water.

He ran his hand through his spiky hair. "It normally takes less than that. So I thought I was putting in work."

The heat was starting to get to me. It felt as if I was melting out in the sun. My body couldn't take anymore. I didn't have a choice; I had to take a chance with Philip inside the house.

I stood from the chair. "Let's go inside to chill. And I do mean chill."

Philip stood with his half-smile on his face. I could hear his friends, even the girls, whooping behind us, indicating they thought he was about to get lucky.

We walked into the house and made our way to the Den. A large TV sat in front of us. I reached for the remote, but Philip beat me to it. He sat it in his lap as he smiled at me. "Too much TV is bad for you. I thought we could talk."

I didn't want to talk about what happened in the alley. It wasn't going to be easy getting him to forget about me saving his ass from those guys whaling on him. I was tempted to start making out with him to get his mind off of it, but I wasn't that desperate yet. "You want to talk about the math test tomorrow? Isn't it against the law to assign a test for the second day of school?"

"If its not, it should be." He moved closer to me on the couch. I could smell his scent. It was intoxicating. He smelled, well, delicious.

I wasn't sure if it was my hormones that were kicking into overdrive, or my Nightling senses slowly rising to the surface. I had a couple more weeks left. I could fight it until then.

I scooted a little away from him. He didn't move closer. Instead, he stared at me as if he was trying to figure out his next move. I had to say something to change the subject. "So is swimming half-naked something you and your friends do a lot?" Great Haven, bring up something sexual.

Philip sat back in the chair. He smiled at me. It looked genuine, and not the playful BS half-smiles he usually gave me. "You would prefer to talk about something sexual instead of talking about what happened in the alley? I'm tempted to take the bait, but we both know nothing physical is going to happen, so I think I want to talk about the alley."

Not like I didn't know it was coming. "Why can't you just be grateful and leave it at that? I saved you. A thank you should be all I hear coming from you."

Philip slowly drank from his glass, his eyes focused on me as he took a few deep swallows of ice water. He pulled the glass of water from his face before he licked his thin lips. "I'm sorry, but I gotta know exactly what happened."

"Why don't you ask the guys from the alley? Oh yeah, you slept with one of their girlfriends. Guess you can scratch him off as a probable BFF." I stood from the couch. "Do I get a tour of the place?"

"Not much to see. We like this place because Larry's parents are never home, plus the neighbors don't mind teenage girls sunbathing." Philip didn't make a move to stand. Instead, he continued to stare at me with his beautiful dark eyes. "You can sit back down. I won't ask you about the alley for the rest of the day. Promise."

I looked around the house. He was right; it really wasn't much to look at. Not trying to sound like a stuck up you-know-what, but for most of the people that went to Lexington High, Larry's place didn't fit in the brochure. I wondered why the Summerbrooke kids hung out around here. Oh yeah, parents never home. That explained it.

I sat down, making sure to sit at the opposite end of the couch than Philip. No matter how much I tried to convince myself how wrong and dangerous I was lusting after a human, I couldn't help it. I'd decided it wasn't anything more than lust, because there was no way I could be falling for this guy. I don't do that.

I started to make another stupid joke when I noticed one of the guys half-pulling one of the girls down the hall to some stairs.

I glanced over to Philip, who looked back at me with confusion. "What?"

"You didn't see that?" I asked.

He looked down the hall where I had been looking a second before. The guy and the half-unconscious girl were gone. "See what?"

I didn't answer him as I stood from the couch and walked

towards the stairs. I heard Philip walking behind me as I made my way to, and then up the back stairs. I felt tempted to kick open all the doors to find where the guy had taken the girl, but I decided to use my newly developed hearing to find them.

I stood in silence with my eyes closed. I could feel Philip standing beside me. He didn't say anything as I used my hearing to scan the rooms for sounds. I pushed everything around me away. I focused on the sounds of the house. I could hear the others coming in from outside, it had become too hot for them as well. I could hear Philip breathing beside me. I pushed all of those sounds out of my head until I got the sound I looked for, or listened for... the sound of a body being lowered onto a bed.

I opened my eyes and pointed at the second room to the right. "There."

Philip tried to take the lead, but I wasn't about to let him beat me inside the room. I didn't think Philip knew anything about what I felt sure was about to happen, but I wasn't certain.

I kicked open the door just as Brian had started lowering his underwear. The unconscious Lindsay lay already naked on the bed.

Brian turned to us with a frown. "Do you mind? This is a private party."

I began to say something, but this time Philip beat me to it. "You got to be joking right? Cause I don't think they drug you when they take off your clothes and lay you naked on a bed in prison."

Brian quickly pulled up his boxers. "Prison, for what? Come on man, you know how Lindsay is. You had it before."

Philip walked towards Brian. He stood face to face with him. "Yeah, but she was wide awake until afterwards." He leaned down to Lindsay. He pulled the covers over her body, giving her some dignity. "Not passed out before."

Brain grabbed Philip and slammed him against the back wall. He placed his elbow at Philip's throat. "I'm not going to jail because of no skank."

I was just about to grab Brian when Philip kneed him between the legs. Brain folded over as his face turned red. Philip then caught him with a solid right across his jaw, knocking Brian out cold to the floor.

Philip turned to me while rubbing his hand. "Four on one, I might need a little help. But one on one single scumbag, I got that easily."

"My hero," I said before I walked up to the unconscious Brian. It was over with; Lindsay was safe, and Brian lay on the floor knocked out cold, but I couldn't help myself. I kicked him in the ribs as hard as I could. Two ribs broke as my foot connected to his side. Brian momentarily regained consciousness, only to fall back out from the new pain.

Philip looked at Brian before he turned to me. "I'm guessing I'm going to have to take them both to the hospital. You want to come?"

"I don't really like hospitals. You think one of your non-rapist friends could give me a ride home?"

I got a ride home from one of Philip's more talkative friends. I tried to ignore the girl until we pulled up to my family's estate. I had to deal with ten minutes worth of questions about how big our mansion was, how many rooms we had, and is there a swimming pool. I answered the questions as quickly as I could without trying to be rude. If Philip and I were going to hang out more, I would have to get used to his friends, and he would have to get used to mine. The latter was a frightening idea.

When I entered the mansion, Vincent tried to question me about where I'd been. I ignored him as I made my way to my room and locked the door behind me. Angela wasn't anywhere to be seen, even though I knew she was in the mansion. I thought she would be waiting for me in my room, but instead she had locked herself in her own. I'd learned from Raffaele that Angela hadn't been out of her room since she got home. It was strange, but I didn't feel like investigating it until the next day.

I laid in my room for the rest of the day waiting for night to come and for my father to burst through the door demanding I tell him where I had been and what I had been doing.

He never came. Instead, when night came, I fell asleep.

SEVEN

The closer I got to Crossing Over; I would begin having dreams about my parents' transformation. We all go through it. No one really knows why we have Dreams Transfers, as they are called, but I'd been told I would have two of them: one about my father, and another about my mother.

The Dream Transfers would be about the night before my parents' eighteenth birthday, and also the day of. I'd been told it would feel as if I lived though my parents. I would feel what they felt; experience what they experienced as if it was happening to me.

I'd looked forward to the one about my mother. My curiosity of her never decreased no matter how many people told me I wouldn't like what I'd find. Everyone told me my mother had been a heartless monster that my father tried to convert into a decent woman. A task he'd failed. She didn't care about the rules; she didn't care about human life; she didn't care about anything except her lust for death. If so many of our kind hadn't feared my father, they would have burned her long before my birth ended her life.

It didn't take me long to realize my first Dream Transfer was about my mother. Constance had told me my mother ran away from her family a year before she Crossed Over. No one knew where she went or what happened to her, only that when she'd returned home, even her own parents feared her.

So as the dream started, I found myself more curious than frightened.

I found myself in London, but not during this time period.

I wasn't a history buff, but from what I knew about my mother, I'd have to say it was the early 17th century. The moon loomed bright above the street. Stars cluttered the night helping to illuminate the old city. All the shops and taverns seemed empty, and a creepy fog hovered in the air.

The streets were filled with the women of the night. They tempted the travelers and the men of wealth and the men who only had enough for them and nothing else in the world. The women took man after man to alleys around the fogged street. The fancy clothed gentlemen snuck into the alleys to partake in the pleasures the women had for sale, and then I realized I was one of those women.

I stood on the side of the dimly lit street wearing a long green dress that covered up most of my pale beautiful skin. My long red hair hung all the way down my back. I looked thin, because I hadn't eaten in days. I felt oblivious to the world around me, yet I belonged to it. I could feel the misery deep in my soul, while standing to the side, holding myself, fighting tears from escaping my heart and aching all over.

The men walked by me as they saw the tears coming from my eyes. I tried to calm myself; I needed to at least accept one filthy offer from one of the slimy men. I was starving, and needed to make enough money to eat, which I hadn't done in two days. I gathered myself, and tried to make myself desirable for the low lives that paid for the warmth of women.

"You don't seem to be good at selling yourself." A man's voice said from in front of me, causing me to look up at the young man standing completely still watching me. I had been so lost in my thoughts I didn't see him approach.

I pushed aside my pain as best as I could. My body needed food, so I had to convince this man I was worth his money. "But what I'm selling is very good." I said with a forced smile.

The man walked to me. "You don't have to do that."

"What do you mean sir?" I asked.

"Act like this is you. I don't want to buy you. Are you hungry? Let me give you something to eat and a place to sleep tonight." The man said with a gentle smile.

His kindness made him look beautiful to me. I thought of him as an angel, if I believed God would send an angel to me. But the man was there, standing in front of me offering what I wanted more than his money. I smiled back at the man, this time it wasn't forced. "Thank you sir," I said shyly.

The man held out his hand for me to take. I did and he led me to an inn across from where we stood.

We walked inside of the inn and to his room. He opened his door and waited for me to enter before he followed, like a perfect gentleman. I smiled at him as I walked past him into the room. He closed the door, then gestured for me to sit on the bed. I looked at the bed, *so he does want me*, I thought as I stared at the bed.

"Don't worry; it is just that the bed is more comfortable than the chair. Have a seat, relax, and tell me what you want to eat." The man said with his gentle smile.

While returning his smile, I made my way to the bed and sat down. He had been right, the bed was comfortable. I didn't want to sleep on the streets again like I did the night before.

"Thank you," I said as I relaxed on the bed.

"Now, what do you want to eat?" He said as he walked to the bed. "You can have whatever you want, then we can talk about whatever is causing your pain. And you can sleep in here tonight if you want." He finished as he sat next to me.

His words caused me to stare at him again. No way someone was being so kind to me and trying to help me. Being alone for the rest of my life had been something I'd accepted awhile back, when I'd decided to leave my family, but the man showed me that maybe I could find happiness from another.

After a few short moments, I started to answer him when I saw him pull something from under the sheet on the bed. I didn't recognize it at first. My mind couldn't accept what was about to happen, it couldn't fathom something like that happening to me. When I saw the knife, for a moment I thought my imagination was taking over again. There was no way this man that had been so kind to me had taken out a knife to harm me. I had to accept it wasn't my imagination when the man slung me on my back. I tried to fight, but he was too strong, and I was too weak even though I was close to Crossing Over.

"Be still, whore." The man yelled as he slapped me a few times.

The fear inside of me screamed for me to beg the man to

stop, to beg the man for my life, but I knew it was hopeless.

I was defeated, but I didn't care anymore, I just hoped it would be quick, with as little pain as possible. A simple and painless death, one quick slash across the throat, but the look in the man's eyes told me that wasn't what he'd planned for me.

When the knife came across my face the first time, I screamed like I had never screamed before. My hand went to my face, but the knife slashed another cheek, then the top of my forehead, and then all over my face. I tried to stop him, I tried to block the knife, but the man was too strong for me in my weakened state. If I had been at my full strength, I could have easily turned the tables on the man, but as I was, nothing could save me. The knife was too sharp, and I was losing so much blood. I screamed and pleaded with the man to stop, but he kept slicing at my face. I cried out for help, I cried out for mercy, I cried out for God, I received nothing except the pain of the knife.

When the man finally stopped, I found myself crying in a pool of my own blood, while choking from my blood, as well. The man laughed at me as I laid there shivering from the pain. He laughed at me as I struggled to breathe. He laughed even harder as he saw I had soiled myself. The sound of him laughing hysterically was the last thing I heard before I finally passed out.

The dream changed.

The man was gone. I lay in an alley, bloodied and disfigured. My clothes were half torn from my thin body, my legs were stained with urine, and my fingers were bleeding from being nibbled on by rats. I resembled something out of a horror story. The night blanketed me, pulling me into its embrace. Then, my shimmering green eyes opened, and all the scars slowly disappeared from my face, returning my beautiful design. My skin became porcelain, and my red hair flowed behind me like fire. Slowly I stood from the ground and vomited everything inside of me as a new hunger tore at my gut. It wasn't just the need for blood, but the need for death. The power surging inside of my Nightling body screamed for it.

With a flash, the dream changed again.

I stood outside of a room, before gently knocking on the old oak door.

When the door opened, a rush of excitement passed

through me when the man standing in front of me recognized me. It was the man who had slashed my beautiful face.

Yes, I had returned for vengeance, but this time no longer weak, I had returned a Nightling.

Restraining myself from attacking him where he stood was hard. I wanted him so bad; I could taste his blood, his fear, his death draining inside of me within seconds. But that would have spoiled my fun, my night of joy, and I wasn't going to allow it to happen.

The man tried to slam the door, but I shoved it so hard it sent him flying through the air. He landed and slid to the rear of the room.

As I entered, I saw a woman come from the back of one of the rooms. The man yelled for her to get out, but the woman wasn't going to leave her... husband. The thoughts of the woman came crashing into my mind.

Yes, the man was married, and he had a child... a baby girl. A little baby girl lay asleep in the next room. The ideas of torment came to me. The things I could do to the man and his family caused a smile to creep across my face.

I grabbed the woman before she made it to her husband and slammed her to the back wall of the room.

"Please, let her go, let her go," the man cried.

"Please, did you say please? That word sounds so familiar. Where have I hard it from?" I mocked as I held the woman to the wall. The woman tried to fight, she tried to free herself, but I was too strong, "yes, I believe it was the word I used as you slashed my face."

"Please, it was me, take me and let her live. Let her go, she did nothing to you, it was me," he pleaded as he stood to his feet.

I hissed at the man so he could get a full view of my fangs. My unnatural porcelain skin shown in the flickering candles along the wall, I wanted him to know I had become a creature of the night. The woman whom he so easily held down and slashed her face had gone. A monster now lived in her beautiful shell.

"You think I don't know who wronged me. You think I will ever forget you. You will be etched in my heart for the rest of my life. Just as the death of your wife shall be etched in yours," I punched the woman as hard as I could in the pelvis, shattering it.

The woman screamed. Her face turned red as I let her fall to the floor. The man ran towards me, he cursed me as he flung his body at me. I caught him in mid air, slung him to the side of the room, and ran to him with my Nightling speed. I held him to the wall as he kicked and yelled.

The sounds of screaming mortals filled the room. The woman lay on the floor crying from the pain rushing through her body, the baby cried from the sounds of her parents being harmed in the front room, and the man screamed in front of me as I pinned him to the wall.

He tried to free himself, but it was useless. He found himself in the grip of an immortal. He was nothing but an infant to me. He was no different than the baby crying in the other room compared to my strength.

The thought of the baby gave me a devilish idea.

"When I am finished with you and your wife, I shall feast on your little child. I shall devour the girl as if she was my unholy communion. First the blood, then the body." I whispered into the man's ear.

He screamed. He kicked me with all his might. It hurt, but not enough for me to release him. I slammed him into the wall harder, causing blood to come from his mouth.

I lunged for his neck and sunk my fangs into his flesh.

Pleasure ran through my body as I felt the man's blood running down my throat. I wanted to end him, to drain him of all his delicious life fluid. But I had other plans. Other plans that needed for the man to live.

With all the will power I could conjure, I forced my mouth away from the man's neck and released him, allowing him to fall to the floor. He was still alive and still conscious. Good, that's the way I wanted him. I needed him to be so weak he couldn't move, but conscious to watch what I had planned to do next.

Very slowly, my attention shifted to the woman. Fear burned in her eyes as she tried to crawl away. The man mumbled behind me as I got closer to the woman. The fear from them both fueled my hunger. The horror of the moment crushed both of their faith. Their hearts were no longer filled with prayers, but with pain and fear. It pleased me. It pleased me to cause so much pain and fear to them both.

My hatred for the woman was as equal to my hatred of the man. The woman loved the vile creature, the fiend who committed such an act of malevolence. The woman loved him and bore a child with him. The woman didn't care her husband sometimes stalked the streets of London for godless souls to torment. The woman felt the evil people deserved the pain her husband gave them, which made my torment of her all the more delightful.

She begged me not to kill her as I stood over her. My dead heart fluttered with pure pleasure as she cried for mercy.

"Do you wish to live?" I asked the woman.

"Yes... please... please... no more... please," the woman cried.

I kneeled beside her, "then denounce God. Denounce your love for him. Denounce his very existence, and I shall let you live."

The woman stared at me, her face twisted in pain. The torment in her thoughts pulsated in my head; I could feel the pain in her pelvis, the fear inside of her growing, she slowly convincing herself the only thing that mattered was to live.

"I denounce him! I denounce his love and his existence."

I smiled to myself, before turning to look at the man staring at me from his half dead eyes. I then smiled at him. He knew what I was about to do. He knew it as soon as I told his wife what to do to save her life.

With one quick motion, I turned back to the woman and lunged at her neck. Her flesh tasted so sweet. Her blood tasted like heaven. The heaven I was sure she would not see.

I drained the woman as she moaned from the pleasure of my bite. Every drop of her blood filled inside of me until she lay on the floor dead.

The cries of the man's child echoed in the room as I slowly stood from over his wife, and made my way to him. Gradually, I strolled towards him, allowing the fear inside of the man to swell, wanting him to feel the terror I felt when he slashed my face, wanting him to see the mask of death he carved into the beautiful face approaching him. I loved the scent of his fear, the smell of his urine as it traveled along his thighs.

I stood over him, kneeled down, and then turned him over on his back. Every part of me wanted to take the man's life, but a new thought entered my mind, a new act of vengeance.

Straddling the man, I stared into his glazed eyes. A slight smile worked its way across my face, as I began clawing at his face. I tore bits of flesh after bits of flesh, until the man under me resembled a thing. He no longer had the face of a man, but an unrecognizable monster. Just the way he left me in that alley.

I leaned into the half attached ear of the man, "now comes the sweetness that is your child." I stood as he mumbled towards me.

I walked to the back room and gently picked up the crying child. A part of me felt sorry for taking the child's mother and father from her. But I felt the man and woman would have only raised the child to hate like them. To treat people who didn't believe as them like animals. The best thing I could have done for the child was killing her parents.

I took the child to a parish nearby, got as close as I could, then left the child wrapped in a blanket in front of it.

I walked from the parish, then threw rocks at the window. When I broke a few, the bishop of the parish opened the door.

While hiding in the shadows, I watched as the bishop discovered the child. He looked around, but I was well hidden. The bishop returned into the parish with the child in his arms. I gave the child well wishes before I left my hiding spot.

EIGHT

I awoke from the dream fighting back the urge to scream. Not that I was frightened, or even horrified by what I had seen. How real everything had felt left me a little unnerved. When they told me about the Dream Transfers, they left out how real everything would be for me.

I rolled out of bed and made my way to my bathroom. I took off all my clothes and took another long cold shower. Afterwards, I quickly got dressed in my brown t-shirt, with Disturbed written across the front of it in white letters, and 'Down With The Sickness' across the back of it. I pulled a pair of clean blue jeans from the floor, and put on my shoes.

By the time I made it down stairs, Angela was waiting in the kitchen for me.

Vincent stood beside her with his same judgmental expression across his face. I didn't like him, and he didn't care. We had an understanding that suited both of us fine.

"Do you want to grab something to eat before we leave?" Vincent asked me.

I walked past him to the door. "I'll get something at school.

A few moments later Vincent drove Angela and me back to Lexington High for our second day of school.

Angela didn't speak as she sat beside me staring out the window. I thought for a glorious moment the entire trip would be in sweet silence, until Vincent shattered that lovely thought.

"So what happened with you yesterday?" He asked without looking at me.

I sighed. "Nothing much. Met a few future victims. That was fun."

Vincent didn't take the bait of my joke. He never did. "Your father was worried about you. It took all my effort to calm him down." He paused for a moment. He seemed to be in deep thought, as if he was contemplating his next words. "Your father has a lot on his plate right now, Haven. It would be very helpful if you would not add more."

I started to say something witty and a little mean, but I had to admit something seemed off about my father lately. Any other time my father would have been in my room as soon as the sun had set, instead no one came, which was very odd. Something was going on with the Nightlings. Something they were trying their best to keep us out of, which meant something I needed to find out about.

Angela and I quickly jumped out of the car as soon as we drove up. Even though Lexington High was filled with the wealthiest of the wealthy, most kids drove themselves to school. We didn't want to stand out anymore than we already had by being seen getting out of a limo.

As soon as I walked into my homeroom, all eyes focused on me. I'd noticed a few glances from students as I walked through the hall. I didn't pay much attention to it on account of my thoughts being clouded with visions of Philip. What he did in the visions I would never tell for the rest of my life.

I sat in the seat next to him. A few of the kids started whispering around us. Instead of using my new hearing ability to find out what they were saying, I decided to try the old fashion way of getting information.

I turned to Philip. "Why is everyone staring at us?"

"Lindsay wouldn't have been the first of Brian's victims. He'd done it before, it's just the other girls were too frightened to come out about it." Philip glanced around the room. "They think we're heroes."

Great, just what I needed. Less than three weeks now before I Cross Over, and I've got kids watching me with admiration. This couldn't get any worse.

"A news crew is on their way to interview us." Philip said to pull me back into the nightmare I found myself being trapped in. I would have preferred to stay in my mother's quest for revenge.

No way would I allow myself to be interviewed on camera. My kind didn't like there being evidence of us living during a time period. I would have to sneak out of the school before the camera crew showed up.

"I heard you broke a few of the perve's ribs." A female voice said from behind me. I turned around into the large, innocent, brown eyes of Olivia Dawson. Olivia had been one of the girls that had decided to befriend the new girl. I remembered when she first walked up to me, freaking me out and slightly intimidating me at the same time. She was tall, a little over six feet, with a slim body naturally designed to be a model of some kind. Her long brown hair hung all the way down her back, and she wore a form fitting navy blue dress. She'd told me the designer, but I didn't remember. My predetermined stereotype of teenage girls had me waiting for her to reenact a scene from 'Mean Girls' on me. Instead, she casually introduced herself, and began telling me about the school as if we were old friends. "You've *got* to show me some moves." She finished as she sat behind me wearing her gray Lexington High Track team sweat suit.

"Nothing to it. Just kick as hard as you can." I said before turning back towards the teacher.

I hoped, but knew Olivia wasn't going to let the subject drop so easily. "Girl, you're like the baddest thing here. I heard you got kicked out of middle school for attacking a teacher. That's why you were home schooled."

Mrs. Henderson, my homeroom teacher, sat quietly at her desk looking through a stack of videotapes.

"Never went to middle school. Never went to any school."

Philip leaned back to whisper to Olivia. "Maybe she beat up all the kids in the sandbox. That's why her parents decided to home school her."

Olivia giggled. "Badass from birth. That would look hella sexy on a t-shirt."

Philip's half smile spread across his face. "Anything would look hella sexy on you Olivia."

She gave him a playful frown. "Don't try to work your mojo on me. I don't want to get on my girl's bad side by flirting with her man."

"He's not my man," I grumbled.

Philip focused his intoxicating dark eyes on me. I squirmed a little in my set as I stared back at him. "Not yet."

Olivia giggled before I turned back to Mrs. Henderson.

The school extended homeroom because of what happened with Brian. We had to watch videos about girls who had been drugged and raped at different events. Some happened at parties, while others happened at festivals, and even a few happened at family gatherings. It seemed no girl was safe anywhere in this world filled with overly sex-crazed members of the opposite sex. And I wondered why I spent most of my life avoiding the human world.

After the extended homeroom, I made my way to my locker, avoiding more of Olivia's requests for fighting pointers. Just as I started to open it, I heard my name being summoned to the Principal's office over the intercom, along with Philip. Crap! That meant the news crew had already arrived at the school.

Olivia smiled beside me. "Time for your fifteen minutes. Don't let it go to your head."

"Olivia, I can't do an interview. There are things... I just can't... I've *got* to get out of here." I said frantically.

She saw the edge in my eyes. She stopped smiling as she looked around the hall. "Okay girl chill. I'll head to the office and see if I can stall them while you make a run for it."

"Thanks," I said with a sigh.

"Philip said you were secretive, but I didn't know you were this secretive." Olivia joked before she headed towards the main office.

I slowly walked away from my locker hoping no one had noticed me. But being considered a hero had its drawbacks, everyone at the school now knew who I was. They all watched me as I walked by them. They thought I was heading to the Principal's office for my fifteen minutes of fame. I had other plans – like trying to find the nearest exit to make my escape.

Unfortunately, because of what almost happened to Lindsay, extra guards were posted at the school. The school board decided to lock the school down for a few days to make the parents feel safer. It didn't register to them that Lindsay had been almost raped off of school property. I really wasn't in the mood to bring that point up.

I was trapped. I couldn't get out of school while the guards stood by every exit, and since the news crew had already made it on school grounds, everyone did their jobs to perfection.

"There's a secret make-out room on the side of the gym." I heard a familiar voice say behind me. I was off my game. I hadn't smelled him this time.

I turned around to see Philip standing behind me with his half smile on his face. "Make-out room? What makes you think I want to go with you to a secret make-out room?" I said as I tried to relax the nerves working overtime inside of me.

Philip's half smile evolved into a full out smile across his beautiful face. "Is that all you think about MJ? Making out with me? Because I was suggesting it would be a great place for you to hide until the reporters left."

I felt a little grateful and suspicious at the same time. "What makes you think I want to hide from the news people?"

He leaned closer to me. My skin tingled as I felt his breath on my bare neck. "You and I both know exactly what you want." Philip leaned back from me. "I ran into Olivia on her way to run interference. Billy is waiting for you in the gym. He'll show you how to get in the room. I'll come and get you after the news crew leaves."

Philip walked away without saying another word.

I made my way to the gym, while kids stared at me as I walked by them. I wanted to blend into the human world, not stand out as a hero. I was going to have to learn how to keep out of the malicious things humans did to each other.

Billy anxiously waited for me on the far side of the bleachers in the gym. He looked around to make sure no one was looking at us before he waved for me to come towards him. I thought he was being a little melodramatic, but played along as I crept closer to him.

He didn't say anything as he led me under the bleachers to a door sitting in the wall. He took out a key, and unlocked the door. He led me into the room, before locking the door behind us.

I looked around at the secret make-out room. The damn room even had a few mattresses stacked up in the center of it. I couldn't believe the faculty didn't know anything about it.

Billy stood in front of me pointing out the different areas as if he was showing off an apartment for a potential buyer. "Over there is a restroom. Over there is the old couch someone brought in a few years ago. And of course, right there is the bed."

I looked around the room. It was like a little apartment inside of the school. It freaked me out. "So Billy, where is the hidden camera?"

He stared at me with confusion etched across his face. "What?"

"You're not going to get me to believe you guys don't have a hidden camera in here to tape your little adventures with young impressionable freshman girls."

Billy stared at me for a moment. Then his eyes lit up with excitement. Obviously, I had been wrong about the hidden camera, but Billy loved the idea of it.

I stepped closer to him. I wasn't Sophia, but I hoped the rumors about me would allow me to intimidate him a little. "Don't even think about it. If I learn you put a camera in this room, I'm going to make sure you pay severely for it."

Billy placed his arms in the air in a gesture of giving up. "Don't worry. I'm too much of a gentleman for that." I didn't believe him at all, but I didn't feel like threatening him anymore. "Are you okay in here alone?"

I nodded yes. He gave the room one last look over; I guessed he tried to figure out the best place to put a camera. He then left me in the room by myself.

I sat on the couch. It felt comfortable, for a couch used for things I didn't want to know anything about.

About an hour later, I heard a slight knock at the secret make out room door. I slowly made my way towards it. When I opened the door, Philip stood on the other side.

"The reporters are gone for now. I told them you weren't really there. That you had left before it all went down. I think they bought it." He didn't enter the room as he told me what had happened in the Principal's office with the reporters. "I think it's safe for you to return to class if you want."

I followed him out from under the bleachers, back to the hallway. I'd missed an entire class while I waited inside that room. I would have to deal with that later, but for the rest of the day, I spent it listening to people congratulating Philip and me as being heroes.

Even though the reporters bought Philip's story of only him being involved with taking Brian down, none of the kids did. Mostly because Olivia wouldn't stop telling people I'd been there. She made it seem like I didn't want to talk to the press because of something in my past. After Olivia got through spreading her story around school, my rep had increased even more. All I could do for the rest of the day was squirm as more and more girls stared at me in awe.

NINE

After the last school bell rang, Angela, Olivia and I waited outside for Vincent to pick us up. I'd allowed Olivia to talk me into inviting her back to our estate. I called Vincent to make sure it would be okay. At first, he seemed to be against the idea, but after a few moments of what I could only guess were deep thoughts, he agreed to Olivia coming by for a little while. I hated having to ask his permission. Unfortunately, I was on thin ice with my family. I had to play it safe for now. At least until whatever was going on with the Nightlings was over.

The thought, of Olivia being in my house with my family, sent shivers up my sweating spine. I didn't plan on her being there when the others awoke. I would think of some reason for her to have to leave before nightfall. She seemed excited about visiting my house. Everyone at school had always wondered about the Vigano estate. Another piece of gossip I'd learned in my two days of attending high school. I'd thought Angela would be the one that stood out at school, but after all the rumors about me were spread around, I'd become the Vigano everyone wanted to know about.

"You know, we can give you girls a ride home?" I heard Philip say from behind me. This time, I blamed not smelling him first on being distracted by Olivia gossiping to Angela beside me, about me. The new rumor had something to do with experimental drugs. Not party drugs, but something like drugs created to cure ADD that had gone wrong, leaving me with super strength and a quick temper. If only!

I turned to see Philip standing behind us, along with Billy.

I glanced over to my side to see a forced smile across Angela's face, and boredom across Olivias'. No way would I allow Philip to come anywhere near our estate. Olivia being there was one thing, but Philip – no way in hell! I had to play it cool, without being too dismissive. "Don't think my father would approve of two guys dropping us off."

The smile left Angela's face, being replaced with relief.

"I can't believe a girl that would take on four guys in a dark alley would be afraid of her father." Philip said as he strolled closer to me.

I hated the way he looked at me. I hated the way he smiled at me. I hated the confidence oozing from him as he stood near me. He felt he had me in his twisted little perverted grasp... the thing I hated the most, is that he was almost right.

I stepped back. "You don't know my father."

"Fathers like Philip. He has a gift when it comes to charming the parental obstacles." Billy stopped in front of Angela.

Angela awkwardly looked away from Billy, while Olivia's large brown eyes glazed with interest at the scene in front of her. I could see a new rumor forming in her beautiful eyes. I wondered if the girl hung around me because I provided front-page material at Lexington High. I would have to deal with that later. I didn't want her to see something at home that wasn't meant for the outside world.

For a moment, I found myself taking in Philip's scent. He smelled so good to me. Again, I couldn't tell if it was my hormones working in overdrive, or if it had something to do with me being so close to Crossing Over? Either way, I needed to learn how to contain myself when I was around him.

I placed my hands in my pockets, while trying to stand in a manner that would project indifference. "Not even worth the headache."

He laughed. I could tell he enjoyed the challenge that was me. From what I'd gathered from the kids around school, Philip normally got what he wanted when it came to girls without much of a challenge. He was a born charmer, along with his supposed vast amount of money everyone said he had, it never took him long to secure another conquest. He thought I would be no exception, but the more I proved him wrong, the more he wanted me. "It's just a ride MJ, what's the harm in that?"

"My father seeing me getting out of a car with two strangers."

"He really wouldn't see it," Angela added to the conversation. "I mean he'd be asleep."

"He hadn't been sleeping well lately. He'd know, trust me." I said as I took my hands from out of my pockets, and wrapped my arms around my waist.

Philip started to say something when the black BMW drove up behind us. Vincent got out of the car and walked around to where Angela, Olivia and I stood. He looked Philip and Billy up and down. I could tell he was sizing them up. He was trying to determine if they were a threat or not.

Even though Vincent was neither a Dayling nor a Nightling, he had developed almost supernatural skills when it came to sizing people up. If he felt something was wrong about a person, even if my father or none of the others picked it up, my father would cut off all contact with that person until they were thoroughly vetted. Normally, Vincent's feelings were right. So we trusted him with our lives.

Vincent turned to Angela, Olivia and me. "You young ladies ready?"

We shook our heads yes before we got into the car.

Philip took a step towards the BMW, but stopped after Vincent gave him a look that would have sent shivers down the devil's spin.

Vincent got back in the car, and without a word pulled away from the school towards our estate.

Angela and I sat in the back of the BMW in silence, while Olivia sat in the front passenger seat. I could tell from how her brown eyes shimmered as she glanced at Vincent, she was crushing real hard for him.

Vincent didn't notice the enthralled teenage super model sitting beside him. He was too busy glancing in the rearview mirror towards me. I didn't need to be able to read minds to know exactly what he was thinking about.

"What?" I asked.

"So who was that young man?" He said while looking at me in the mirror.

"A guy from school. You do know guys go to school right? Shockingly with today's grammar, but they do."

Vincent stared at me for a quick moment. He then returned his eyes to the road. I sat in the back seat for the rest of the ride in silence. Olivia continued to glance at Vincent while he ignored her. And Angela gazed out her side window obviously contemplating something. I didn't know what was going on in her head. And to be truthful, at the moment I didn't really care. I had things to figure out for myself.

Like what the hell was I doing with Philip? If I did decide to get in a relationship with him, it could only last for less than three weeks. Once I Crossed Over, it would be impossible for us to be together. The blood lust would be too much for my new body to handle. I would want him in every way, which could end up getting him killed.

We pulled up to the estate. I jumped out of the car, grabbed Olivia by the arm, and pulled her into the mansion and up to my room before Vincent could ask me more questions about Philip. I passed my little brother as I walked up the stairs. He grunted at me – his usual greeting – then continued walking with his headphones on. I could hear the latest Disturbed song blasting from his iPod.

I flopped on my bed, lay on my back, and stared up at the ceiling. I thought about my father. The unusual stress that had consumed his face the last time he was in my room. Something big was going on. Something the others were trying to keep from us Daylings. I wanted to help. No matter whatever it was, I wanted to be a part of it.

Can't lie, a part of me would rather spend time trying to figure out what was going on with my father than trying to understand my feelings for Philip. I would have to enlist Angela in my plans. I still didn't know what was up with her in the car. I would talk to her about that later. But first I needed to get some sleep. I never knew high school was so damn boring. I had to fight to stay awake a few times during the day. If it wasn't for Philip sitting next to me looking so cute, I might have missed out on the exciting mating rituals of eastern pigeons in biology class.

I got out of my bed, walked to the bathroom and splashed water over my face, trying to shake off the grogginess I felt. I had to know what was going on with my father and the others. The best way to investigate them would be when they were all unable to move.

I finally remembered Olivia had been with me when I

walked out of the bathroom. She'd sat leisurely on one of my leather couches. She glanced around my room, obviously trying to remember every detail to report back to the masses at school. Maybe inviting her over had been a mistake. I would have to figure out a way to get her to leave quicker than I'd first thought.

I walked over to the couch in front of Olivia. I flopped on the couch as I sighed. "So what do you think?" I asked as I waved my hand around the room.

She continued to take the room in for a moment. She then focused on me. "Not what I'd imagined."

I released a slight laugh. "What? You thought I had weapons along the walls? A dojo type feel to the room?"

Olivia crossed her long legs in front of her. "Yeah." We both laughed. "So what's with your driver?"

I frowned at her. "Don't go there. Nothing good is there."

She smirked at me. "He's sexy. You got to admit that."

I rolled my eyes. "Vincent is attractive. He's a good-looking man. Sexy is a whole other thing. I'm not going there."

Olivia allowed her long thin frame to sink into my couch. She tried to look innocent as she looked around my room again. "What about Philip? You think he's sexy?"

I rolled my eyes again. I'd been interrogated by centuries old creatures of the night. Olivia had no chance at breaking me. "I think Philip thinks he's sexy. I think a lot of other people think that as well. Do you think he's sexy?"

She focused her brown eyes on me. "I think you two would make a sexy couple." I stared to say something when I heard her phone ringing. Some hip-hop song I didn't recognize escaped from her pocket, before she pulled out her iPhone, and answered it. "Hello? Yeah I'm with Haven. Her room is pretty cool, not at all Batcavey."

I tried to ignore the fact of her sitting across from me, gossiping about me to someone on the phone. I turned from Olivia, to see Raffaele staring at her through my door. I quickly got up and walked towards him. "Need something?"

Raffaele reluctantly pulled his eyes from the teen super model sitting on my couch. "Introduce me."

I laughed. "You really can't be serious. Goodbye Raffaele." I closed the door in his face. When I turned around, Olivia was on her feet. "What's up?"

"Sorry, got to go. But I would love to come back and hang out with you another time."

"No prob. I'll walk you out." I said as I reopened my bedroom door. Raffaele had left, and was nowhere to be seen as I led Olivia down our stairs, to the front door. Obviously, she'd seen all she wanted to see. I wondered how she would embellish everything at school? "Do you need a ride home?" I asked as I opened up the front door.

She shook her head no. "Got it covered. See you tomorrow at school." And then Olivia was gone. I watched her for a moment as she made her way down our walkway, while pulling her iPhone back out, and talking to someone on it. I strained my ears, barely making out something like, *girl they're loaded. And everyone here is gorgeous. Plus, I got this vibe that they're all scared of Haven. It's crazy.*

I closed the door with a sigh. I made my way to Angela's room and tried to open the door, but it was locked. Anybody else, that wouldn't have made my spidey senses tingle, but Angela never locked her door.

I knocked on the door. I had to wait a few minutes before she opened it. She looked a little nervous as she moved out of the way to let me in.

"What up Haven?" Angela had a bit of uneasiness in her voice. "Where's Olivia?"

I looked around the room for any type of clues, wondering if she was hiding a guy under the bed or in the closet. Slowly I made my way towards her bed. "Left. She got a call from someone and had to leave. You know Angela, if you have a secret, you can always tell me right?" I stopped at the foot of Angela's bed. I made sure I didn't take my eyes from hers.

She tried to force a smile across her face. "What are you talking about?"

I quickly dropped to my knees and looked under her bed. Nothing was there except a few shoes and a box of thong underwear Sophia had gotten for Angela on her fourteenth birthday. I was the only other person that knew about the inappropriate gift. I might one day use that if Sophia continued to harass me.

When I looked from under the bed back at Angela, she frowned at me. "What are you doing?"

I stood from the floor. "You've been acting weird every

since we left school. What's going on?"

She walked over to her bed. She sat on the edge and continued to frown at me. "Why do you think everything is your business?"

"Whatever. But I told you about the human I got the hots for." I said before I sat on the bed next to Angela. "Anyway, I didn't come in here to find out what's going on with you. Have you noticed how strange the Elders have been acting?"

"You mean the closed meeting last night? They've done that before."

"Yeah, but my dad was acting like he was distracted. I mean that's the only way I could explain why I didn't get killed for staying out all night."

Angela turned towards me. Her face no longer bore a frown. "Yeah, and when they sent everyone searching for you, it was like they were terrified something had happened to you. Like they were frightened about something."

I tried to remember the last time I'd seen my father scared. And to be truthful, I never had. Even when Uncle Myron tried to push for more power, my father would always stay cool and collected. He never showed emotions during times of stress. But the other night, when he told me that he missed my mother, he was definitely showing emotions.

I stood from the bed. "Okay, are you going to help me find out what's going on?"

Angela looked down at the floor, her telltale sign again. "Give me a few hours alone. Then I'll help."

"Fine," I said before I walked out of her room. I had something to take my mind off of Philip. I planned on finding out the Nightlings' secret. I figured the only person I could ask, that didn't have the ability to rip me into little pieces, sat downstairs in our kitchen.

Normally Vincent wouldn't be over while the Nightlings slept. So when he headed towards the kitchen when we first made it back to the estate, I figured he knew something about what was going on.

I found Vincent and my brother sitting at the kitchen table talking. My brother wore an oversized Florida Marlins jersey, with jeans and tennis shoes.

As I got closer to the table, I could make out bits of their conversation. They were talking baseball, a subject I knew nothing about. Batting averages and on base percentages meant as much to me as an Intel Processor to the Amish.

As soon as I stood in front of the table, my brother cut his eyes towards me, picked up his half eaten bowl of cheerios, and walked away after mumbling later to Vincent.

"So what did you do to him?" Vincent asked as he looked up at me.

I sat in the seat my brother had vacated. "His hatred of me is embedded in his genes. When he was born, he looked at me and frowned."

Vincent laughed. His deep blue eyes reflected in the kitchen light. I had to admit it, he was truly gorgeous, but I wouldn't call him sexy like Philip. I shook the thoughts of Philip out of my head. This wasn't about him. I'd have all day tomorrow to pine over him.

"Why did your friend leave?" Vincent asked.

"Something came up. You know how your kind is. Always on the move." I sat up in the seat. "If I asked you a question, would you give me a straight answer?"

Vincent placed the half eaten sandwich on the plate in front of him. He wiped a few crumbs from his mouth. "Depends on the question."

"Something is going on with my father and the other Nightlings. I want to know what?"

He sat back in his seat. His blue eyes focused on me with enough intensity to burn a hole in my face. "Wrong question. Whatever your father is dealing with is for him to deal with. Stay out of this Haven. You will only make it worse."

I wasn't going to give up that easy. "Make what worse?"

Vincent leaned towards me. His eyes were still burning with intensity. "Lets talk about your little friend at school. What's going on with you and Philip Flowers?"

I almost jumped from the chair. How in the world did he know Philip's name? I felt so confused and shocked I must have sat with my mouth open for a few minutes before I could gather my thoughts. But even after I finally closed my mouth, I couldn't find my voice. It took all the energy inside of my body to force out, "how do you know about Philip?"

"Did you really think your father would send you and Angela to school without someone watching both of you?" Vincent reached in his pocket and pulled out his iPhone. He pushed a few buttons before flipping the front screen towards me. "Can you explain these?"

My mouth fell back open. I couldn't believe it. The screen slowly went through a slide show of Philip and me at school. There were pictures of us at lunch, in different classes, in the library. All of them had one thing in common, it was clear we were flirting with each other in each shot. And then came the money shot, a picture of me getting in a yellow jeep with Philip and leaving school.

My shock quickly changed to anger. I couldn't believe my father would have me spied on. It was a complete invasion of privacy. "How dare he? How dare you help him? Who I talk to is no one's business but mine. And where I go during the day is also no one's business. I was back before dark."

Vincent placed the iPhone in his pocket. He nonchalantly leaned back in his chair and grabbed his sandwich. He took a bite of his ham and cheese on wheat as he stared at me. "You're his eldest child, the future leader of this family. He had to make sure you were safe these last few weeks before you Crossed Over."

"Safe from what? High school boys? Remember I'm a Dayling, I'm stronger than anybody at that school." I said as the anger continued to build inside of me.

He slowly placed the sandwich back on his plate, before wiping his mouth again. "Maybe so, maybe not. You still haven't answered my question, what is going on between you and this high school boy?"

I jumped from the chair. "None of your business."

Vincent looked up at me. "I've told you, your father has a lot of things on his mind right now. I would like to deal with this without his involvement. But that depends on you."

I wanted to take a swing at his smug face. I could take him out without breaking a sweat. He was a fighter, everyone who worked for my father who knew about us were. It didn't matter though; I was way stronger and faster than him. It wouldn't take but a few moments to clean that smugness from his face.

The wonderful thoughts of beating him unconscious slowly left my mind, if I touched Vincent for doing what my father asked him to do, I would never be allowed to leave the estate again. The bastard knew I couldn't touch him. "He's just a guy. I thought he was cool, and he thought I was cool. We went for a ride in his cool jeep. Nothing more." I forced out through clenched teeth.

Vincent folded his arms in front of himself, as he looked me up and down. "Then why are you getting so defensive? And why did my source tell me it looked as if you two knew each other when you met at school? And what's this about you breaking some kid's ribs?"

"Who is this spy of yours? Obviously they didn't see what they thought they saw. And I have no idea about some kid getting his ribs broken." I said as I glared at Vincent.

"I'm only trying to protect you Haven. The more you lie, the harder it will be for me to do that." He said with an even tone.

I lost it. Before Vincent or even I knew what had happened, I had him pinned against the wall snarling at him. I wouldn't have fangs until after I Crossed Over, but that didn't mean I couldn't bite a plug out of his neck. Surprisingly, Vincent didn't seem at the least bit nervous. He relaxed in my grip while gazing into my eyes. I didn't see fear or anger or any emotions in his blue eyes, just emptiness.

I released him after I gathered myself. He straightened out his clothes as he sat back in the chair. "Now, since you've gotten that out of the way, shall we continue?"

"I don't care about you or your spy. You can show those pictures to my father and tell him whatever you want," I said before I turned around and stormed out of the kitchen.

TEN

I stormed out of the house, down the driveway, and through the large gates. I started up Bannerman Road with fumes escaping from my head. Each day felt hotter. My skin boiled from the heat. I could feel beads of sweat rolling down my back trying to keep my skin cooled off, it didn't work. The heat wave made it harder to breathe. I'd heard weather reporters saying to bring in all pets from this type of heat. I still couldn't believe there were people who didn't believe in global warming. It was obvious to me as I walked in the scorching sun.

I wanted to turn around and sling Vincent against another wall. I wanted to go back to the house and rip him apart. My mind became clouded with violent desires. It was the change growing inside me. I would have to learn how to control my anger.

It wasn't like I didn't have something to be angry about. I couldn't believe my father had that wannabe Calvin Klein model keeping tabs on me. I couldn't believe he had a spy at school watching me. I wondered who the spy was. For a moment I thought about Angela. She knew about Philip and me, but she knew everything from me saving him in the alley that night and staying at the hospital with him. If she were telling on me, it would have been a whole other type of conversation. She was acting strange, but I didn't think it was guilt from ratting me out. No, Vincent had someone else watching me at the school.

All I wanted was three weeks of peace before I turned into a blood drinking, sun allergic, mind reading, ill-tempered immortal. My father and his pretty boy lackey had to go and ruin it. I wanted to scream at the top of my lungs, but I was using all the energy I had to move my legs through this pounding heat.

My shirt stuck to my body. My jeans seemed to have shrunk two sizes. And my feet felt as if I was walking across a trail of hot coal. The only thing keeping me moving was the anger inside of me. No matter how much I tried to calm myself, each time I thought about Vincent my anger would return ten times worst.

I remembered the first time I met Mr. Calvin Klein. I was twelve, running around our old house in LA playing with Angela. He and my father were in our study talking about stocks and bonds and other business deals I didn't know anything about. My father invited me into the room to meet our human liaison, Vincent Mitchell. I thought he was the most beautiful person I'd ever seen. His deep blue eyes kept me frozen in place as he smiled at me.

Fast forward five years later, and now I wish I could stick something through those blue eyes.

I'd been so lost in my thoughts of killing Vincent; I didn't hear the car creeping behind me at first. Normally I could tell when I was being followed. But this time I didn't see the black Explorer until it came right beside me.

For a moment I thought it was Vincent or one of his men, so I debated making a run for it. My legs were feeling like bags of cement on account of the blazing heat. I didn't know how fast I could move. I thought I could at least out run a human even in my weakened state.

The SUV pulled closer to the sidewalk. The back window of the Explorer slowly retracted. I readied myself to at least curse out whomever Vincent had sent for me, even if I wasn't in any shape to make a run for it. But to my surprise, sitting in the back seat wasn't one of Vincent's men, but someone I hadn't seen in a long time.

"Isn't it a little too hot outside for a midday stroll, *Lis*?" I heard the guy sitting in the back of the SUV say in is French accent.

I froze for a moment as I stared into his dark blue eyes. His long blond hair was pulled back into a ponytail revealing his thin beautiful face. His freakishly white teeth were gleaming in the sunlight as he smiled at me. All I could do was whisper his name. "Sébastien?"

He opened the door of the SUV. He didn't make a move to get out, but moved over so I could get in.

Once I climbed into the Explorer and closed the door behind me, he motioned for the driver to go.

Sébastien then turned to me. "Would you like for me to turn the air up? You must be near death in this unbelievable heat."

I slowly shook my head no. The last time I'd seen Sébastien de LaVigne we were both fourteen-years-old playing on his estate located on the outskirts of Bordeaux, France. He was obnoxious, egotistical, and plain and simply a pain to be around. But I didn't remember him being so gorgeous.

"You must be wondering why I am here?" Sébastien said as he sat back in his seat.

It took me a moment to gather myself. I wondered if my sudden obsession with beautiful guys had something to do with me being so close to Crossing Over. I blamed every new feeling in my life on me getting closer to becoming a Nightling. "Kinda, I guess, yeah."

"I was sent to make sure your family was safe."

"Why wouldn't they be?"

Sébastien's blue eyes squinted at me. He then glanced towards the driver, who looked back at us after I'd asked what seemed to be an odd question to them. "Surely your family has heard of what's going on around the world? We are all in danger."

Even though I'd said I didn't want the air to be turned up, the driver had turned it up anyway. My body was quickly cooling off, clearing my mind enough for me to think. Something was going on with the Elders back at home. Obviously I'd been right about it being something big. They'd chosen to leave us Daylings out of it, but it seemed Sébastien's family had informed him of the danger. The only way I would learn what the hell was happening would be by getting the information from Sébastien.

"What danger are we all in?" I asked as I moved my sticky hair from in front of my face.

Sébastien glanced back at the driver before he turned back to me. "*Mes* excuses, I'd thought you were informed on the situation."

"I guess you're going to do that now."

He slowly shook his head no. "I'm sorry, but if your family hasn't told you, then it isn't my place to do so."

I leaned closer to him. I stared deep into his exotic blue eyes. "When the time comes, I'm going to be the head of my family, and you're going to be the head of yours. Don't you think we should start working together now? So there won't be any hard feelings when that time comes."

Sébastien started laughing. "*Mes excuses Madame Lis*, I would never want to make an enemy of you." He looked at the driver. "Continue to drive around for awhile, while I talk with *Madame Lis*."

The driver shook his head in agreement as he turned the Explorer down Thomasville Road.

Sébastien then turned back to me. "Do you know about the Mântuitors?"

I slight shiver passed through my body. I'd heard of the Mântuitors all right. They were the secret group of humans who knew we existed and wanted to end our existence.

The way the story about them had been told to me was like this: In the early 12th century, a crazed Nightling was discovered by a group of peasants in a small village. The Nightling had been feeding on the local young girls of the village, and had been captured by some of the girl's family.

The discovery of the Nightling was passed along to a Cistercian monk. The name of the monk was never said, but he informed a Cistercian abbot, Bernard of Clairvaux.

Bernard of Clairvaux had a strong place in The Knights Templar, and commissioned that a separate group of Templars be formed to handle this new threat. And from that, The Holy Sect of Mântuitor was created to hunt down and destroy all of the blood-drinking creatures of the night.

For centuries, the Mântuitors tracked down Nightlings and killed them. They discovered the Nighling's weaknesses. They even discovered the existence of Daylings. They live for one thing and one thing only, to rid the world of all blood-drinkers.

The shiver continued throughout my body as I thought of all the horrible stories about the Mântuitors. But they had hunted my kind since the 12th century; I couldn't understand why everyone was all of a sudden so scared of them.

"The Mântuitors have been a threat to us for a long time, so why is everyone so jumpy now?" I asked as I refocused on Sébastien's blue eyes.

"Someone has betrayed us. The leaders of the Mântuitors know about all the families. They know all of our names, and most of our whereabouts." Sébastien said with an even tone.

I suddenly realized why my father looked so stressed out. Our sworn enemies knew who we were and where we were. I couldn't understand why we weren't making a run for it. A panic began to build inside of me.

I could feel Sébastien's soft hand graze my cheek. He was close to Crossing Over just like me. He was less than two weeks away, and I could feel the power growing inside of him as his skin caressed mine. I was right about him and I one day being the leaders of our families. I couldn't freak out in front of him. I had to prove my father wrong for not trusting me with what was going on.

Even though I didn't want to, I moved my face from Sébastien's hand. "So why isn't everyone relocating? If the Mântuitors know where we are?"

Sébastien pulled his hand down to his lap. "Some families have tried to relocate. Some of them were still found and destroyed. We have no idea as to who is working with the Mântuitors and what all they know. So everyone is being cautious about what to do next."

I looked away from him for a moment, needing to work out everything in my head. There were a few things I needed from Sébastien before I returned to my father and confronted him with the information. "How do we know all of this? How do we know we've been betrayed?"

"We have a few spies in the Holy Sect. Even some of them have lost their lives warning us about the new danger. Whoever is working with them knows all of our secrets."

I turned back to Sébastien. His blue eyes were glowing in the daylight. His flesh had already begun to change. It looked more porcelain than usual, almost as if it had started to harden, even though it still felt soft. "If everyone is a suspect, then why are you here to see my family? How do you know it wasn't one of us?"

"Our families have gone back for centuries. Your father and my father have been best friends for nearly five hundred years. If we cannot trust each other, then there is no hope for the future of our kind at all." He said without taking his eyes from me.

I couldn't tell if he was trying to trick me or assure me. The problem that he could be doing either started to become a little much for me to handle. I needed to go home and talk with my father. I needed to find out exactly what he knew, and why the hell he hadn't told me.

Sébastien's father had trusted him with the truth. Maybe I'd been wrong, maybe Sébastien was going to be the future head of his family, but I was not. Maybe Franklin would skip me in succession. Maybe that's why I'd been kept out of the loop.

I couldn't feel sorry for myself while I sat in the back of the Explorer with Sébastien. I would have to ask my father if what I felt was true, no matter the answer.

"Can you take me home now?" I forced out while trying to quell my emotions.

"Of course," Sébastien turned to the driver. "To the Vigano estate Simon."

The driver, a human named Simon, drove back to the mansion. I didn't say another word to Sébastien as we rode back to the estate. He didn't try to speak to me as well; I guessed he could feel the pain growing inside of me. I couldn't believe my father wouldn't tell me something as serious as this was going on. I couldn't believe they would keep this from the next in line.

As the black Explorer pulled up to my front gate, I saw an unfamiliar car waiting outside of it. It was a black Chrysler XR, with tented windows and a Florida State Seminoles tag on the front of it.

Sébastien turned to me after he noticed the car. "A friend?"

I shook my head no. "Never seen that car before in my life."

"We will stop here. Simon and I will check it out." Sébastien said as the Explorer began to slow down.

I'm not brave by any meaning of the word. I took on those guys in the alley because I knew I could beat them, but taking on trained Mântuitors was a whole other thing. Yet I wasn't about to be the stereotypical damsel who needs to be protected. Sébastien was just as young as me with the same strength and speed. He was only a week older than me. If I wanted to prove I would be able to lead my family when the time came, I couldn't allow someone else to fight my battles for me. "No, keep going. We'll see who that is to-gether."

Simon glanced in the mirror towards Sébastien. Sé-bastien turned to me. "You do not have to do this."

I continued to stare at the car. It didn't seem like a ride I would imagine a secret sect of vampire hunters to roll in. "I'm fine."

Sébastien motioned for Simon to continue.

We pulled along side the Chrysler. Simon made sure Sé-bastien's side was next to the little sports car.

When the Chrysler's driver's side door opened, and the driver stepped out, my heart almost leapt out of my chest.

"Philip," I gasped as my spiky haired prince leaned against his car staring at Sébastien.

I opened the door of the Explorer and jumped out of the SUV. I quickly made my way towards the Chrysler as Philip and Sébastien continued to stare at each other without speaking.

I found myself standing in between their staring contest. I turned to Sébastien first. "Thanks for the ride, and the in-formation. Are you going to stay here while you're in town?"

Sébastien's blue eyes seemed to be filled with anger for a moment. Then they softened as he focused on me. "If your family wouldn't mind."

"Of course not," I said before I walked to our gate and punched in the code to open it, then moved out of the way for Simon to drive Sébastien in.

As the SUV started to pass me, Sébastien leaned his head out of the window. "Are you sure you do not need my assistance?"

"I'm fine. I'll see you inside." I said.

I watched the Explorer slowly make its way inside of my family's estate before the gate closed behind it.

I turned to Philip, who continued to lean against his car with his half smile on his face. "Old boyfriend?" He asked.

"How did you find out where I lived?" I asked as I walked towards his car. "And how many cars do you have?"

"First, how I found out where you lived? I got my sources. Remember I'm the star athlete." Philip winked at me. "Second, you'll have to come by my house and check out how many cars I have for yourself." He wore a black tank top, with extra long mesh shorts and basketball shoes. He looked as if he was on his way to play ball. "Now, you still haven't answered my question."

I stopped in front of him. "None of your business. Anyway, I thought you liked girls with boyfriends."

He laughed. The sound of him laughing brought back all those warm feelings I had for him. The sound of him drove my senses crazy. I stood in the smothering heat and took him all in again. I could fully smell his scent now. I could almost taste him on my tongue.

"What's going through that head of yours?" He asked, bringing me out of my moment of fantasizing.

I stood beside him. "Is there any reason you're here Phil?"

He leaned his head back as he said 'ouch'. His chest flexed a little under his tank top. His arms were also surprisingly muscular for his thin frame. Actually, his entire body looked pretty chiseled. "Low blow, MJ. Low blow." He stepped from his car, and stood directly in front of me. He gazed into my eyes, obviously trying to entice me. "Just wanted to see if you were busy tonight? Billy's having a party, wanted to know if you were up for coming and protecting me from all the angry boyfriends that are going to be there?"

If it wasn't for everything I'd learned from Sébastien, I'd have melted right there in front of him, but instead I had a lot on my mind. "I don't know. Family issues have come up. I might be busy tonight. So you might have to protect yourself from all the jilted boyfriends looking for you."

Philip reached behind me for his car's door handle. Our bodies brushed against each other as he pulled the door open, forcing me to move forward. "If you change your mind, you know where I'll be."

I watched as Philip got into his Chrysler, turned on the little sports car, and then sped away with dirt spitting up in the air. Any other day, I would have jumped in the car beside him, but I had to talk with my father.

I punched in the code to the gate, and then walked in.

ELEVEN

I walked inside of the house. The cool air instantly began its work on my skin. I stood at the bottom of the stairs for a moment to give my body time to fully enjoy the cold air.

It didn't take me long to hear them talking in the Oriental sitting room.

I walked into the room. Vincent and Sébastien stood by the piano talking. Vincent saw me, and immediately stopped. Sébastien looked up with frustration in his beautiful blue eyes.

I walked over to them and stood in front of Sébastien. "I think we should go talk with my father."

"He didn't want you involved with this Haven." Vincent said.

"Too late for that," I said as I turned to walk out of the room. "You coming Sébastien?"

Neither of them said a word, but both of them followed me through the library to the lower level. I made my way to my father's chamber just like I'd done before. Except this time I had more on my mind than staying out all night and my attraction for a teenage boy. Our world could be crumbling around us. Not to mention, my father obviously didn't trust me enough to let me in on it.

I opened my father's chamber door without knocking. To say my hurt feelings were rapidly turning into anger would be a major understatement. I was ready to tear into my father and whoever else thought I was too weak to be let in on the impending disaster.

My father lay still in his bed as before. His eyes instantly opened as soon as we entered the room. Vincent stood behind me, while Sébastien stood a safe distance away. Even though he knew my father couldn't move during the day, I could still sense the fear coming from him.

"We need to talk." I blurted out as I stood to the side of my father's bed.

His powerful dark shimmering eyes slowly moved towards me. Fear began to form inside of me, but I pushed it away as I stared into his eyes. "Is that how you greet your father?" He forced out through clinched teeth.

"Is keeping life-altering secrets how you treat your daughter?" I asked as I glared at him.

My father's eyes rolled over Vincent, and then Sébastien. The blue-eyed heir to the de LaVigne family shrunk a little as he stood by the door. "Yes. If those secrets were not her concern."

I took a step closer to the bed. My footing had become quieter. The predator in me slowly crawled to the surface. "Not my concern? The Mântuitors are killing our kind. One of us is helping them. If I'm supposed to one day lead this family, shouldn't I be involved with this?"

"You said you wanted to live the last three weeks of your Dayling life as a normal human girl, mio fiore dolce. I didn't want to take that from you. I figured we would be safe until you Crossed Over, then I would tell you what was going on."

My heart began to calm in my chest. Even though we were in grave danger, and there was no telling what my father would do to Sébastien for telling me the truth, I felt relieved to find out my father didn't keep everything from me because he didn't trust me. He had tried to honor my wish to live as a human for three weeks.

I pulled the side chair closer to his bed. Even it felt lighter than it did the last time I'd been in my father's chamber. I sat in the chair, and gently placed my left hand over his right hand, doing my best not to move it. "I know now dad. And I'm glad I do. I can help with this."

My father forced a smile across his porcelain face. His eyes then focused on Sébastien again. "Sébastien, come closer."

Sébastien slowly walked towards the bed. He held his head down as he crept across the chamber. He didn't make a sound as he stopped at the foot of my father's bed, unable to look at my father. "I'm sorry, sir. I didn't know she wasn't to be told."

"What is done is done. You two will one day run the most powerful families in our society. I'm glad you're finding a way to work together now. But first we must figure out how to save all of our kind from this new threat." My father focused his eyes on Vincent. "Any new news from our source inside the Mântuitors?"

Vincent stepped closer. He kept his head slightly bowed in a sign of respect. "I'm sorry to say sir, the Duncan family have all been destroyed."

My father let out a muffled sound of pain. Sébastien looked at Vincent with disbelief. I couldn't control the emotions working their way through my body. I'd known the Duncan family for as long as I've lived. They were as close to us as the de LaVigne family. I couldn't stop myself from thinking about little Lucile Duncan. She was three years younger than me; with ambitions beyond being a blood-drinking fiend like the rest of us. She wanted to help the human world become better. She didn't care about the blood lust that came with Crossing Over. She felt it could be controlled long enough for us to live among a large number of them without losing ourselves. I brushed her off as being a naive child. She couldn't save the world for Nightling and human kind. Now, she would never get the chance to prove me wrong.

I looked down at my father. I could see tears building in his eyes. Then I saw nothing. It was as if he'd pushed his pain completely out of his body. "Sébastien?"

Sébastien looked down at my father. "Yes sir."

"What is your father's plan?"

"Actually, he sent me here to find out yours. We can't trust using phones. They might have them tapped. So from now on we must have face to face talks." Sébastien said as he began to regain his composure.

My father stared up at the painting above his bed. "You should go back. Tell your father I believe we should combine our families for better protection. You and your family should come here and live with us until we can handle this."

"Do you think that is wise sir? Having the two most powerful families in the same place might become an irresistible target for the Mântuitors." Vincent said.

I had to admit, a part of me agreed with him. If we all stayed away from each other, some of us could probably make it out of this alive, but if we gathered together as a single group, we'd be playing into their hands. But there was an upside to it.

My father's eyes moved back to me. "What do you think Haven?"

I was taken off guard for a moment. Unable to believe my father had asked me for advice. I felt honored and scared out of my mind at the same time. "I agree with you dad. It's risky, but we would have a better chance defending ourselves if we're together. Taking out two families at the same time might be a little much for the Mântuitors."

My father's eyes rolled back to Sébastien. "It's settled. Advise your father of our plan. Get his perspective of it."

"From some of the things I've heard him say, I believe he's thinking the same as you." Sébastien said. "I'll go home at once. I'll have the other Daylings and our human associates make the preparations for my family's journey as quickly as possible."

"If there is nothing else, I would like to speak with my daughter for a moment please." My father said before Sébastien and Vincent bowed their heads and walked out of the chamber.

I sat in the chair next to my father in silence. I stared at his pale and almost lifeless face. I wanted to ask him again when the last time he'd fed was, but I figured this business with the Mântuitors was taking everything he had.

I've only spoken to my father during the day on a few occasions. Each time I find myself disturbed by his helplessness. During the night, he was one of the most powerful Nightlings ever. Not only was he 6'4 and over two hundred pounds of muscles, but he had the face of a warrior.

He and Sébastien's father were the only two of our kind that had fought in a human war. They both were soldiers in Fifth Italian War with France, which meant they were on the opposite sides of the war.

My father had convinced my grandfather, Gareth Rota-Vigano, to allow him to fight in the war before he Crossed Over. My grandmother didn't approve of it, but grandpa Gareth gave his blessings to his sixteen-year-old heir.

My father told me about the first time he'd taken human

life. He was assigned to the front lines. Men were dying all around him, French and Imperials alike. The blow of a battle-axe gutted a young Spanish soldier – who my father had befriended – in front of him. Men were crying out for mercy as cannons exploded around them. This was the age of the Renaissance; not only were philosophies and art being redefined, but also warfare. Man had developed new ways to obliterate each other. No longer were they wearing armor, fighting face to face, but now they stood twenty or more yards away firing bullets or cannonballs.

A French soldier had broken my father's unit's flank and was heading straight for one of his friends, a human by the name of Luigi. My father reacted without thought. He grabbed a pike lying next to him and ran to Luigi. My father was filled with fear. He thought he would not reach the frightened Luigi in time before the French soldier ran him through with his bloodied sword.

As the French soldier lunged for Luigi, my father swung his pike. He blocked the sword before it penetrated Luigi. Luigi fell to the ground unable to move from fear. The French soldier turned to my father. My father took a step back, but kept his footing just as he was taught. The soldier attacked wildly. He was hurt, and my father said his eyes looked as if he had gone mad. My father blocked his attack and countered with an attack of his own. Neither of them would give ground to the other. Cannons exploded around them as they continued their death dance.

My father said he could hear soldiers dying in the distance. But he was determined not to meet his end in battle. There was too much he wanted to do in his life. He wanted to visit Florence and talk poetry. He wanted to run through the streets of Rome barefooted. He wanted to fall in love.

He waited for the soldier to make a mistake. My father was growing tired. He said his arms felt as if he had swam the Mediterranean Sea. His body ached, but his mind wouldn't allow him to drop his guard. And then it happened. The soldier tried to end their stalemate with an all out lunge. My father moved to the side and came down on the soldier's back with the pike. As the soldier tumbled to the ground, my father rammed the pike through his spine. The soldier lay below him dead.

My father was a hero to the world of humans. He was

even a bigger hero in our world. No vampire, Dayling or Nightling, had done what he'd done. That is, until Sébastien's father joined the French army and never lost a battle.

The two Daylings never met on the battlefield. But legend has it they met a week after they Crossed Over and went at it. Who won between Lazzaro Rota-Vigano and Jean-Paul de LaVigne is still a mystery in our community. It depends on which one you ask. They became best friends after their fight, and the rest is history.

"Are you listening mio fiore dolce?" My father said bringing me out of my thoughts.

I focused my eyes on him. "Yeah, I'm listening."

"When Jean-Paul arrives, he and I will be spending a lot of time trying to figure out who has betrayed us. I think you and Sébastien should be in charge of all the Daylings." He said.

"But what about Sophia? Didn't you leave her in charge of us?"

"Sophia is to assist you and Sébastien in any way you both need." He very painfully moved his head towards me. I could see the agony racing through him as he stared at me. "You and Sébastien are the future. You're no longer a child Haven. It's time I give you more responsibilities."

I couldn't believe how much those words meant to me. I didn't know I wanted to hear my father say that to me. It meant he trusted me. I loved being trusted by the greatest warrior of the vampire community. "I won't let you down dad."

He forced another smile across his face. "I have no doubt about that. Now, as for your interest in spending your last few weeks as a Dayling in high school must be revisited."

I stood from the chair without thinking. A panic began to build in my chest. I didn't want to give up on my chance of spending more time with Philip. No 12th century religious fanatics were going to take that away from me. "Every Dayling has a choice as to how they will spend their last month before they Cross Over. I don't think its right that I have to suffer because of what's going on. I have a right."

My father's eyes seemed to dilate in front of me. His stare became piercing. I could feel a light pressure pushing against my temple.

"What are you doing?" I asked, even though I knew the

answer.

His eyes relaxed a little. "What are you hiding from me Haven? Why are you so passionate about being around humans? I've always thought you hated the mortal world."

I slowly sat back in the chair. The sun was still out, so he didn't have enough strength to read my thoughts as he tried. The thing I realized, when the night does come, he will not only have the strength, but he will attempt to read my thoughts again. Vincent already knew a little about Philip. I figured the best thing I could do, would be to come clean to my father about my spiky haired prince. Not everything of course, but enough to keep him from pushing into my mind. "I met this guy. I think I like him."

"A Dayling?"

I slowly shook my head no.

I've heard the pain a Nightling felt if they moved during the day was like having electricity flowing throughout their entire body, being set on fire, stabbed, and being ran over by an eighteen-wheeler all at the same time. So when my father rose from his bed, and placed his face in front of mine, I almost had an accident all over his chair. Adding to the sudden fear encasing my body, was the fact that my father's fangs were gleaming in my eyes has he snarled at me. "You have developed feelings for a human a few weeks before you Cross Over? Do you know the danger you could place yourself in?"

I was frozen in place. I'd never seen a Nightling move in the day before. There was a story about my father being so pissed at my uncle, he moved across a room at him while the sun had been up, but a part of me thought it had all been exaggerations to fuel my father's legendary status. Feeling his breath so close to my face while the sun still blazed outside, caused me to rethink a few of the legends about my father. Also, I'd never seen him flash his fangs at me. I couldn't do anything except sit in silence.

"Do you?" My father's voice boomed.

"I didn't plan it, dad. You have to believe me." I forced out while still staring at his bared fangs. "I'm not in love with him. I just like being around him. I want to spend my last days as a Dayling hanging out with him. Also, there's this girl I'm cool with at school. She was over here earlier. I just wanted to feel human for a little while. But once I Cross

Over, I plan to never see either of them again."

Truthfully, I didn't really know what I was going to do about Philip once I Crossed Over. Giving up Olivia wouldn't be as hard as giving up Philip. I hoped my father couldn't tell that while he stared at me with rage in his shimmering dark eyes.

After a long moment of silently glaring at me, he relaxed as he fell back into the bed motionless. He returned to resembling a lifeless corpse as all Nightlings do during the day. "There is too much going on for me to worry about you and your crush. Be careful with this boy." He painfully took hold of my hand. "The day before you are to Cross Over, you will break it off with this human, with all your human friends. Or I will send Sophia to *end* your crush for you." He released my hand. "I must rest until Jean-Paul's family arrives. Leave me Haven."

When my father called me Haven, and not '*mio fiore dolce*', it meant he was pissed at me beyond words.

I stood from the chair. I slowly made my way to the chamber's door. As I placed my hand on the doorknob, I stopped and turned back to face him. "Oh, yeah, I forgot he asked me to join him at a friend's party tonight. I was wondering if I could go?"

I heard a low growl come from my father's bed. Then I heard him whisper, "I shall talk with you tonight."

I opened the chamber door, walked out, and made my way through the library and up the stairs to my room in no time. It's amazing how fast you can move when you are motivated by fear.

As soon as I opened my door, I saw Angela sitting on my bed. She didn't look that well as she sat fidgeting.

I closed the door behind me, made my way to my bed and sat beside her with my hands folded in my lap.

Angela slowly turned to me. "So, Haven... I think I'm gay."

TWELVE

We sat in silence for what felt like half an hour. It was a lot to process in one day. I'd admitted to my father I had a thing for a human, a gorgeous Dayling I used to be friends with popped up out of nowhere, a secret sect of vampire hunters were killing families all over the world because one of us betrayed the rest, and oh yeah, my cousin thinks she's gay.

Angela broke the silence. "Are you going to say something?"

"I told my dad about Philip." I mumbled.

Angela stood from my bed. "What? Why? Are you crazy?"

I pushed myself farther on the bed, before folding my arms around my balled up legs. I couldn't answer Angela's question about my sanity. I wished I could blame everything on me getting closer to Crossing Over to my father, but who am I kidding... I'm as good as dead.

I sighed as I gazed up at her. She had her worried look on her face again. "So why do you think you're gay?"

Angela's face softened a little. "Not important anymore."

"Very important. It's a big deal."

She sat back on the edge of the bed. "Your father tearing you apart is a big deal. Me finding another girl attractive isn't."

"So there's a girl? You've already found a girl?"

Angela pushed herself to the back of the bed where I sat. "Kinda. I met her at school today. We've been talking on the phone since I got home."

I thought for a moment. "Was it the girl that showed you around?"

"What? No, I got better taste than that." Angela said with a frown. "I met her in English class. She's really cool, Haven. Not to mention really sexy."

"She would have to be to land a hottie like you."

"I haven't been landed yet." She said with a smile.

It felt nice sitting with my cousin talking about silly things. I missed those times when everything seemed so simple. I would sit in my room, reading whatever book I'd picked up, then spend time harassing Angela about the greatness, or lack of greatness, of the book. I didn't have to worry about my father killing me because of feelings I'd developed for a human, or being hunted by lunatics with swords. At least I think they still used swords. I wasn't sure how Mântuitors killed my kind these days.

A knock on my door startled Angela and me. At first, I thought it was my father, but the facts that the sun was still out, plus I was certain he wasn't going to knock when he comes for me, calmed the sudden fear that had started building inside of me.

"Come in," I yelled.

The door opened, and Sébastien strolled in. His hair was no longer tied in a ponytail, but hung behind his ears as he made his way to the foot of my bed. "Hello Angela. You are as beautiful as I remember."

"I think she was like eight the last time you'd seen her." I said sarcastically.

Sébastien smiled at us. "She was a rare beauty even at the age of eight."

I leaned over to Angela. "Are you still sure you're gay?"

Angela pulled her lust-filled eyes from Sébastien. "Maybe I'm bi." She turned back to Sébastien. "So what brings you to our side of the world?"

Sébastien looked at me with confusion. I turned to Angela. "Yeah, I forgot to tell you that one of our kind betrayed us all to the Mântuitors and they are hunting down and killing families all over the world. We're on red alert."

The worried look I've gotten used to returned to Angela's face. "What? When?"

I looked to Sébastien. He took the cue. "We learned of their aggression a few weeks ago. The Draken family and now the Duncan family have all been annihilated."

I could feel the sadness encompassing Angela as she sat

beside me. She had friends in each family, we both did. It wasn't fair. Both families were filled with good people. Yes, they were vampires, but nothing like how the movies depicted our kind.

The Drakens weren't even wealthy like the rest of us. They'd chosen to live like middle classed American families. It was twelve of them in all, including three Daylings. One of which was one of Angela's best friends, outside of our family of course. Now they were all dead, and for what? Some ancient war we had nothing to do with and want nothing to do with. It's funny; the Mântuitors go around massacring innocent families, yet they consider themselves to be the good guys. I was starting to remember why I never got involved in the human world.

"So what is the plan?" Angela obviously tried to fight back tears as she spoke.

Sébastien placed his hands in his pockets. He looked like the perfect gentleman as he stood in front of us dressed in his gray suit. "I was speaking with Vincent. My family shall take the jet here as soon as the sun goes down. When they arrive, we shall look after the Daylings. They are not to know what is going on."

"You called? I thought you were supposed to go yourself? What about the phones being tapped?" I asked.

"I used a disposable phone Vincent had. I called a human liaison and arranged everything that way."

"Your family is coming here? How many are there?" Angela asked.

Sébastien took his hands out of his pockets. He slowly sat on the edge of my bed facing Angela and me. He moved his long blonde hair out of his face. His exotic blue eyes seemed to mesmerize Angela and me at the same time. If it wasn't for my feelings for Philip, and Angela's mystery lesbian lover, things could have gotten really interesting in my room. "Fifteen in all. Four are Daylings, including myself. Five Elders and six under the age of two hundred."

In our world, you have to be over two hundred years old to be considered an Elder of a family. And even that doesn't guarantee you a spot at the head of the table. You have to be voted in by the already existing Elders. The vampire world is just as political as the human world.

"Vincent and I believe it will be best if we keep a low profile until we have this situation under control." Sébastien said with his deep French accent.

Angela looked over to me, then to Sébastien. "Sorry, I got school."

"Yeah, and I have a date. Kinda." I whispered.

Angela and Sébastien both turned to me. "A date?"

"Yeah, I was invited to a party tonight. Thinking about going."

Angela began to smile. Her entire face glowed as she stared at me. "I thought you didn't do teenage parties?"

"Things change. You should know that better than anyone." I said as I stared at her.

"I guess I do. So what time is this party?" Angela unfolded her arms.

"Don't know. Sometime tonight." I said honestly. Philip didn't give me a lot of details. I would have to find out more about this party on my own. "Olivia should know. Maybe I'll give her a call."

Sébastien stared at Angela and me with disbelief swimming around in his blue eyes. "We are being hunted by the Mântuitors, and you two plan on attending a party? Do you both know you are mad?"

I unfolded my arms as I sat up in the bed. "We're teenagers." I pulled myself to the foot of the bed. I climbed out and stretched. "You're more than welcomed to come if you want. It's up to you."

Sébastien stood from the bed. He made sure he stood close enough to me for me to smell his wonderful scent. I didn't know if it was some type of cologne he'd gotten, or his natural scent, either way, it was intoxicating. "I think I shall help with the plans to save us all from being killed."

I slapped Sébastien across his shoulder. It felt strong and solid. The change was working it's way though his body. "Your call. I'm party bound tonight. Too much stuff on the mind."

Sébastien gave me a disappointed look before he bowed at Angela and me. He left the room without saying another word.

Angela stood in front of me. "He'll get over it. Do you want me to call Olivia and find out what time this party starts? I'm sure she knows."

"Go for it." I leaned closer to Angela. "It's not Olivia is it?"

"Noooo! Don't hurt that brain of yours trying to figure it out Haven, you'll meet my girl tonight at this party. More than likely she'll be there."

"Your girl?"

Angela blushed before she walked out of my room.

I was alone at last, nothing but my thoughts and me. I didn't know how I was going to handle my father. I didn't know how I would handle Philip at the party. And I didn't know what to do about this sudden attraction I felt for Sébastien. I wanted to deny it, but there was something going on between us, something more than just wanting to save our people from being killed by the Mântuitors.

I sat in my room alone for hours. I didn't even notice the sun had gone down. The closer I got to Crossing Over left me with the ability to feel the change in the atmosphere. I had been way too lost in my thoughts to be aware of the sunset.

That is, until I looked up at my door and saw my father standing at my entrance. He wore a black three-piece suit, with a long trench coat that hung to the floor. His grayish dark hair hung behind him. His hard porcelain Italian face seemed to glow under the halogen lights.

I jumped to my feet as soon as I saw him. Before I could blink, he stood in front of me face to face. Thankfully, his fangs were not protruding from his mouth. I could see the anger in his dark eyes. I could also see the restraint inside of him working it's hardest to keep him from doing something he would regret... like killing his only daughter.

"How long have you been seeing this human?" He growled at me.

"I'm not seeing him father. I met him at the party Sophia dragged me to a few nights ago. I like talking with him is all." I said as I took a step backwards.

My father matched every step I took backwards, forwards. "Did you spend all night with him?"

"Kinda. He got hurt. I made sure he was okay." I said deliberately leaving out the part about me saving his life in the alley. I felt the same slight pressure against my temple again. The sensation I felt when my father tried to get into my head. I turned away from him. "I can't believe you're trying to read my thoughts. Why don't you just ask me what you want to know?"

The pressure left immediately. I turned to see all the rage out of my father's dark shimmering eyes. It was replaced with sadness. He stood in the middle of the room resembling a man with the weight of the world on his shoulders. To a point, I suppose he did. My father and Jean-Paul were two of the most powerful Nightlings around. Our two families were looked at as being kind of the appointed heads of the vampire community, along with an African family named the Ali-Kufurus. We had to find a way to stop the Mântuitors before another innocent family was killed. Maybe Sébastien was right. Maybe I should spend more time on how we're going to get our people out of this mess, than going to a party just to see a guy I could never have.

"I'm sorry dad. I should've never gotten myself into this situation. I'll stay away from him if you want." I said as I stood in front of my father.

He stared at me for a moment in silence. His dark eyes changed from agony to delight. His face almost seemed to beam with a hidden source of joy. I didn't know what was going on with him. I liked seeing him like that. It was as if he had begun experiencing some type of moment of happiness in the middle of all the madness around us. "You are so wonderful mio fiore dolce. No matter what happens, I want you to know I love you. Enjoy your time with the human." He placed both his hands gently on my shoulders. "Be careful."

I felt a light kiss on my forehead before I found myself standing alone in my room. I didn't know what had just happened. I had expected a flogging of some kind, maybe even being slung to a wall or two, but I wasn't expecting what had happened.

I walked out of my room heading down the stairs towards the kitchen. The kitchen was surprisingly empty. I grabbed a sandwich out of the fridge, along with a soda. I sat at the table to eat. As each day passed, I was growing closer and closer to losing the ability to enjoy a good sandwich and soda. I was excited about the powers I would gain, but I didn't like having to give up turkey on wheat, with mustard and mayo.

"Hello, little one." I heard a voice say from behind me.

I knew who it was before I even turned around to see

him. Something I wasn't planning on doing anyway. He was the fiend I had to call uncle. "Hello Myron."

Myron strolled over to the seat in front of me. His short blonde hair sat on top of his head perfectly in place. Myron was born in 14th century England. He was a master swordsman and hunter. He was the second in command to my father, and second to my father in strength in our family. He didn't keep it a secret his desire to replace my father as the head of the family, which meant my father, my brother and myself were in constant danger as long as he lived. Jean-Paul had suggested that my father kill Myron to get rid of his potential threat. My father believed Myron knew better than to harm us on account of the other families. They would hunt him down and destroy him if he went against our laws.

"When are you going to call me Uncle Myron, little Haven?" He said with a wicked smile on his glittering porcelain face. Unlike my father, it seemed Myron hadn't missed a meal. He wore a long sleeved button up white shirt that hugged around his muscular frame. He also wore loose fitting cream kakis. His shimmering eyes gleamed as he stared at me.

I tired not to frown at him. Unfortunately, I had a bad poker face when it came to Myron. "When hell freezes over, Myron."

He pretended my words hurt him. "Why such hostility? I only want what's best for our family."

"You only want what's best for you." I said before I took another bite of my sandwich.

Myron sat back in his chair. His fake frown had left from his face. He replaced it with a fake smile. "I didn't want this bitterness between your father and me to spill over to our children."

I almost choked on the turkey in my mouth. I'd been certain for a while the only reason Sophia and I never got along with each other is because Myron made sure the bitterness between him and my father spilled over to their children. The only reason Angela and I are close, is because Angela and Sophia share the same mother, but fortunately not the same bastard of a father.

Very rarely did female Nightlings become fertile again after having a child. It was normally a one-time thing. I'd heard stories of a Nightling have three kids over a five hundred year span. I've even heard stories of Nightlings having twins and even triplets. I've never met one before, but it was a part of our mythology.

One of the reasons, one of the main reasons Myron hated my father as much as he did, had to do with Franklin. Myron and Constance were married for a long time, but she was never fertile during their relationship. Then Constance and my father had a moment of passion, and here came little Franklin. Myron took it harder than I thought he should have. Yeah he and Constance were together and Myron and my father were brothers, which in a way made the whole thing dirty on my father's part, but come on. It's time to move on. Myron and Constance were no longer together when it happened.

I stuffed the rest of my sandwich in my mouth. I then swallowed down my soda with a few big gulps, and let out a long burp before I stood from the table. "I would love to sit here and lie with you some more, but I have something to do."

"Hot date tonight?" Sophia said from the entrance of the kitchen.

I looked over to see her. She was dressed even sluttier than she was the night of the party at Eliot Little's house. She wore a cut off t-shirt with the words 'tongue the girl' written in red across her chest. It was obvious she didn't have on a bra underneath the shirt. She had on hip hugging bandless jeans, revealing she didn't have on any underwear at all. For shoes, she had on black high heel boots.

Her father didn't seem to mind her attire as he stood from the table and greeted her with a kiss on the cheek. "Going out tonight sweet heart?"

"Nigel and I are chaperoning the little ones tonight at this party. Myrene is also joining us, along with monsieur de LaVigne." Sophia said with a smile.

I couldn't believe it. I wanted to spend time with Philip, but not only was the evil witch of the east and her lackey coming, but Sébastien would be there too. I wasn't sure I wanted Philip and Sébastien in the same room with each other. The thought of it left me a little stressed.

Myron gazed at me with a malicious smile. "Enjoy. And do be safe."

Sophia winked at me as soon as her father left the kitchen.

THIRTEEN

It didn't take us long to find the house. Olivia texted the address to Angela before we'd left. Of course she planned on meeting us at the party. The idea of Philip being around my 'family' had started to freak me out enough, but with Olivia my panic kicked into another gear. Olivia would be too curious about things she shouldn't be curious about. I would have to spend time I'd planned on spending with Philip, keeping Olivia from getting herself in more trouble than she could handle.

Simon drove us in my father's all white Avalon. He wanted to join us in the party, but Sophia insisted, in the extremely unpleasant way she insists, that he didn't. Sébastien assured Simon he would be fine before we all exited the Avalon.

There we were; three Daylings and three Nightlings walking into another high school party, except this time we were invited, which was one of the many strange things about the night.

Sophia turned to us as we reached the door. "No one is to leave alone. You three Rugrats must stay together at all time." Sophia's shimmering dark eyes focused on me. "No sneaking off with any human fun buddies."

Nigel laughed as he stood beside Sophia. Angela giggled, while Sébastien stood beside us without an expression on his face. Myrene stood beside Nigel looking as serious as always.

Myrene was the oldest of us at the party: she'd been born in 1942, which meant she looked as if she was in her early twenties like Sophia, on account of Nightlings aging every twelve years after they Cross Over. Myrene was almost six feet tall, with a muscular frame and a thin exotic face. She looked completely African, even though she had some Italian blood running through her. She was a Vigano after all.

Her mother and my mother were friends. Myrene's mother, Majaji's entire family had been destroyed when she was still a baby. A human associate helped Majaji to escape, but slave runners later killed the human. Majaji grew up never knowing what she was until her eighteenth birthday when she Crossed Over and surprised her masters. She wandered around for fifty years until she came across a family lead by a Nightling known as Axum Ali-Kufuru. Axum took Majaji into his family.

During that time, Axum, my father, and Jean-Paul were best friends. About two centuries later Majaji got pregnant from a Vigano Elder, my cousin Hugh Vigano. Myrene stayed with her mother's family for a while, until a Mântuitor killed Majaji. Myrene could have continued to live with the Kufuru family, but decided to join the Vigano family to be with my mother. I've always felt she hated me because of my mother's death.

Regardless of Myrene's feelings about me, she loved my father deeply. She would protect me for him, and only for him. I was certain that's why she was with us at the party. I couldn't imagine another reason why she would follow Sophia, who she hated more than me, and Nigel, who she hated a little less than me, anywhere. I didn't believe I needed a bodyguard, but if it meant I could see Philip, I would have to deal with it.

Sophia knocked on the door. Billy's house was a little bigger than Eliot's. It wasn't the size of our estate, but it did have three-levels, except all of its levels were above ground, instead of one being below.

As the door opened, the same blend of techno hip-hop blasted from the decked out house. The party took place on the first floor. Billy explained the rules to us as he hopelessly stared at Angela. We were only to venture around the first floor. The indoor pool was in back, where most of the party-goers were at, and there were three restrooms located on the first level.

We followed Billy to the back where the pool was. It had to have been a hundred teenagers running around in bikinis and swimming in the pool. Of course alcohol was all around, not to mention I could smell weed in the air.

Sophia's eyes lit up as she saw a group of guys staring at her. Nigel whispered something in her ear before they stalked over to the group of teenagers.

"So this is an American party?" Sébastien said as he stood in front of me an Angela.

Unfortunately for Sébastien, Angela and I were scanning the crowd for the two people we'd come to see. I didn't know what Angela's mystery girl looked liked. I didn't really care as I tried to find Philip in the swarm of bodies.

Sébastien snapped his fingers in front of me to get my attention. "Looking for your human lover?"

I frowned at him. "He's not my lover."

"Not yet, but you wish for it."

I walked past Sébastien. "I don't think that's any of your business."

He walked beside me. "It isn't, just curious."

I stopped and turned around to face him. He stood in front of me dressed in his custom-made light blue Armani suit. I couldn't believe he'd put on a suit for a house party. I also couldn't believe he would wear a suit in the smothering night air. Obviously, nothing stood in the way of Sébastien's high society style. "Listen, I'm wondering why you come to this thing anyway? Shouldn't you be getting everything ready for your family's arrival?"

Sébastien's blue eyes flashed with real pain. He slowly ran his hand through his long blonde hair. "If you do not want me here Haven, then I shall leave."

I sighed. I didn't mean to hurt his feelings. I didn't know what I wanted exactly. I wasn't looking forward to hanging out with Philip and Sébastien at the same time, but it didn't look like I had a choice in the matter. "I don't want you to leave Sébastien. Honestly, I don't know what Philip is to me."

"Philip? Is that the name of the human?"

I rolled my eyes at the way Sébastien said human. "Yeah, that's the name of the guy. Are you sure you want to hang out with Philip and me? You don't want to mingle and sweep a human off her feet with your French charm?"

The pain had gone from his eyes. I could see his usual playfulness return. "That wouldn't be a challenge. And Sophia said we should all stay together."

At that moment, I realized Angela wasn't with us. She must have wandered off while Sébastien and I talked. I scanned the party, but couldn't see her anywhere. A slow panic started to build inside of me. "Did you see where Angela went?"

Sébastien looked around the room with me. Everything at the party was just like Eliot's party. Half-naked teenagers danced to music as sweat dripped from their bodies. No one seemed to be paying attention to anything except the people they were dancing with. It seemed as if everyone was in a trance of hormones. Just your stereotypical party I guessed. At least this time they didn't have the disco ball. Enough people joked about that to keep it locked away for at least two more decades.

"Got her." Sébastien said beside me.

I followed his eyes to a spot at the back of the room. Angela stood off to the side watching an Asian girl dance. The girl had long black hair, a small curvy body, and smooth looking skin that was visible through her strapless black top. She wore tight fitting black pants and high heels that made it seem as if she was about to tip over. Her hands were in the air and her eyes were closed as she danced to the music.

"Interesting," Sébastien said as he noticed how Angela stared at the dancing girl.

"What? Girls dance with each other all the time." I said as I started towards Angela.

I could hear Sébastien laugh, even though the music pulsed louder. "I know that look in Angela's eyes. I've had that look."

Any normal human wouldn't be able to see the lust in Angela's eyes the way we could. I'd noticed it also, but hoped Sébastien didn't. I wasn't sure if Angela was ready for anyone else to know how she felt about this girl.

Angela didn't even notice Sébastien and me standing beside her as she continued to watch the girl dancing alone. I wondered why Angela didn't join her. In today's time, no one really did think twice about two girls dancing with each other.

Sébastien informed Angela of our presence. "*Elle est belle*, Angela."

She turned to us with a blush forming on her face. "What?"

"She is beautiful." Sébastien said with a wink.

Angela shot me a nasty look. I slowly shook my head no. "Wasn't me. It's written all over your face." Angela looked down at the floor. I walked up to her and placed my hand on her shoulder. "Hey, it's nothing to be ashamed of."

She looked back up at me. "If Sophia found out."

Sébastien stood beside me in front of Angela. "No one cares what Sophia thinks. She has no real power."

The music changed. A slowed tempo came from the speakers. Also, I finally noticed that even though Eliot's disco ball had been banned, his multicolored flashing lights weren't. The blue and red lights flashed across the Asian girl's face as she made her way over to us. I must admit she was one of the most beautiful girls I've ever seen. Her slim curvy body seemed to glide as she walked over to Angela.

"Hey," she said as she gazed into Angela's eyes. Angela looked down to the floor as she smiled. The Asian girl looked over to Sébastien and me. "Who are your friends?"

Angela looked up. She looked from the girl to Sébastien and me as she introduced us. "Guys, this is Mu-Lan. Mu-Lan, this is my cousin Haven and a friend of the family Sébastien."

We all shook hands. Mu-Lan's hands were as soft as they looked. Angela had good taste; I'd give her that.

Mu-Lan looked at me. "I've heard a lot about you, an independent outcast right?"

I looked over to Angela before I returned my eyes to Mu-Lan. I never saw myself as an outcast. "I don't know if I would describe myself like that."

"I would." Sébastien said with a smile.

Mu-Lan smiled as well. "I didn't mean it as an insult. I think it's cool. Everyone at school is always whispering about the mysterious Haven. And Angela always talks about you. She looks up to you."

I turned to Angela with a smile. She frowned at Mu-Lan. "I wouldn't say I look up to Haven."

I wrapped my arm around Angela's shoulders. "Admit it, I'm your hero."

Angela moved from under my arm. Mu-Lan stood beside her and then placed her arm around Angela's shoulders. Angela didn't move from under her arm.

Mu-Lan looked from Sébastien to me. "You two make a cute couple."

"We're not a couple," I said. Not that I didn't think about

it. If it weren't for Philip, I would have definitely made a move for Sébastien. It was just too complicated to think about. I came to the party to have some fun. So that's what I planned to do.

The song changed to another fast paced, techno beat. Mu-Lan grabbed Angela's right hand and dragged her out to the dance floor.

I looked over at Sébastien as he watched the two girls seductively dancing to the music. "Having fun over there?"

"*Absolument*," Sébastien said with a smile in his deep French dialect.

I shook my head before I started scanning the room for Philip again. He'd asked me to come to the party, so it didn't make sense he wasn't anywhere to be found. I wondered if he had got caught in another alley. Knowing Philip, he could be getting his butt kicked right now.

Sébastien must have been able to sense the uneasiness running through me. He stared at me with concern. "Is there something wrong?"

I looked from the crowd to Sébastien. "I can't find Philip. He said he'd be here."

"Maybe he is." Sébastien said as he continued to watch Angela and Mu-Lan dance.

I didn't know if I was starting to feel worried or angry. I wasn't sure if Philip asked me to this party because he wanted to spend time with me, or to play around with me. Either way, I wasn't going to look for him anymore. If he wanted to be with me, he'd have to find me.

I turned to Sébastien. "I'm going to the restroom."

He turned from the girls. "Is it wise to go alone?"

"Angela is busy, and you're not coming with me. I'm fine; I'll be back in a minute." I turned to walk away.

Sébastien grabbed my arm. "Wait." He pulled out his iPhone and made a call. A moment later a voice was on the other line. "Haven has to use the restroom and Angela is busy." He said in the phone.

"Who is that?" I asked as I pulled my arm from his grasp.

He didn't have time to answer. Myrene popped up behind me. "Let's go."

"I don't need an escort to the restroom." I hissed out. I understood we were on high alert because of the Mântuitors killing our kind. I wasn't going to allow them to make me afraid of going to the restroom at a party. I've been taking care of myself for a while. My father was the head of the family, which meant he was busy with family issues most of the time, leaving me on my own to take care of myself. I didn't like they had a spy watching me at school. And I really didn't like being escorted to the restroom.

Myrene didn't seem to care about my outburst. She stood in front of me with her arms crossed in front of her chest. She wore a simple white shirt and jeans. Her hair was in braids, and she wore somewhat large earrings. Her shimmering dark eyes gleamed in the flashing blue and red lights. I thought Sophia was intimidating, but Myrene had her beat hands down.

I still wasn't going to give in so quickly. "I don't need or want anyone to hold my hands while I use the restroom."

"I won't be holding your hands, Haven. I'll just be waiting outside of the stall." Myrene said without cracking a smile.

Sébastien on the other hand did more than smile; he let out a slow laugh as he watched Myrene staring down at me.

I frowned at him before I turned back to Myrene. "You're not coming with me to the restroom."

"Then I guess you don't have to use it anymore. Or are you planning on going right here in the middle of the party?" She said, again without a smile.

I felt the pressure building inside of me. I really had to go. I wasn't ready to give up this fight yet. I wasn't going to allow Myrene to control me, just like I didn't allow Sophia to do so. "If I did, are you also supposed to clean it up?"

Myrene took a step towards me. Sébastien stopped laughing as he realized the seriousness of the situation. "I don't know who you think you are, but I'm not your servant. You're not the head of the family yet... thank god."

I took a step towards her. "One day I will be. Then you'll have to clean up more than just my piss."

Sébastien tried to get between us. "Okay, lets everyone calm down." He turned to me. "Haven, there is a real threat out there. We must look after each other."

I turned to him. I understood what he said. He was right. We had to play it safe while the Mântuitors were kicking their war against us into overdrive. But I wasn't about to back down. "All I know is that she isn't about to go with me to the restroom."

Before Myrene or Sébastien could say anything, Angela returned from the dance floor laughing with Mu-Lan. "What's up," Angela said as she saw the tension growing between Myrene and me.

Sébastien breathed a sigh of relief. "Haven needs to go to the restroom. No one is to be alone, so she needs someone to go with her."

Angela looked from Myrene to me. She quickly caught on to the situation. "Okay, I'll go with her."

Mu-Lan looked at the four of us with confusion. "Why does she need someone to go with her to the restroom?"

Angela turned to Mu-Lan. "I'm sorry I didn't tell you. I kinda didn't want to. My family has received a few death threats. No one is to be by themselves until this is taken care of." Angela gently squeezed Mu-Lan's hand. "Do you still want to hang with me tonight?"

Mu-Lan brushed her hand through Angela's long hair. The Asian beauty smiled at Angela. "Of course."

I turned to Myrene, who stared at Angela and Mu-Lan with disgust. "You can leave now."

She frowned at me. Her dark eyes sent an uncontrollable shiver through my body before she disappeared into the crowd.

I turned back to Angela. "I really got to go."

Angela forced herself away from Mu-Lan as she followed me through the crowd of partygoers. I could feel the teenagers' sweaty bodies knocking up against me as I hurriedly found the bathroom. I was nervous the entire walk. I thought with my luck, there would be a long line outside of it. It seemed my luck had turned for the good, because no one was waiting for the restroom.

I quickly opened the door. Angela and I didn't completely understand the rule about no one is to be alone, so she walked in with me. She closed and locked the door as I snatched down my pants and released my bladder with a satisfying sigh.

"Are there any Nightlings at the house you get along with?" She asked as she turned her back to me.

"Besides my dad, nope." I said as I started to feel better and better. "Why do you have you're back turned? You know you wanna look."

"You're not my type. Plus, family... ewww." Angela said.

I laughed as I finished up. I cleaned myself, pulled up my pants and quickly washed my hands.

Angela turned to face me. "So is this weirding you out? Seriously?"

"In less than three weeks, I'm going to be sleeping all day and drinking human blood. Nothing is really weird to me." I said with a smile.

Angela smiled back. I could see the joy forming in her head as she realized I was telling the truth. I didn't care who she dated. I just wanted her to be happy.

FOURTEEN

We made our way out of the restroom back into the smothering party. You would think with it being as hot as hell outside, Billy would have turned on the A/C in the party. But that would have meant not enough sweating girls for the guys to gawk at. Maybe Angela had the right idea about switching teams.

At least I thought that for a moment, until I saw Philip standing next to Sébastien and Mu-Lan. His half smile crept across his face as he saw Angela and me making our way towards them.

"So you decided to come after all? Left your lightsaber at home?" Philip said as soon as we stood in front of him.

"Sorry, don't speak Geek Latin." I joked. "You're late."

The smile across Philip's face widened, I didn't realize until then how I had made a mistake by pointing out his absence from the party. "Missed me I see."

I rolled my eyes. He was right. I did miss him, and it was eating me up inside that I did. "I just wanted you to be stuck at this lame party if I had to be stuck at it."

"We can leave if you want?" Philip said.

I looked from Sébastien to Angela. I knew leaving wasn't an option. Sébastien would call in the cavalry on me before we made it to the door. I wondered if that's why he decided to come to the party, to keep an eye on me as well. I could see my father asking him to spy on me, along with Myrene. And I could see him excepting my father's request.

I looked over to Mu-Lan, who was staring at Angela. "I'm heading to get something to drink, you want something?"

Mu-Lan shook her head yes.

Sébastien spoke up before Philip could. "I can go and get the drinks Haven."

I rolled my eyes again. He was trying to be a gentleman, it was in his blood, but I didn't need him or Philip to get macho on me. "I will get the drinks. You guys hang out around here." I turned to Angela. "You thirsty?" She shook her head yes also. I turned to Sébastien and Philip. "What about you two?"

"I'm good," Philip said as he put his hands in his pockets. He wore a short-sleeved light red silk shirt, with dark blue khakis. His hair sat in its usual spiky place on top of his head. I inhaled deeply, taking in his full scent. I finally realized what he smelled like. The smell coming from Philip reminded me of a freshly picked strawberry from my time in Italy. I could almost taste the juices running down my throat as I would bite into one of my family's strawberries as I walked along our Italian estate while the sun comfortably hovered above me.

Sébastien took a step closer to me. He whispered just loud enough for me to hear him over the music, making sure the human's couldn't. "I should walk with you to get the drinks Haven."

His warning tone pulled me out of my memory. I was becoming very annoyed with him. "I think I can get drinks and come back over here without getting attacked."

I turned around and walked away before Sébastien could respond. I didn't need him to be my babysitter. I didn't need a babysitter. Between him and Myrene, my night had become more frustrating than fun.

I walked through the crowd to a table covered with drinks. I'd heard stories about not drinking from drinks you didn't fix yourself. Since this was only my second human party, I didn't know if it was safe to take the already poured cups of soda from the table, or look for some unopened cans.

After a few seconds of deliberating, I decided to go with the cups on the table. I walked to the table and took three drinks, one for each girl. When I turned to walk back over to the others, a man stood in front of me.

The man had short black hair, with a thick beard and mustache. He wore all black, which was strange considering the heat. He looked to be in his mid twenties, which was also strange considering this was a teenage party. And I could see his muscles bulging from his tight black outfit.

The man didn't say anything as we stood eye to eye. He stared at me with a blank expression on his face.

I decided to break the silence. "Can I help you?"

The man continued to stare at me with a blank expression. He looked me up and down a few times before he finally spoke. "You have not Crossed Over yet. You're still a moroii."

My heart almost leapt from my chest. Only Mântuitors called us moroii instead of Daylings, which only meant one thing, I was in deep trouble.

I tossed all three cups into the man's face before I sprinted away. The man recovered quickly and ran behind me.

Being a Dayling meant I was naturally faster than any human. I had to maneuver through a few partygoers, but I wasn't worried about the Mântuitor catching me. I wasn't clear as to where I was running, since in my panic I didn't run back to the others. The only thing I knew was that I had to keep running.

After making my way to the side door of the house, I reached in my pocket for my phone as I slung open the door. I had to warn the others that a Mântuitor was at the party. It wasn't until I felt the heat from outside did I realize how stupid I'd been. There wasn't much the man could do to me in a crowd of teenagers, but outside in the wide open, I was dead meat. Not to mention the Mântuitor knew he couldn't catch me in a foot race, so why did he make himself known?

I felt the blow to my side at the same time I realized just how brainless I'd been. I hit the ground hard as another Mântuitor came at me. I rolled over and jumped to my feet as quickly as I could. Fear began to run through out my body as I looked around at the ten men and women, all dressed in black, rushing towards me.

I swung at the first one that made it to me; the guy ducked my punch, and caught me across the jaw with his right fist. Blood spilled out of my mouth before I felt a foot snapping one of my ribs.

Air rushed out of me as I backed away. The Mântuitors kept advancing on me throwing punches and kicks almost as fast at a Dayling. There were too many of them, and I wasn't a fighter. It didn't take me long to realize how dead I was after I caught another fist to the side of my head.

I dropped to my knees. I tried to stand, but the pain racing through my body took all the strength out of me. Both of my eyes were swollen, and I began choking on my own blood.

My desire for a human had caused me to attend a party crawling with Mântuitors waiting to kill me. I thought my luck had changed for the good because of the restroom being freed when I had to go real bad in the house. I should have known something was up. No way could my luck have changed enough for me to have a perfect night. I would die before I had a chance to kiss Philip. I couldn't believe I was about to die, and all I could think about was kissing Philip. Maybe death wouldn't be so bad. At least I'd be away from these damned new feelings inside of me.

Through my blurred vision, I was barely able to make out the blade that one of the female Mântuitors snatched from her waistband. The blade was long, with a small curve to it.

The female Mântuitor brought the blade down with amazing speed towards my neck. I'd wondered how Mântuitors killed my kind. I was moments away from finding out.

The blade never finished its slash. I heard the female Mântuitor scream before I felt blood splashing across my face.

I could hear the other Mântuitors turn from me towards their attackers. Although my vision continued to be a little hazy, I could see the carnage happening in front of me.

Sophia, Nigel and Myrene were fighting the Mântuitors.

Myrene had the arm of the female Mântuitor in her hand, the blade that was about to cut off my head was still in the Mântuitor's hand, while the female screamed in pain on the ground. Myrene tossed the arm at a male Mântuitor as he attacked, knocking him off guard or a moment, giving her the moment she needed to rip his windpipe open.

Myrene moved with speed and viciousness as she attacked another male Mântuitor. The guy had his blade in his hand. He moved with swiftness and awareness around him also. It was obvious he was a skilled fighter. A regular human wouldn't last two minutes against an angry Nightling. This guy gave Myrene all she could take as he sliced her across the arm.

She didn't pause from the pain as she slashed at the man's throat with her now elongated finer nails. Instead of cutting the man's throat as she planned, she caught him across the shoulder, causing him to scream in pain.

I looked from Myrene towards Nigel. He was fighting two Mântuitors at once: a male and a female. The crazy thing about it, I could almost swear I saw Nigel smiling.

The male Mântuitor attacked. He came at Nigel in full speed. Nigel almost didn't dodge the guy's fist in time, but before he could counter the male's attack, the female caught him in the ribs.

I saw Nigel flinch as the pain of the blow took some wind out of him. When the female tried to land another punch, Nigel drove his elbow into her kneecap. The female Mântuitor screamed in pain as she dropped to the ground.

Nigel didn't have time to block, or brace himself, before the male Mântuitor caught him across his left temple. The Mântuitor gave Nigel the quickest, and most powerful, back kick I had ever seen. Nigel flew back and crashed into a golf cart sitting a few feet away. I'd learned when we first moved to Summerbrooke that some of the wealthy residents liked to drive around the neighborhood in golf carts. Rich people, that's all I got to say.

Nigel looked up to see both the male and the injured female Mântuitor coming to finish him off. I was afraid he wouldn't be able to defend himself against the charging Mântuitors, but with one swift movement, Nigel jumped to his feet, grabbed the side of the golf cart, and slung it like a baseball bat at the two shocked humans. The golf cart crashed into them both, sending their crushed bodies flying through the air.

I felt close to losing consciousness as my eyes rolled over to Sophia. She had a Mântuitor in her arms draining his blood. The man flayed in her grasp as the blade he carried slowly dropped from his hand.

Sophia released the dead man's body, and turned to the three Mântuitors creeping up behind her. She growled at them, showing off her blood stained fangs. Her left arm had a nasty cut in it. I could see the blood flowing out of the wound. Sophia didn't seem to pay the wound any attention as she glared at the humans.

The man I'd seen in the party stood in the middle of the

carnage. He pulled a silver sphere out and pushed a button on the side of it.

I'd heard of a weapon that imitated a high frequency sound only Nightlings could hear. The weapon supposedly made Nightlings feel as if knives were being shoved inside their ears. I didn't believe such a weapon existed, until I saw Myrene, Nigel and Sophia drop to their knees grabbing their ears. I could see blood coming from Myrene ears as she screamed from the obvious pain she felt.

It was over. There was no way they could defend themselves against the remaining Mântuitors. There was nothing I could do but watch the Mântuitors kill members of my family, before killing me also.

The man with the thick beard and mustache seemed just as surprised as me, as one of the Mântuitor's knives exploded from his chest. The man looked down at the blooded weapon before he slowly fell to the ground dead.

Sébastien then quickly stepped on the silver sphere, crushing it into little pieces. He rushed over to me as the others quickly recovered.

He leaned down to me. "Are you okay?"

"No," I forced out as Sébastien took me into his arms.

"Time to go," I heard Sophia say as she snatched me from Sébastien's grasp.

The next thing I knew, I felt the wind rushing through my hair. My entire body hurt from the attack, plus the massive amount of blood I'd lost left me feeling light headed, but I couldn't help but feel a sense of joy at the thought of being alive.

The wind increased as I felt us swooping lower to the ground. It was so hot out; even the wind burned my skin. It felt as if my body was being dangled in front of a giant hair dryer. My ears stung from the sound of the city quickly passing below us.

Finally, we came to a stop. Sophia dropped me to the ground a little rougher than she had to. I didn't complain as I slowly tried to get up.

I felt a hand on my shoulder. "You shouldn't try to stand yet." Sébastien whispered.

"I'm fine," I lied as I tried to straighten myself up.

I forced my swollen eyes open. Everyone was there. Myrene, Nigel and Sophia were bleeding from different places on their bodies and faces. Angela stood beside Myrene staring at my swollen face, and the nasty cut on her sister's arm. I could see the full panic in Angela's eyes. No matter how often they fought, Sophia was still her sister. Seeing her injured was taking its toll on Angela quickly. Not to mention seeing me bleeding all over the place.

Sophia stopped attending her wounds as she noticed the emptiness in her sister's eyes. She walked over to Angela, and for the first time I'd ever seen, she took Angela in her arms and hugged her for a few moments. When she released Angela, Sophia gazed into her eyes. "Are you okay?" Angela slowly shook her head yes. "Good, now snap out of it runt."

That was the Sophia I knew. I could feel Sébastien's strong arms around me as I wobbled a little. I gathered myself again, trying not to fall.

Nigel was the only one who didn't have gloom written over their faces. He smiled as he reached in his pocket and pulled out a pack of cigarettes. "Now that was what I call fun."

My attempt at standing wasn't going well. The world spun around me. I couldn't deny enjoying the feel of Sébastien's body against mine a little, but it wasn't enough to keep me vertical. "I think I need to sit back down." I whispered to Sébastien.

He gently lowered me down to the ground. It wasn't until I sat down that I noticed we were on top of a building. I looked around with my hazy vision. It took me a moment, but I realized we were on top of one of the dorms at FSU.

"I don't think we should go home yet," Myrene said as she held a piece of her shirt to a wound on her stomach.

Sébastien didn't leave my side as he stared at Myrene. "You guys are hurt." He gestured towards me as he continued, "some more than others. We need to get help."

"What if they're tracking us? Mântuitors have a nasty habit of doing that." Nigel answered through a cloud of smoke.

Sophia pulled a cell phone out of her pocket. "I agree, but we have to warn them just in case." She pushed a button and placed the phone to her ear. Some one answered the other line after one ring. "It's me, Sophia. The house of Vigano code word is *giglio*." Sophia waited for a moment, and then continued. "I need to speak with Vincent." Again another moment passed. "Vincent it's Sophia, we were attacked at the party... yes everyone is alive... it was about ten Mân-tuitors. Some of us are hurt pretty badly... yeah; *la pequeña princesa* is the one hurt really bad. We don't think it's smart to come home. We're not sure if we're being tracked. Any safe houses close to FSU?" Sophia listened to Vincent on the other end of the phone. She looked over to me before she spoke. "Gotcha. See you soon." She hung up the phone. "There's a safe house not far from here. We need to leave now.

Sophia made her way over to me. She quickly picked me up. Pain rushed through my body as she snatched me from the roof of the dorm. I felt the wind racing through my hair again before I could complain about the pain.

Again, I felt my body being ripped through the air with light speed. I almost passed out this time. My body wasn't taking the trip as well as it did the first time around. Maybe the fact that I had survived occupied my thoughts enough the first time to help my body deal with the pain of being transported by Sophia. I no longer thought about the fight, so my body was able to concentrate on the hell it was in while traveling to this safe house Vincent told Sophia about.

Slowly, I felt myself losing consciousness. I tried to fight the darkness pulling at me. Maybe it would be good for my body if I slept a little? Maybe it would be, or maybe not? I remembered movies' saying it's bad to sleep if you have a head wound. And I had several head wounds.

We landed just as I started to get closer to losing my battle with the abyss. Sophia placed me on the ground with the same gentleness she used when she picked me up to start the trip: none.

Everyone landed beside us. Myrene carried Angela, while Nigel carried Sébastien.

Sébastien rushed to my side as soon as Nigel released him. He again became my crutches helping me stay on my feet.

I looked around trying to figure out where we were. Nothing looked familiar to me. I didn't see anything but the warehouse in front of us.

Sophia stepped to the door of the warehouse. She knocked twice then waited. The door opened and a man carrying a machine gun stood at the entrance. "I am Sophia from the house of Vigano. The code word is *giglio*."

The man glanced over all of us. He moved out of the way so we could walk in. I leaned into Sébastien as we entered the warehouse first.

It was dark inside. It was also completely empty. A few conveyer belts sat unused around the warehouse. It looked as if it had been abandoned for years.

The man closed the door after Myrene walked in last, filling the empty room with a loud screeching sound. He turned to Sophia. "The stairs are over to your left. Follow them all the way to the bottom." The man said in a German accent.

Sophia led the way to the stairs. Sébastien all but carried me beside her. I tried to help him out by walking as much as I could, but my ankle, my foot, and basically my whole left leg hurt like hell. It didn't take a doctor to know it was broken.

I limped as far as I could down the stairs. Sébastien picked me up midway and carried me the rest of the way down. At the bottom of the stairs was a door. Sophia knocked on the door twice like before, and said the same code before it opened.

As soon as we stepped through the door, three women rushed towards me. They took me from Sébastien, and sat me in the wheel chair they brought with them. I looked around the room in amazement. It looked just like a hospital lobby. It even had the same bland pictures around the walls like a real hospital.

I felt myself falling asleep again as the women pushed me towards a room. This time I didn't fight it. I allowed my body to fall into the abyss, away from the pain.

FIFTEEN

As I slept, I felt another Dream Transfer come over me, which could only mean one thing, I was about to see my father's last day as a Dayling, and his awakening as a Nightling:

I walked through a forest heading away from my family's villa in Milan. My hair hung all the way down to my back. My over six foot height was impressive for a teenager in the mid 15th century.

I took everything in as I walked through the forest. I took in the beautiful sights of all the trees, and the way the sun shone down on the ground, and the grass swaying in the slight breeze. I held my hand out to feel the heat of the sun on my skin, wanting to enjoy it for the last time.

My youngest sister followed behind me as I walked. I knew she was there, I knew she'd been following me since I left the villa.

She skipped beside me wearing a long white gown.

"And what do you want Maria?" I asked in Italian.

"You've been back from the war for two whole days now, brother. And yet you have not told me a thing about it. How many French soldiers did you kill?" Maria said.

"I do not remember." I answered as she continued to skip alongside me.

"I do not believe you. You are large and powerful, you must have killed hundreds." Maria said mockingly.

"War is not a thing to mock. It is the worst of all things that exist." I said half-serious and half-teasing back.

I tried to hide the regret I felt for all the lives I'd taken during my time in the Fifth Italian War.

"Don't tell me the great Lazzaro Rota-Vigano is growing weak in his old age," Maria said before she tripped me, and then took off in a full sprint.

I gathered myself, and then chased behind my little sister. We laughed as we ran to the border of our estate.

The estate sat on the edge of Lake Maggiore. A flash of me sitting under my favorite tree, and staring out into the lake entered my mind. It had been at this spot where I would sit with Jean-Paul, when the de LaVigne family would visit, and talk of all the rumors spreading through Milan. We would talk of all the new inventions and the new philosophers. Times were enchanting to me then. Everything felt innocent.

Maria and I fell to the ground laughing under a large oak tree.

"It is good to see you do that again," she said as she calmed herself.

"It is good to do that again," I said, laying back.

We sat under the tree for a while in silence. I allowed the sun to wash over my face. I felt the slight breeze covering me as I closed my eyes and listened to the sounds of nature all around us. It was such a lovely day, I thought. Such a wonderful day.

"Are you ready for your party tonight?" Maria asked.

"Do I have a choice," I clinched my eyes closer together.

The dream changed.

Night had come, and I walked through the night dressed in what I felt was my best attire. I had on the cleanest breeches I owned, with Trunk hoses that were attached to the bottom of my doublet with laces.

When I reached the other edge of my family's estate, where the party took place, the scene awed me. It seemed more than just my family had shown up for my party, and my family had gone all out.

Music filled the air as young men and women, along with the children and the elderly danced around a large fire. About ten musicians were playing as people gathered around them and sang songs, about the hard lives they've led, or the greatness of our kind, or the hardship of war, or just some silly song that they'd learned as children.

The stars in the sky helped to illuminate the scene along

with the large fire. And the cool breeze made the night more magical than any tale I had ever heard. Everyone and everything looked beautiful and filled with life. Laughter and jokes and tales about good times with loved ones filled the air along with the songs. I loved every minute of the festival.

I walked among the different families of immortals, and soaked up the atmosphere, and the gazes of the women, and the gazes of the men that courted the women. I walked until my eyes came upon a young girl standing alone.

She stood just a few feet away from the fire wearing a long cap, with a heart-shaped outline around her face, with her hair brushed up over the pads. Each time the fire flickered; her beautiful face would become revealed to the world around her, more importantly, to me. She had long brown hair and beautiful light blue eyes.

"She is mine, little brother." I heard Myron say as he stalked up behind me. He stood perfectly still. His arms crossed behind him as the light from the fire reflected from his porcelain skin. He wore a long brown cloak that hung to the ground as his shimmering eyes focused on the woman.

I didn't turn around to face Myron. Instead, I continued watching the woman being bathed in the light of the fire. "Who is she?"

Myron stepped beside me. He had a devious look on his face. "Constance Larkin. Her family has promised her to me in a way to unite our families." Myron took a sip from a glass of blood he held in his hand. "The fun I shall have with her brother."

Myron and I made our way over to Constance.

I stood in silence.

Myron stood with his smirk on his face. "Why do you stare into the fire with such intensity my love?"

"In the fire is the secret of eternity. The fire is not good or evil, nor is it driven by malice. It feeds on the air around it because it needs the air to continue to burn. It needs the wood and the leaves and everything else that gets in its path of hunger. It can destroy so much and yet provide so much at the same time. And with enough to consume, it can last forever. But it never does, because sooner or later someone will put it out, after it has served its purpose, or to protect something else from it's hunger." Constance said as the flames created shadows around her beautiful porcelain face.

"And it is pretty to look at."

We all began to laugh. I bowed my head to her as Myron introduced us. I then excused myself from Myron and his betrothed.

I stood in the shadows and watched as Myron and Constance continued to talk, every once in a while, Constance would glance over in my direction.

The dream changed again.

That night I awoke from my sleep, in a little shack on our estate, as the butt of a musket slammed across my forehead. I rolled onto my knees and jumped back landing against the wall. When I looked in front of me, I saw five Mântuitors standing in the shack laughing. The Mântuitors wore black robes, with black gloves and black boots. They wore chest armor, with their symbol painted across it in red: a cross overlapping an M in the middle of a circle.

I felt my blood running down my porcelain face. My mind was confused. I didn't know what had happened or what was going on. Then I focused on one of the Mântuitors, seeing the sight of Maria being shot and decapitated by the man. I almost fell to the ground as the vision assaulted me.

"It is time for you to join your family, demon," one of the Mântuitors said. "All of your kin shall be purged from this world."

The blood coming from my forehead stopped. I gazed at the Mântuitor that had been talking. My dark eyes shimmered in the dim shack. The Mântuitors stared at me as if they'd seen Satan himself. The fear in their eyes pleased me more than I thought possible. I growled at them while showing off my newly developed fangs.

Power rushed through my body, along with an intense thirst.

The youngest Mântuitor dropped his musket. He was out of the shack faster than the others had a chance to call for him. The four remaining Mântuitors pointed their muskets at me and fired.

As the bullets passed through my body, I become angrier, ignoring the pain rushing through me as I focused on vengeance.

Instinctively I lunged at the first Mântuitor and snapped his neck. Two of the last three Mântuitors tried to run, while the other one tried to reload.

Before the first Mântuitor reached the door, I stood in front of him. I tore a large plug out of the man's neck. He fell to the ground strangling from his own blood.

The next retreating Mântuitor stopped and backed away.

The Mântuitor with the musket continued to try to reload it as I lunged at him. Before the man knew what had happened, I had him on the ground drinking his blood.

I stopped feeding and stared at the remaining Mântuitor with blood dripping down my face.

"Please God. Please don't hurt me," the man said as he began to weep.

I rushed towards the trembling Mântuitor and shoved him into the back wall. As he fell to the floor, I stomped on his head, crushing his skull.

"Lazzaro," Myron called as he burst through the shack door, dragging the dead body of the fifth Mântuitor. He dropped the corpse next to the one with his throat ripped open. "Are you okay brother?"

"What of the others? Are there anymore left" I demanded.

Myron walked over to me. He placed his hand on my shoulder. "I'm sorry brother, but they are all gone."

"What of the other families?" I growled.

"They are safe. They left after the party. It was only our family left in the villa. I wasn't there when the Mântuitors came. I showed up after. Everyone in our family is gone Lazzaro."

"No!" I screamed as I turned away from Myron. I took a few steps, then looked around the room finally taking in the horror I'd committed. And strangely, I felt satisfaction. I looked at my masterpiece of carnage, and I felt a small sensation of delight, until I thought about little Maria.

"No," I screamed again as I stumbled out of the shack. I felt confused and frightened, but not frightened for my safety, but frightened for the safety of others. I had become a monster now, not because I had Crossed Over, but because I was capable of more acts of malevolence than what I'd done in the shack.

Lot in a type of madness I walked through the forest on my family's estate gazing at the world around me. I could hear the sounds of creatures I never knew existed, I could feel the shift of the wind as it swirled around me, I could smell the scent of death coming from my family's villa.

I stopped where I stood, dropping to my knees as I thought about my family.

The anger inside of me grew more and more as I heard the sounds of the Mântuitors laughing. I could hear them, around my family's villa, laughing as they set it on fire, with the dead bodies of my family inside of it.

"Yes, you hear them too. They laugh and mock as our family burns inside of our villa. Come little brother; let's show them the vengeance of their demons." Myron grabbed me, and a split second later we were standing at the top of a hill, looking at the Mântuitors standing around our family's villa as flames engulfed it.

Ten Mântuitors stood around the villa in all, some with muskets, while the others had crossbows and swords.

"Come, this is the perfect night for creatures of the dark. And a perfect moment for a feast." Myron said before he went after the men with the muskets.

Without warning, two were laying on the ground dead. Myron attacked with the savagery of a wild animal. He ripped and bit into the flesh of the shocked Mântuitors. Not a single musket fired before all holding them laid on the bloodied grass dead. He killed four Mântuitors in all, leaving me with the remaining six.

Without thought, with only rage and pain in my heart, I ran at the two Mântuitors with the crossbows first.

A single arrow ripped through my left shoulder. I snatched the arrow out and shoved it through the eye of the Mântuitor who shot it.

The second Mântuitor shot his arrow at me. It missed. Before he could reload, I snapped his neck, leaving the four Mântuitors carrying swords left.

They were frightened. I could smell the fear coming off of them, but they were warriors, even though they knew they were facing death himself, they would not retreat. A part of me admired them for it, but admiration or not, they were not going to live past the night.

They surrounded me thinking if they attacked at the same time, then maybe they would be able to take me. I studied the closest one. He seemed to be the bravest. That meant he would be the first to die.

I attacked the boldest Mântuitor first, not giving the

group a chance to advance on me. He swung the sword wildly. I moved out of its way, came up behind the man, and bit down on his neck all in one move.

Just as I had thought, the other Mântuitors hesitated as they saw their leader killed so easily. I took the sword out of the dead Mântuitor's hand and finished off the rest with ease.

I turned to the burning villa as Myron stood beside me. I knew what burned inside of it. My family was truly gone. I had nothing left except my hate, which I had in abundance.

SIXTEEN

I slowly regained consciousness inside of a room in the underground hospital. Everything gradually began to come into focus. The rooms in the underground hospital were the same as a regular hospital... bland. I almost started crying when I saw a picture of a garden in front of me.

"*Mio fiore dolce*," I heard my father say beside me. I looked over to his porcelain face. He didn't do a good job at hiding his worry, it was reflecting in his shimmering dark eyes. "You have finally awoken."

The last sight of my father in the Dream Transfer flashed in front of me. Rage and hatred had covered his face, and not the worry that enveloped his face as he stared at me. I tried to sit up in the bed. A rush of pain knocked me back down. "How long have I been asleep?" I felt my father's hard, yet warm, hand on the side of my face. His eyes stared at me as if he was trying to memorize every line in my face. I felt a little exposed as he gazed at me. I forced a half smile across my face. "I'm fine dad. Really. How did you get here?"

He sat on the side of the bed. He never took his eyes from me. "I arrived last night, a little after you. You've slept through the day."

"How is everyone else?"

"Everyone is fine. Their wounds weren't as bad as yours. And Nightlings heal quicker." My father said as he began to gently stroke my hair.

I reached and took his hand into mine. "I'm fine dad. I'm just ready to go home."

"In an hour. I'll have everything arranged to escort you

back to the mansion."

"Has Sébastien's family arrived yet?" I asked as I tried to sit up again. This time I accomplished my task, not without battling a little pain, but not as much as before.

My father stood from the bed. He wore a black t-shirt and black pants. To see him out of the house without a three-piece suit on looked odd. "The de LaVigne family is settled in. Also what's left of the Ali-Kufuru family."

I almost jumped out of the bed. Three families living under the same roof was going to be interesting. "What happened to the Ali-Kufuru family? Is Uncle Axum okay?"

"Axum is alive. He lost most of his family. Only four others survived with him." My father turned away from me. "Unfortunately Amina wasn't one of the survivors."

A sharp pain spread through my body. Amina was Axum's only child. She was older than Sébastien and me, but we all hung out with each other when we were younger, mostly because our fathers were so close with each other. Amina had been a Nightling for sixty years. Sébastien and I looked up to her. I couldn't believe she was gone.

My father sat back next to me. "I don't want to know what Axum is feeling Haven. You must be careful from now on."

Before I could answer, my father disappeared out of the room. I felt glad for the solitude. I needed time to think about everything. My world was coming apart. I had almost been killed at the first party I'd ever been invited to, and one of my closet friends had died. Nothing would to be the same for me.

The door to my room opened, breaking my solitude. Sébastien slowly walked in with a forced smile on his face. "Glad to see you awake."

I shifted my body in the bed. Sitting up in the angle I sat in had become a little uncomfortable. "Kinda wish I was back asleep."

Sébastien made his way to my bed, his long hair loose behind him. He slowly sat on the side of my bed as my father did. "You heard about Amina?" I slowly shook my head yes. "I can't believe she's gone."

"Yeah, me either. I'm sorry Sébastien, but I don't want to talk about that now. I'm not ready." I said trying to get him to change the subject. I didn't want to grieve for Amina in front of him. I didn't know why I felt self-conscious about him seeing me upset, but I did.

"Did your father tell you they found and killed the remaining Mântuitors from the party?"

I shifted my weight again and tried to hide the pain from sitting up, just like I tried to hide the pain of Amina's death. "No. I hope they ripped the bastards apart."

Sébastien gave a low laugh. "I imagine they did."

My mind finally fully awake, "wait, what happened to Philip?"

Sébastien seemed to be hurt when I said Philip's name. "He's fine. We left him at the party with Angela's friend."

I let out a sigh of relief. I didn't want anything to happen to Philip or Angela's new *girlfriend*. But, I didn't understand how Angela and Sébastien were able to leave them behind so easily though. "They didn't try to follow you guys out?"

Sébastien stood from the bed. He gave me a devilish grin. "After we saw our Nightling escorts rush out the door, Angela and I excused ourselves. We never returned after we walked out into the middle of the fight."

"He must think I ditched him," I thought out loud. I didn't have time to stress about Philip. I would have to deal with him another time. The main focus had to be the Mântuitors that attacked us. How the hell did they know we were going to be at that party?

My father walked into the room. For a moment, a flash of him back on his villa tearing into the Mântuitors entered my mind. It went away as quickly as it came. My mother and my father both suffered on the night they Crossed Over, I was so hoping I didn't inherit their bad luck.

My father patted Sébastien on the shoulder with a slight smile across his face. He turned to me. "Everything is being taken care of. We shall leave shortly."

I sat in the room for another twenty minutes in silence. My father stood in front of my door, like a centurion guarding his queen. His stance seemed tense and ready for anything. The attire he wore exposed his towering frame; he looked to be readying himself for war. Which I guess, he was.

Sébastien sat next to my bed. He didn't say anything to me during the time we waited. Again, I felt glad. I wasn't in the mood to talk either.

When they came for us, my body had started to feel a little better. Daylings healed quicker than humans, not as quick as Nightlings of course, but it would have taken a human girl more than a day to heal from the ass-whooping I took from the Mântuitors. Next time, I would be ready.

We quickly made our way out of the warehouse flanked by guards. Most were humans, with a few of the house of Vigano mixed in. Sophia, Nigel and Myrene walked with the other Nightlings, while Angela and Sébastien walked beside me.

After exiting the warehouse, we walked to a large SUV. There were four other cars with the SUV. Two cars were in front, while the other two were behind it.

I got into the SUV with my father and everyone who was with me at the party. We sat in silence all the way back to the mansion.

There were more guards at the mansion as we entered the gates. Even with the extra guards, I didn't feel safe until we entered the mansion.

Myron waited inside the mansion, along with Uncle Jean-Paul de LaVigne and Uncle Axum.

Jean-Paul looked the same as I remembered him. He had long blonde hair like his son, a chiseled masculine face, with an even more chiseled masculine body. He wore a long white trench coat, with a white t-shirt and white pants, and finished off the ensemble with white boots. His light blue eyes seemed to glow as he saw his son walk through the door.

In the blink of an eye, Jean-Paul moved to his son. He grabbed Sébastien in his arms and lifted him off his feet. I could see the embarrassment etched across Sébastien's face. His father didn't seem to care what anyone thought as he held his son in his powerful grasp.

Axum stood in silence as he watched Jean-Paul and Sébastien. He had on a large leather jacket that fit tightly over his large muscular body. His complexion was an odd type of bronze, and his head was shaved bald. His eyes were exotically light brown. Those eyes of his always made me understand why he was a ladies' man. Except for tonight, his eyes were empty and hollow.

I walked, or more like limped, up to Axum and wrapped my arms around him. His body felt hard, yet I could feel the weakness inside of him. His world had been Amina. I couldn't imagine the type of pain encompassing him.

As I hugged Axum, I glanced over to see Uncle Myron taking Sophia, and even Angela, in his arms. He hugged them both with relief in his face. For the first time I could remember, I didn't see a devious smirk across his face. I wondered if the man truly had a soul. I mean he was there for my father after their entire family had been killed.

My father's voice pulled everyone's attention to him. "Angela, to make room for some of our new quest, you will move into Haven's room. If you do not mind of course."

Angela smiled at my father. "I don't mind."

"Thank you. We are going to have more humans living here than normal as well. We need them for our daytime protection. Also, no one is to be away from the mansion alone." My father looked from Angela to me. "I'm sorry, but you two can no longer attend the school."

Great, my short time in the human world had become even shorter than I thought. I wanted my last three weeks to be spent with Philip. But now with less than that left in my Dayling life, I would be confined to this mansion. It wasn't fair. I started to complain, until I felt Axum's grip around me tighten. I guess it could be worse. I could be dead.

"Those of you who were involved with the battle last night should get some rest." Jean-Paul said.

The older Nightlings shook their heads in agreement. There was no use trying to resist the wills of Elders. There was definitely no use trying to resist the heads of three different families.

Axum released me. I kissed him on the cheek before I made my way up the stairs. Angela followed behind me, along with Sébastien.

Sébastien walked to my brother's room. He stopped and turned to me before he walked in. He smiled at me. I smiled back, and then he disappeared into the little runt's room. I couldn't believe Franklin didn't come downstairs to make sure I was okay. We had our issues, but he was still my brother. The runt must really hate me.

"Haven," I heard my name being called after Angela walked into my room. I turned from Angela, and stared into the beautiful shimmering blue eyes of Constance. "I would like to have a quick word with you."

I looked at Angela, who shrugged her shoulders; before I closed my bedroom door; leaving Constance and me to talk in private. "Sure."

Constance stood in front of me without moving. Her skin was a sparkling porcelain masterpiece. "I am glad that you and the others are well. Your brother was worried."

I sighed. "No he wasn't."

Constance smiled at me. "Give him time Haven." She leaned in closer to me. Her movement had been so quick I almost didn't see it. "Be careful."

And then she was gone.

I opened my door and limped into my room. Constance wasn't only known for her beauty, but also for her insanity. Since she had Franklin, Constance would rarely go out or be amongst the others. Myron blamed my father for her mind state as well.

Angela sat on one of my couches in the dark. I made my way over to her and sat down across from her. I didn't turn on the main light, instead I turned on a lamp I had sitting in the center of the table that sat in between my chairs.

We sat in silence for what felt like hours. Both of us were in our own worlds. I thought about Philip, while I was sure Angela thought about Mu-Lan.

I wondered if Philip would understand my world. If he would be willing to join me in hiding while a group of religious fanatics hunted my people down? Or would he be willing to live with me once I Crossed Over, and had to stay out of the sun? Or would he be willing to put up with my crazy Nightling aunt who creeped everyone out? I didn't know the answer to those questions. And since I was going to be trapped inside the mansion for a while, I didn't think I would get the answer.

Angela's cell phone rang, breaking the silence in my room; she looked at the number before she answered it. "Hey, sorry about last night." From the sound of her voice, it had to be Mu-Lan on the other end of the line. "No everything is fine. Haven got into another fight so we had to leave."

I couldn't believe she blamed everything on me, but in a way, I guess that's what happened. I wondered if I could use the same excuse with Philip? Yeah, I went to get the drinks and a group of kids jumped me for no reason. We had to leave because I got my ass kicked pretty good.

It's not like that would be a lie, just not the complete

truth, since it wasn't a group of kids, and the reason was because I'm a Dayling. Something I wasn't sure if I would ever reveal to Philip.

Angela stood from the couch and walked to my bathroom with the phone to her ear. She closed the door behind her for privacy.

I wanted to talk with Philip, but I realized I didn't know his number. I had no way of contacting him. I could have kicked myself for my lack of dating skills. The exchanging of numbers should have been the first thing I did.

All of a sudden a realization hit me. My kind has great memories if we concentrated on what we were trying to remember. Back at the hospital, the night Philip got attacked; he told the nurse his number. All I had to do was concentrate on that night and remember what he said.

Clearing my head was harder than I thought it would be. There was a lot going on in there. Thoughts of grief, pain and fear were clouding my mind. I had to push it all away to remember the number Philip gave the nurse.

After ten minutes of trying, finally it worked. I remembered that night, and I remembered the number. I picked up my iPhone, not wanting to use the house line in case big brother, AKA Vincent, was listening.

I dialed the number and waited. My hands were actually sweating as the phone rung a few times. Finally a woman answered it with a, "hello."

"Yes, is Philip there?"

The woman on the other end of the phone called Philip's name. I sat in silence for what felt like an eternity waiting for him to pick up the phone. Then I heard him whisper something to his mother, before I heard his voice on the line. "Yo, this Philip."

"Yo, this Philip? What type of greeting is that?" I joked, trying to seem relaxed.

He laughed on the other end of the phone. "Mara Jade? You always ditch guys at parties?"

"Naw, got into a thing with some of the guests. Guess that's what I get for messing with a playa."

Philip laughed again. It sounded like he was sitting down as he talked. "See, I can't imagine any girl getting the best of you MJ. You need to come with something better than that."

"One girl I can handle, ten is a little much for me." I said.

Again, wasn't like I lied, just left off the part about it being a group of trained vampire hunters. "So what you up to?"

"Homework. All of the teachers asked about you today. It seems you made a good impression with them. So why you missed school?"

"Didn't you hear me say ten girls jumped me? I was a little banged up today, thank you for asking." I sat back in the couch. The lamp from the table set the mood for me. I wished Philip was in the room with me instead of over the phone, but it would have to do.

"I can't see ten girls getting the best of you. So you can keep that lie for the teachers. I'm going to unlock the secret about you MJ. Eventually." Philip said with his arrogant tone.

That was one of the many things that were different between Philip and Sébastien. Philip was way more arrogant than Sébastien. Sébastien has a gentleman's presence to him. Philip has that bad boy thing working for him. I didn't want to think I was falling for the same trap every girl before me had fallen for. But I couldn't deny it; the bad boy with a pretty boy's face got to me.

"How long did you stay at the party after we left?" I asked.

"Not long. Talked to that Asian chick for a minute. Did you know she's into your cousin?"

"Yeah, they're on the phone now. What did you two talk about?"

I swore I could 'hear' Philip's half smile on the other end of the phone. "Wouldn't you like to know? So is your cousin using the same lie to her that you told me?"

"First off it's not a lie," I said. "Secondly, yeah Angela is telling her about me being attacked by ten girls."

"From the little time I spent talking to your cousin's girl, I think she's smart enough to see through that." Philip said. "See, if I was your cousin's girl, the first thing I would ask is, why didn't anyone see ten girls attacking your cousin? One girl taking on ten girls at once, the entire party would have stopped for that. Hell, one girl taking on a single girl would have stopped the party."

"They chased me outside," I said.

Again, he laughed at my lie. "And no one saw ten girls chasing after you?"

"One girl chased me outside while the others waited."

"You took on four jocks in an alley, but you ran from one girl? I would hate to see this girl."

I thought about trying to lie some more. But I wasn't stupid, and neither was Philip. He didn't believe a word I said. Might as well change the subject. "Did we have a lot of homework?"

"More than I thought for the third day of school. If you want I could bring the assignments over and we can do them together?"

I so badly wanted to say yes to Philip's suggestion. I couldn't. We were on DEFCON 1 at the mansion. Not to mention there were too many Nightlings around to allow Philip to come over. "Thanks, but I don't think that would be a good idea. My dad is in a mood."

Philip was silent on the other end for a moment. He then said, "Is it that dude that was with you at the party? You two got a thing?"

"Who? Sébastien? He's a friend of the family. We've known each other since we were little kids." I said.

"I've been with girls I've known since we were little kids."

"You've been with all kinds of girls." I joked. "There's nothing going on between me and Sébastien. He's just a really good friend."

"Good. You coming to school tomorrow?"

"Naw, don't know if I'm coming back. My dad's thinking about putting me back into home school again."

"Cool. Then I'll be by, and pick you up after I get out of school tomorrow. See you then."

Philip hung up the phone before I could say anything. I thought about calling him back and telling him I can't leave the house. I thought about it, but that would be listening to that smart part of my brain.

I hung up the phone just as Angela walked out of the bathroom. We exchanged half smiles as she made her way to my closet and pulled out the extra covers.

All of a sudden my iPhone rang. I thought it was Philip for a moment. But then I recognized the number, before I answered it. "Hello Olivia."

"So what happened to you guys? I looked for you at the party?" She said over the phone. She sounded annoyed.

Even though Philip didn't fall for my lie, maybe Olivia would. "Got jumped outside of the party. I had to go to the hospital, but I'm fine."

Olivia paused for a moment. "Who would be crazy enough to fight you?"

That damned rep of mine was starting to get on my nerve. "I didn't know the girls. They must have been from another school."

"Why did they jump you?"

"Don't know. They didn't say before they started swinging."

Another pause came from the other end of the line. It seemed no one believed me. And I thought I was a great liar. "I didn't hear about a fight." Olivia said with the same disbelief in her voice as Philip had.

"No one saw it. They caught me when no one was around. Listen Olivia; I'm still a little tired from what happened. Can I call you tomorrow?"

"You're not coming to school tomorrow?"

"I don't know if I'm coming back at all. My dad's pretty upset about the whole thing. He's thinking about putting me back in home school."

Another long pause came from the other end of the phone. I began to wonder what was I going to do when I Crossed Over and had to explain to people why my skin and eyes seemed to shine a little more, and why I couldn't come out during the day anymore. "Okay," Olivia finally whispered with curiosity humming in her voice. "I'll drop by sometime this week to see how you're doing."

Olivia hung up before I could respond. Great! Philip and Olivia in my house along with two other families of Nightlings.

SEVENTEEN

I was dreaming. The crazy thing about it, it felt like a Dream Transfer. But it couldn't have been, because you only get two of those, one of your mother and your father.

I felt crazed as I made my way through the hot night air completely naked. I couldn't seem to escape the heat wave even in my dreams. It was so unfair. Why couldn't I dream of a snow trip with Mario Lopez?

I moved with an unnatural speed. My feet barely touched the ground as I maneuvered around large oak trees, and leapt over tall fences I occasionally came upon. I didn't know where I headed or how I moved the way I did, I only knew I had to keep running.

Suddenly I stopped, causing fallen leaves to scatter in front of me. I sniffed the air. Something sweet lingered in the breeze. A smell I had never smelled before. It called to me like a dog in heat, jumpstarting an instinct I never knew I had.

Quickly I made my way to the source of the aroma.

I was in a park. It resembled any ordinary park found anywhere in the world. It had a broken down basketball court, along with a merry-go-round and a small swing set.

But the aroma came from a bench sitting to the edge of the park.

Slowly, I crept to the bench without making a sound. My breath evaporated in the air as I stood over the bench. I hungrily gazed down.

An old homeless man, trying to sleep in the smothering heat, lay on the bench. His face was rough, with patches of gray hair scattered around it. He also had long gray hair that draped to the side of the bench. He wore a filthy t-shirt, with pants cut off at the knees to form shorts. And the smell, the glorious smell, came from a small wound the man had on his right knee. I couldn't take my eyes from the little drops of blood dripping from the wound.

My eyes gradually made their way from the man's luscious knee, to his pulsating exposed neck.

I stood transfixed on the man's neck, watching his veins enlarge as the delicious blood flowed through them.

Without thought, I had my teeth inside of the man's neck. He didn't wake as I drunk his blood, instead he let out a slight moan.

As I drank the man's blood, I became overcome with a pleasure like nothing I had felt before. My entire body felt as if it was on fire as the life liquid entered me. I gnawed at the wound I made, begging for the blood to come quicker. I didn't want it to stop.

But the blood stopped flowing from the wound. Nothing was left inside of the man. I had drunk him dry, leaving an empty dead shell in front of me.

I stepped away purring and began laughing hysterically. I felt strong and filled with life. I was enraptured in a type of bliss like nothing I could explain. It was wonderful, that is, until I realized what I had done.

Oh my God! I killed someone. I didn't know what to do. The ecstasy was gone. Nothing was left except an overwhelming sense of terror.

I ran from the park with the homeless man's blood smeared on my face. I ran as the hot night air wrapped around my naked body.

I stopped again, except this time I fell to my knees, staring at the leaves on the ground. Everything became blurred. But I could see the red bloodstains dripping from my face onto the leaves. I vomited, releasing some of the homeless man's blood.

I couldn't move, no matter how much I wanted to, my body felt molted to the ground.

Finally, I fell over to my side. In the distance, I could make out the figure of a man coming towards me as I slowly faded into the darkness trying to cover me.

I awoke from the nightmare covered in sweat. I also felt a little bit of guilt for the pleasure I felt from drinking the man's blood. It had been a dream, nothing but a dream. It couldn't have been a Dream Transfer. It had to have been a simple nightmare.

I decided to keep it to myself.

I was in my bed while Angela slept on one of my couches. I told her she could sleep in the bed with me, but she mumbled something about me tossing and turning too much as she sprawled out on the couch.

I woke up before Angela and walked to my bathroom as she continued to sleep. I took care of all my hygiene, along with a long cold shower. When I emerged from the bathroom, Angela was placing the covers back in my closet. She gave me another half smile as she made her way into the bathroom.

She was being very odd. Angela normally would be talking my head off. She was hiding something from me again. Unfortunately, I was too busy hiding my own secrets to figure out hers. I had a few hours before school let out. A few hours to figure out either how to turn Philip away, or sneak out of the mansion while it was being super heavily guarded. If I planned on having a real date with Philip, I would need to come up with something fool proof quickly. Any slip ups, and I wouldn't just find myself imprisoned in the mansion, but in my room.

I put on my normal outfit, a white t-shirt and blue jeans, before I sat on my couch. The light from the sun illuminated my room enough for me to leave the lights off. Not to mention, it was too hot to have lights on anyway.

I thought about watching a little TV while I tried to figure out my next move. I changed my mind because I didn't feel like finding the remote. I lost it a week ago, although I swore Franklin hid it to torment me. I wouldn't put anything past the little runt.

I could hear the shower starting in the bathroom.

I sat back in the couch thinking about Philip. Something bothered me from the conversation we'd had. The same thing had been bothering me since I realized I was attracted to Mr. Cocky. He was a lot more experienced than me. He'd been with tons of girls, while I've been with no one at all. I wasn't planning on jumping into a physical relationship with him soon, but even a hanging out relationship would be more than I'd ever had. I couldn't count the times I hung out with Sébastien. We were little kids. Also, we mostly talked about family stuff.

Sébastien and I would spend most of our time together trailing behind Amina trying to feel like we belonged among the Nightlings.

I still couldn't believe Amina was gone. She was so beautiful and strong and smart. She was also the kindest Nightling I'd ever met before. Most Nightlings were like Sophia, dark and deadly, but Amina had a kind soul. The Mântuitors didn't care. They didn't care if she was a good person or not. They only cared about killing all of us. I wondered what they would do if they got their wish and destroyed all of my kind. They were too filled with hate to retire to a farmhouse or something. They would find another species to obliterate.

Poor Amina. *I hope all the bastards that hurt you burned in hell.*

I stood from the couch and made my way over to my chest. After pulling out a comb, I walked back to the couch, sat down and began combing my hair. It was still wet from the shower. I loved the way it felt to comb my hair while it was damp. Something about it soothed me. And my mind definitely needed soothing.

My body still felt a little sore from the major butt kicking I'd taken. It was funny how Philip saw me as this bad-ass-fighting-chick. I took out those four jocks in the alley because they were teenage boys. They didn't have any fighting skills beyond using their size to get the advantage. Mântuitors are way better fighters than high school jocks.

I wanted to learn how to defend myself better. I planned on asking my father to teach me some moves as soon as the sun went down. Until then, I was going to figure out how to escape the mansion. I might as well stop kidding myself. I knew I was going to leave with Philip when he showed up. I didn't know how I was going to do it, but I would figure it out.

Angela came out of the bathroom at the same time I heard a knock on my bedroom door. Angela was fully dressed as she emerged from the bathroom, so I advised the person knocking on my door to come in.

Sébastien stepped inside my room. Another Dayling followed behind him. Her name was Rachel Ali-Kufuru. She was two months away from crossing over.

Rachel stepped into my room and stood with her back to my door. She had light brown skin, with long curly hair and beautiful brown eyes. She wore a long black dress that hugged her slim body. The dress wasn't slutty like Sophia's normal attire. It had a sense of dignity to it.

Rachel smiled at me. I returned her smile with one of my own. "How is everything Rachel?"

Sadness built up in her eyes. Sébastien looked away as Rachel exhaled a long breath. "My dad didn't make it. He died with Amina."

I'd forgotten Amina wasn't the only member of Axum's family that had been killed by the Mântuitors. Eleven members of his family were killed, leaving only him and four others, including Rachel. It was senseless, all the murders the Mântuitors were committing, yet we were supposed to be the monsters.

"I'm sorry, I didn't know." I said.

Rachel moved her curly hair from her face. "Anyway, I heard about you and a human. I had to ask you myself about the details."

I saw Sébastien out the corner of my eyes. He looked hurt again by the mention of Philip. "Nothing to tell. Our first date was cut short by me almost being killed."

Rachel walked over to the couch in front of me. Angela already sat on the couch, so Rachel flopped beside her. Rachel turned to Angela with a smile. "Nice to see you again, Angela."

Angela didn't look at Rachel as she talked. "Sorry to hear about your dad."

Rachel's expression turned to sadness for a moment. She then pushed the sadness away as she looked back at me. "Will there be a second date?"

I shrugged. "With everything going on around here, I don't know."

Rachel's eyes gleamed a little. "Would you like to have a second date?"

Sébastien continued to stand in the shadows to the rear of my room. I looked over to him. "What are you doing? Why are you standing over there instead of sitting with us?"

He smiled. "It seems like its girl talk time. I'll stay over here."

Rachel turned to Sébastien. "Come on Bastien. Don't be a wuss."

Sébastien placed his hands in his pockets, his long blonde

hair hanging behind him. This time he wore a more casual white t-shirt, and cream-colored khakis. He slowly strolled over to my couches. He reluctantly sat next to me on the couch I sat on. "Happy?"

"Completely," Rachel joked. "Back to you Haven. Do you want a second date?"

I could feel myself blushing from the question. I hated myself for it. "Yeah, I would like a second date, one where no one tries to kill me. No dancing. Maybe some hand holding."

Rachel and Angela giggled with me. Sébastien shifted a little on the couch. It felt strange to have this moment with them. Rachel's father was dead, Amina was dead, and I was almost killed, yet we sat like your average teenage girls talking about a guy I had a major crush on. It was the life I wanted to live for the last three weeks as a Dayling.

Rachel turned to Angela. "Any guy caught your eye yet?"

This time Angela shifted in her seat. "No... no guy."

"Come on Angie, I bet you can get any guy you want."

"Maybe it's not a guy she wants." I mumbled out.

Angela shot me an evil look. Rachel looked at me with confusion. She then looked back at Angela. "Wait, what was that about?"

"Nothing. Haven was just being Haven." Angela said while still staring at me with daggers in her eyes.

Rachel turned back to Angela. "Come on. What's going on?"

"I don't want to talk about it right now." Angela said defensively.

Maybe I'd made a mistake hinting something about Angela and guys. I wasn't sure. I didn't think Angela should feel uncomfortable about it, but since she did, and I'd brought it up to Rachel, I decided to dive on the sword for Angela. "Anyway, I was plotting a prison break. Anyone in?"

Every one stared at me. I small smile crept across Rachel's face. "When?"

"Today. Around four."

"Got plans?" Sébastien said with acid in his voice.

"Yeah." I stood from the couch. "I don't want to let the Mântuitors keep me locked inside this mansion." I looked down at Sébastien. "I have less than three weeks left before I Cross Over. You got less than two. It's our right as Daylings to spend our last month anyway we want."

"Yes, as long as it is safe." Sébastien's light blue eyes focused on me. "Are you willing to risk your life to be with this human?"

I couldn't answer his question. I didn't know exactly what Philip meant to me. We hadn't spent enough time with each other for me to say I would die for him. That's why I needed to escape, to see if he was the 'dying for' type. "I'm talking about a day out on the town. Let's face it; with all the tension around here, we need this."

"I'm in," Angela said.

Sébastien turned to Angela with shock across his face. I, on the other hand, wasn't shocked at all. I was convinced Angela wanted to get out of the mansion just as badly as I did, maybe even more.

Rachel smiled at Angela, before she turned to Sébastien. "Come on Bastien. Don't be the odd man out. Not to mention I think these two have hot dates, so I'm going to need someone to hang with."

It became my turn to get a little jealous. It was a quick sensation of pain and anger. I tried to deny I felt it. I couldn't lie to myself. I didn't like Rachel and Sébastien hanging with each other alone. It didn't make any sense. But nothing made sense lately.

"Okay, I'm in." Sébastien said.

"Great, time to brainstorm." I said as I sat back down.

It took us almost until four o'clock to come up with a plan. It wasn't a great plan, but it was something that could work.

First thing we had to do was get our human guards off our trail. They would check on us every twenty minutes like clockwork. It was their order. They didn't want to deal with the consequences if they didn't follow those orders. So we had to figure out how to keep them from checking on us for the rest of the day. Sébastien, with his studies to become the next leader of his family, knew of a ritual that took hours to complete, and no humans can be around while you do it.

It became Sébastien's job to convince Vincent that we were doing the ritual as a way to deal with grief. The ritual was designed for that, and I was even thinking about doing it once we got back, but I wasn't sure Vincent would go for it.

Surprisingly, he did. Sébastien convinced Vincent to tell the guards to check on the others and leave the four Daylings in my room alone for the rest of the day.

Next, we had to figure out how to get out of my window,

through the estate and over the gate without setting off any alarms.

Rachel took care of the alarms. She used my computer to hack into the system. She set up a backdoor for us to use once we returned. She put the alarms on a fifteen second delay. With our super speed, we should be able to make it out of the mansion and to the gates.

The gates were going to be the problem. They ran on a separate line than the mansion's alarms. We couldn't shut them off. We were going to have to find a way over them without touching them. The thing about it, none of us could jump that high, at least not yet.

It was 3:30 when we decided to make our move. Angela called Mu-Lan, so someone could be waiting for us on the other side of the gate. Mu-Lan must have deep feelings for Angela to ditch school to help us out. I wondered if Angela would ever have the guts to tell her about what we truly are.

As soon as Rachel finished hacking the system and setting the alarms to shut off for fifteen seconds, we were off.

We made it out my window in no time. We used our hearing to time the rotation of the guards, so we were able to avoid them easily.

The yard wasn't hard to maneuver. It was a straight shot from my window to the gates without anything in our way. A few trees were scattered around, but they were better protection for us than obstacles.

Sébastien made it to the gate first. Not because he's faster than us girls, but because that's the way we set up the plan.

Sébastien stopped in front of the gate and turned around. Rachel got to him first, and in a full sprint, she ran straight towards him. Sébastien readied himself to help push her farther in the air. As soon as Rachel got to him, Sébastien cupped his hands, and pushed as hard as he could after Rachel placed her foot in them. She cleared the gate with room to spare.

Angela made it to Sébastien next. Angela did the same as Rachel, and was also propelled through the air and over the gate.

I almost lost my nerves as I rose my foot up to place in Sébastien's cupped hands. I thought about seeing Philip's half smile to keep me moving. I placed my foot in Sébastien's hands, and the next thing I knew I found myself in the air flying.

Sébastien put everything he had into slinging me in the air. He had no choice, on account of our bad plan. I had a piece of cloth tied to my ankle. As I left Sébastien's hands, he grabbed onto the cloth, and jumped behind me. The plan was, from the power of me leaping from his hands, along with him jumping a little, it should give us enough to make it over the gate.

I was honestly surprised when it worked. It didn't work by much, if Sébastien wouldn't have moved his feet just as he passed over the gate, it wouldn't have.

I hit the ground and rolled. My t-shirt got a couple of grass stains in it, but all in all everything seemed fine.

We stood on the other side of the gate laughing and giving each other high fives. Everyone was as shocked as I was that it worked. I think we all thought that Sébastien and I would never make it over the gate without setting off the alarms. We thought we'd be in deep trouble, waiting for the human guards to round us up.

Instead, we found ourselves waiting for Mu-Lan to pick us up. We didn't tell Rachel who Mu-Lan was to Angela. We explained her as being Angela's 'good friend'.

I stood on the side of the road thinking about the chance I was taking with meeting up with Philip. Sébastien's question echoed in my head, was I prepared to die for this guy? I hoped it wouldn't come to that. I just wanted to hang around and have some fun. I wasn't looking for proving my feelings by giving up my life before I Crossed Over.

It was still hot out; actually, it felt hotter than the day before. I didn't know if each day my body found it harder to be out in the sun, or if the world was spiraling into hell, either way I was ready for Mu-Lan's air-conditioned car. At least I hoped it was air-conditioned. Since I'd never ridden in it before, I didn't know.

I slowly turned to Angela. "Um, does Mu-Lan have A/C?"

Angela turned her head to the side with a puzzled look on her face. "I don't know. I hope so. It's hot as hell out here."

I looked down the street. I could see the waves of heat rising from the road. With my luck, I was betting she didn't.

EIGHTEEN

A few moments later, I found myself riding in the back seat of Mu-Lan's air-conditioned light blue Escalade. I thought with the gas prices being what they were, and going green being the new trend, the number of Escalades on the street would decrease. To a degree I suppose they had, obviously Mu-Lan didn't get the memo since her Escalade was a 2010.

We drove out of Summerbrooke with the A/C on full blast. I enjoyed the cool air as it flowed all over my body. I really, *really* hated the heat.

Mu-Lan had 2pac's 'Me Against the World' pumping through the speakers. Sébastien stared out of the window, with his head slightly bobbing to the beat. Rachel kept looking from Mu-Lan to Angela, working out what we didn't tell her in her mind. The thing about Angela and Mu-Lan was that they gave off a type of heat towards each other, it wouldn't take someone long to figure out something was up with them.

"So how did you two meet?" Rachel asked over the music.

Mu-Lan turned 'So Many Tears' down to answer Rachel. "At school."

Rachel sat in the middle of Sébastien and me. This gave her a perfect spot to gauge both Mu-Lan and Angela's responses. "Right. Not in class though, since you're a senior and Angela is a junior?"

Angela shifted a little in her seat. I didn't understand why Angela hadn't figured out that Rachel had already realized what was up with her and Mu-Lan. Either Angela was in denial, or pretending to be in denial. "We met at lunch. Mu-Lan saw me eating alone. She came by and sat with me and we became friends."

"With the way you two look, I bet you both had to fight the boys off the entire lunch period." Rachel said.

Sébastien lightly shot Rachel an elbow. When she turned to him, he gave her a frown to stop. Rachel frowned back.

Mu-Lan looked in the rearview mirror at Rachel. "Okay, you obviously know there's more to Angela and me besides friendship. Does that bother you?"

"It bothers me Angela didn't tell me herself." Rachel said as she looked from Mu-Lan's eyes to Angela's eyes.

"I'm not ready to tell anyone." Angela said as she frowned at Rachel.

Mu-Lan laughed. "Naw, she's a newbie. When I was a newbie, I went through this whole trying to figure out what it meant to be attracted to a girl thing. She's still trying to understand her feelings, so she doesn't want to tell anyone what she's feeling yet."

"She could have said that." Rachel said.

"Would you give it a rest?" Sébastien said half-annoyed. "She didn't tell you. Get over it."

"Someone is in a mood." Rachel said to Sébastien.

He turned back to staring out the window.

Mu-Lan glanced in the rearview mirror at me. "I'm supposed to take you to Philip's crib."

"What?" I said in mild shock. I'd agreed to go out with him, but he didn't say anything about hanging at his place.

"I saw him today at school after Angela called. I told him I was picking you guys up. He told me where to drop you off."

Rachel turned to me with a devilish smile. Angela even turned all the way around in her seat to smile at me. Sébastien grunted in the corner.

"Well, well, well," Rachel started. "It seems your man has plans for you."

"Shut up okay." I said as I sunk in the seat.

Rachel and Angela quickly forgot about their little battle to join together against me. I folded my arms in front of me, and planned to give Philip a piece of my mind once I saw him. How dare he make plans without asking me first? I wouldn't be that easy to control.

It didn't take us long to make it to Philip's house. He had a gate in the front of it, but not as tall as ours. As soon as Mu-Lan pulled up to the gate, it opened for us to enter.

We pulled up to the three-story house. It was white all over, with large windows around it. It didn't look as old as ours.

I looked out of the window of the SUV and saw Philip standing outside waiting for me. He walked over to the Escalade with a smile on his face. I opened up the door and got out. I tried to frown at him. I tried to be angry; instead, I smiled back like an idiot.

Philip walked over to the front passenger side door. "Nice to see you again, Angela. Don't worry, I'll make sure your cousin won't get into anymore fights today." Angela smiled back at Philip. He looked at Mu-Lan. "Nice ride."

"Thanks, nice house," she answered.

Philip looked in the back at Sébastien. "What up man?"

"Nothing much," Sébastien mumbled.

Philip then focused those beautiful dark eyes on Rachel. "Don't think we've met. Name's Philip."

Rachel smiled at my spiky haired prince. I didn't like the feeling I had in my guts. Rachel had lost her dad and her best fiend on the same night. She was also my friend that I loved very much. But I didn't like the way she looked at my men.

My men? I had to gather myself. What the hell was I thinking?

"My name's Rachel. Take care of my girl there." Rachel winked at Philip. "If you know what I mean?"

Philip tapped on the side of the Escalade's door, before moving away so the massive SUV could pull off.

As soon as the SUV drove out of Philip's estate, I turned to him. "Nice of you to ask me over."

"What? Last second change of plans." He reached his left hand out for me to take it. "Plus you don't have to worry about getting into fights around here."

"I don't know. Your gardener was giving me the evil eye when we pulled up." I said as I stared at his hand.

Philip reached for my wrist. He gently grabbed it. He started pulling me behind him. "Come on MJ. You can pretend you don't want to be here while we're cooling off in the house."

I walked behind him as he led me inside of his mansion. It was almost the size of my family's place. The entrance was large, with a large room to the right.

Philip pushed open the door to the room to the right. It had oak furniture all around it, with paintings of the great out doors adorning the walls. It even had light animal sounds coming from hidden speakers.

We walked to one of the oak couches and sat down. I looked around the room while soaking up the animal sounds. "That's just creepy."

Philip laughed. "I'll be sure to tell my mom."

I gave him a playful frown. "That's not what I meant... dork. It's just all so interesting." I felt a little strange commenting on the strangeness of Philip's sitting room, while I hid the fact that I was a Dayling trying to hide from vampire hunters.

Philip sat back on the couch. He stared at me in silence for a moment. "I haven't figured you out yet MJ. But I'm working on it."

"Work all you want. I'm a mystery worthy of Doctor Jones. See, I got some Geek Latin stored away." I joked.

"I guess we should get down to business." Philip said.

"Business? This is business?"

"Everything is business. Some business is just more pleasurable than others."

It was my time to laugh. "Does that ever work? I'm only asking, cause I'm trying to make up my mind on the brain power of my generation."

Philip gave me his half smile. I could tell he was in full charmer mode. "Has anyone ever told you you're a bit of a snob?"

"You just *now* getting that? A little slow to the draw there aren't we fella?" I sat back on the couch and looked around the room again. Everything seemed as normal as I'd thought it would, except for the animal sounds of course. The paintings weren't anything special, but everything in the room had an expensive look to it. Even the couch we sat on felt expensive. "So what's the plan? You got me here."

"That was as far into the plan as I got. I'm working on where to go from here." Philip joked before he stood from the couch. "You want something to eat?"

I stood up beside him. His 'extremely pleasant' strawberry scent almost knocked me back down. These newly developed senses of mine started to become a pain.

He walked out of the oak sitting room as I followed behind him. I sat at a counter, while Philip walked to the refrigerator and grabbed some sandwich meat and two sodas. He walked back to the counter, placed the meat and the sodas on it, and then got some bread, along with mustard and mayo. Philip began making two sandwiches. "You can tell a lot about a person based on how much mayo they like. So how much do you want?"

"Light mayo please."

He pretended to be calculating my request for light mayo in his head. "You know, that answers a lot of questions I had about you."

"Spending today with you has answered a lot of questions I had about you. You're insane." I joked as I reached for one of the sodas.

He finished making my sandwich, cut it in half and then gave me the two halves. "Light mustard as requested my lady."

Now came the hard part. I'd never been out with a guy before, so I didn't know the rules on how to eat a sandwich in front of a guy you liked. I knew there were rules to all of this; I just didn't know the rules. Sophia said something about not eating at all while out on a date, but that wasn't going to happen, on account of me being hungry.

I played around with the sandwich before I picked it up. I'd never cared what anyone thought about my feeding habits before. Normally I would be halfway done with the sandwich by now. Since meeting Philip, I'd noticed a few new behavior changes I was experiencing.

"Tell me you're not afraid to eat that in front of me? You're disappointing me MJ. I thought better of you than that." He said as he took the freshly made sandwich he had in front of him. He bit down on the sandwich, as mayo poured out of the bread onto his cheeks.

I took his lead by biting into my sandwich. I didn't swallow the whole thing like normally, but I was at least eating it.

"Do I make good sandwiches or do I make good sandwiches?" Philip gleamed to himself.

I looked around the kitchen trying to imagine myself living there. Could I really see myself eating sandwiches, playing house with Philip in this marble kitchen? Sad thing about it, yeah, I could see it.

I heard them before Philip did. I didn't know exactly whom it was walking towards the kitchen, but I could hear two different footsteps slowly making their way towards Philip and me. I started to say something to him; instead I decided to keep my mouth closed on account of not wanting to answer how I could hear footsteps coming down a hall covered in carpet.

When the rear door to the kitchen opened, I pretended to be just as surprised to see the man and woman walking in as Philip.

The man standing at the kitchen door looked to be in his mid forties, with two gray patches on each side of his dark hair. He looked like a man that came from money. He had a type of sophisticated air about him. He wore a gray sweater and khakis. The sweater caught my attention because of the suffocating heat outside, along with the fact the man didn't seem to be uncomfortable in it. No way he wasn't burning up inside.

The woman looked absolutely beautiful and also dignified in her stance. She had long brown hair, a thin face to go with her thin frame, and dark brown eyes. Her middle-aged skin had a hint of a tan to it, not at all pale like the man.

Both of them stood at the rear entrance of the kitchen staring at Philip and me. Oh yeah, as for me, I sat frozen in place with a mouth full of a ham and cheese sandwich with light mayo.

"Mom, dad, I thought you guys were going out for the day?" Philip said breaking the silence.

Great first impression Haven, they will definitely be inviting you to all the social dinners in the future. If you could have a future with a human, but that's a thought for another time, now I had to deal with mommy and daddy walking in on Philip and my lunch date. It wasn't like they walked in on us doing anything scandalous. It wasn't like they walked in us getting to know each other in the carnal sense. Nope! We were just having sandwiches. So why did I feel naked as Philip's parents stared at me?

Philip's mother took a step towards us. "So, Philip, are you going to introduce us to your friend?"

Philip seemed nervous as he looked from his parents to me. I began to get the feeling he wasn't ready for the whole meet the parent's moment we were having. "Sure, mom dad, this is Haven. Haven, these are my parents, Donna and Richard Flowers."

Philip's mother looked me up and down again. That feeling of being naked intensified as Mrs. Flowers obviously judged whether or not I was good enough for her son. Finally, she smiled at me as she extended her slim hand. "Nice to meet you, Haven. Such a pretty name for a pretty girl."

I could actually feel myself blushing all over as I took Mrs. Flowers hand in mine. "Thank you, Mrs. Flowers." I looked at her outfit; it was a sleeveless flower designed dress that came down to her ankles. She wore yellow high heels on her feet to match the dominant color of her dress. I thought about giving her a compliment on her outfit. That's what you're supposed to do to women right? My people skills needed a little practice. I didn't think Mrs. Flowers would believe a girl wearing a stained white t-shirt, jeans and Converse tennis shoes would truly appreciate her sense of style.

Mr. Flowers didn't say a word as he stared at me with his emotionless dark eyes. I couldn't read this man. I couldn't decide if he was plotting to kill me, or simply annoyed with my presence in his kitchen.

"So, Haven, do you attend Lexington High?" Mrs. Flowers said to break the tension of Mr. Flowers' silence.

"I did for a couple of days. Trying to talk my dad into letting me come back, but we'll see." I could feel Mr. Flower's eyes burning through me. I couldn't figure out what this guy had against me. Obviously he decided I wasn't good enough for his son as soon as he walked in the kitchen.

"Why wouldn't he allow you to go back to school?" Mrs. Flowers asked.

"She's home-schooled mom. The two days she spent at Lexington were the only days she's spent at any school." Philip said joining the conversation.

"I thought about trying home school for Philip, but I couldn't pass up on eight hours of freedom." Mrs. Flowers joked, causing me to relax a little. Having one out of the two parents to be cool is about as much as you can ask for I guessed. It would have been too much for me to ask for both of them falling madly in love with me. Oh no, I'm Haven Vigano; my luck doesn't work like that. "So what are you two kids planning on doing today?"

I looked towards Philip. I wondered the same thing as Mrs. Flowers. Philip gave his mom a more innocent smile than the devious ones he gave me. "A quick walk, then a dip in the pool."

"How am I supposed to go swimming? I didn't bring a swim suit." I said as I stared into Philip's eyes.

He tried to give me the same innocent look. "I was going to figure something out."

"Right," I said sarcastically as I understood his plan. I wasn't shocked, I mean he was a teenage boy; I was only a little surprised he thought it would work with me. Especially since it didn't work the first time he tried it.

"I think I can find an old swim suit for you to wear Haven." Mrs. Flowers said as she gave her son a displeasing look.

"Great," Philip started. "Lets start walking."

I gave Mrs. Flowers a smile, and she returned it with a warm smile of her own. Philip started out of the kitchen while I followed behind him.

Mr. Flowers' voice froze us in mid step. "I didn't catch your last name Haven?"

I turned towards the emotionless man. His dark eyes were staring at me. "Vigano, my name is Haven Vigano."

"Is that Spanish?" Mrs. Flowers asked.

"Italian. I'm part Italian and part English."

"A beautiful combination," Mr. Flowers said with a slight smile. His smile wasn't as warm as Mrs. Flowers.

"Thank you," I said before I turned to follow Philip out of the kitchen door.

NINETEEN

I understood the genius of Philip's plan. It felt so hot outside; I would have been willing to go skinny-dipping to cool off from the suffocating heat wave. I could feel the sweat running down my body as we walked down his street. We passed mansion after mansion, some with different types of gates, while others had tall trees hovering above the driveways.

We walked in silence at first. I could tell Philip felt guilty about how his father treated me back at his place. I was still dealing with the whole idea of being introduced to the family. It had been an experience I wasn't looking forward to experiencing again.

For the most part, I spent the silent part of our walk thinking about home. I wondered if Vincent would keep his agreement with Sébastien, or would he send someone in to check on us no matter if it meant disrupting the grief ritual. Knowing Vincent the way I did, I bet the posse had already assembled and rode out into the blazing sun.

Vincent had been with my family for ten years now. He started when he was fresh out of college looking for a gig with an investment firm my family used. Three years into his employment, he was brought into our world, and made our Chief Human Liaison. My life hasn't been the same since. Vincent, for some odd reason, believed Chief Human Liaison meant keeping 'me' in check. Whenever I got into trouble, Vincent would be right there to catch me in the act. I even tried to bribe him once, after I'd stolen the keys to my uncle's Porsche back in New York, and decided to go for a little ride. I offered Vincent two months of blissful smart-aleckless remarks. I found myself not only getting into trouble about the car, but also trying to bribe Vincent. My father didn't like the path his thirteen-year-old daughter was heading down.

"What's going on in that head of yours?" Philip asked, bringing me out of my thoughts of Vincent.

I looked over to him slowly walking beside me. He had his silly half smile on his face. "You couldn't handle what's going on in my head. A whole army of you would hold up their hands in surrender from a smidgen of what's going on up here." I tapped the side of my head.

Philip placed his hands in his pockets. He seemed to relax a little after he did it. "I don't think you're as complicated as you think you are. Interesting maybe, but not complicated."

"The non-complicated, interesting girl; has a nice ring to it."

"Hey, the main office receptionist quit today. She was at Lexington as long as you were." He said as he completely relaxed into his normal self.

"What do you mean?"

Philip squinted from the sun. "She was new. Guess she didn't like the job."

Well, that's one mystery solved. She had to have been Vincent's spy. That's also how he got us enrolled so easily in school.

Philip looked away at an old mansion as we passed it. I thought I even saw him take in a deep breath as if he was trying to savor every moment of our walk. "Sorry about my dad back there." He turned back to me. "He's normally not like that."

I didn't know what to say to him. I could lie and say it didn't bother me that his father had looked at me as if I was a pimple on the prom queen's nose. Or I could be honest and say how much of a jerk I thought his father was. "It's cool. I would have done the same thing if I'd caught my son alone with a floozy."

Philip stopped and reached for my arm. "You're not a floozy. And my father doesn't think you're one either."

I smiled at him. "Wasn't talking about me. Was talking about the last girl your parents caught you in the kitchen with."

Philip smiled. "Oh her, yeah she was a bit of a floozy."

I stood there staring at his smile. My body felt warm all over. It might have had more to do with the increasing heat pounding around us than my raging hormones, but I had to admit being able to stare at Philip's smile was worth the price I would pay once Vincent's men caught up with me.

I started to say something when I noticed a white van coming down the street. Normally a white van driving down a street wouldn't catch my attention. The thing about this particular white van was that I couldn't hear what went on inside of it. My super Dayling hearing had increased each day I got closer to Crossing Over. I was at the point of hearing muffled sounds coming from cars. Like a radio, or people talking, or even the A/C blowing. Even if everyone inside of the car was silent and not listening to music, there was no way they were driving in this heat with rolled-up, tinted windows without the A/C.

I turned back to Philip. My heart pounded in my chest. We were going to have to make a run for it, and I couldn't tell him why. I really hated the Mântuitors. "We need to get out of here. I can't say why, but we need to get away from that white van."

He looked towards the white van with his eyes squinted. He looked back at me, and then looked around at the different mansions around us. "Okay, hold onto my hand."

He held out his hand for me to take it. I took it in my hand, knowing full well I should be the one leading this escape. I could pick him up and run a lot faster than him, but I wasn't ready to reveal myself yet, so instead I allowed him to lead the way.

Without saying another word, Philip took off in a full stride towards a gray mansion. I ran beside him with our fingers interlocked. I didn't turn around to see the van speed towards us. I didn't have to, since I could hear the tires squeal out on the road.

Philip chose a mansion that didn't have a gate for us to climb. It was a good idea; except for the part about there was nothing to slow the people chasing us down either. For a moment, I thought maybe Vincent's men were chasing us. Unfortunately, Vincent would never send his men in a white truck with tented windows. He would want me to see them coming.

Philip and I ran up the driveway full speed. At least Philip ran full speed, I, on the other hand, had to slow up a little so I could stay beside him.

I could hear the van turning down the driveway as we made it to the mansion's front door. Philip turned the door-knob, to my surprise, the door opened right up.

We jumped in the mansion and locked the door behind us.

I turned to Philip. "How did you know it was unlocked?"

He looked out the peephole. "The Johnsons! They never lock their door."

"That's not smart." I said as I peeped out a window.

"Good thing they aren't, or we'd be stuck out there."

I saw five men jump from the van. They were dressed from head to toe in black. They made their way towards the front door.

They were definitely Mântuitors. I had to figure out how to get Philip and myself out of this quickly. I didn't want him to die because of me. I also didn't want to die in this strange mansion. "We need to find a way out of here."

Philip turned to me with a smile across his face. He grabbed my wrist and pulled me towards the back of the mansion. We passed through a long hall until we got to a wall in the back. The wall was covered in a large painting of President Bush, the Second.

I looked towards Philip. "Oh great, I'm going to die in the house of a republican."

He gave me his half smile. "You were going to make out with a republican." He touched a spot to the side of the painting. A door opened in the middle of it. We ran through the door and allowed it to close behind us, just as the Mân-tuitors crashed through the front door.

We stood in a room in silence. The room had video moni-tors all over it, along with guns and other 'end of the world must haves.' Like walkie-talkies and food rations.

"I don't know if I'm safer in here or out there. You people are crazy you know that?"

Philip made his way to a seat in front of the monitors. "Coming from the girl who has five guys dressed in black, driving a white van chasing her."

I walked over to the monitors and sat next to him. "That's not crazy, that's just living dangerously."

The entire mansion was like Big Brother After Dark. Every

room, bedroom and bathroom could be pulled up by the monitors. It even had sound.

"Tell me, does Mr. Johnson invite a lot of girls over here for candy?" I asked as I looked at one of the Mântuitors pulling out a dagger.

Philip frowned at me. "This is his safe room. All of us rich republicans have them."

"For the day when you overthrow the government? Good to know." I watched as the Mântuitors made their way from room to room.

Philip studied the monitors. "Why do we have to overthrow what we already control?"

"You guys lost, get over it." One of the Mântuitor's took out a small device. I didn't study up on my fanatic religious assault group gadget guide, so I didn't have a clue what the device was for, but since the guy holding it planned on killing me, I decided it wasn't good. "Is there another way out of here?"

Philip turned to me with a smile. "Of course." He stared back at the monitors. "But don't you wanna see what they're going to do?"

"Not really," I said as the man started mashing buttons on the device. "So can we go now?"

"Why don't you go out there and get your Mara Jade on?" Philip said as he started typing something on the keyboard in front of us.

I looked at the men on the monitors again. I wanted to hurt them real bad. I wanted them to pay for Amina and Rachel's father and every one of my kind they'd killed over the years. Still needed to be trained before I could take on five Mântuitors alone. "They can fight a little better than your average basketball jocks."

Philip stopped typing on the keyboard. He stared at the man with the device on the monitor. The man tossed the device to the floor and motioned for the other men to leave the mansion. Philip then pushed enter on the keyboard before he stood. "I'm thinking its time for us to leave."

I stood up beside him as a trapdoor opened on the floor. "Again, are all of your people this paranoid?"

He took my hand as he started down the stairs of the trapdoor. It was dark, with a single light illuminating at the bottom of the stairs. Philip couldn't see anything as he felt the wall while we made our way down. I could make out a little with my heightened vision.

We made it to the light and walked into a tunnel. Philip typed in a code in a keypad beside the entrance of the tunnel. A blast door slammed down behind us. "Come on," Philip said as he started down the tunnel.

We walked in silence for a few feet, and then the tunnel began to shake a little as if something exploded over it. *Goodbye Johnson's mansion*, I thought as we continued down the tunnel.

"So, you gonna tell me what's going on?" Philip said.

"Overdue rentals. I meant to take them back a week ago." I said while trying to think up something to tell him.

He stopped in his tracks. He turned to me. The tunnel had little lights on the ceiling leading to the end of it. "I've just saved your ass this time. I think I deserve to know what's going on."

"I agree, you deserve to know," I said as I stared into his dark eyes. "Still can't tell you. At least not yet." Philip turned from me heading towards the end of the tunnel. "So, how did you know about all of this?"

"Mr. Johnson and my dad are friends. He showed me everything and gave me the codes in case of an emergency."

"Protecting a damsel in distress would be an emergency." I tried to change the mood with a joke. The reality though, everything was dead serious. I had no idea how the Mântuitors kept finding me. It didn't seem possible they were driving around hoping to get lucky, and then happened across me. Maybe they knew about Philip and me? If so, Philip wouldn't be safe anymore.

We made it to the end of the tunnel. Philip opened a door that led to stairs going up. We walked up the stairs and out of another trapdoor in the floor of a small outhouse.

He closed the trapdoor behind us. "Now what?" He asked as he walked to the only window in the outhouse.

"Now I make a phone call," I said as I pulled out my iPhone and dialed Angela's number.

After two rings, she answered while still laughing. "Hello?"

"Yeah, sorry to bother you, but I'm going to need you to come and pick me up." I said in the phone.

I heard Angela whisper for Mu-Lan to giver her a minute.

"You can't wait one more hour?"

I sighed. I didn't want to disturb Angela's happy time, but I had no choice. "Our friends showed up while Philip and I were walking. You know, the ones who dress in all black. They blew up a mansion trying to kill us."

She was silent for a moment. "Are you both okay?"

"Yeah," I turned to Philip. He leaned against the wall watching me. "You know where Sébastien and Rachel are?"

"Yeah, we'll swing by and get you and Philip first. I'll call Sébastien and warn him about what happened to you. So where are you?"

I handed the phone to Philip for him to tell Angela how to get to where we were. After Philip stopped talking to Angela, he hung up my iPhone and handed it to me.

We stood in silence for what felt like hours. Only a few minutes had passed, but each second slowly ticked away like everything moved in slow motion. I thought about trying to make a joke again. I quickly decided not to as I saw the look on Philip's face. He was gearing up for an argument. I'd seen that look way too many times on everyone I've every talked to. I could literally see the storm building in his eyes.

"Okay, enough is enough. I want to know what's going on!" He said as he stood from the wall.

"Sorry, can't tell you that." I answered.

He walked towards me. He didn't storm over or explode like I thought he would do. He moved slowly, and kept his tone low and even. "Listen Haven, whatever is going on, I'm a part of it now. I cost my father's friend his place. Not to mention, I would have been in the mansion when those guys blew it up. It didn't seem like they cared too much about killing me to get to you."

I moved towards him to meet him halfway. "That's why I can't tell you. You've already been placed in way more danger than I wanted to place you in." We stopped only inches from each other. I could feel his breath. I could smell his strawberry scent. Everything became intoxicating. I wanted to take his arms and wrap them around me and... I turned from him to gather myself. I didn't have time to fantasize about a guy I almost got killed.

Philip's hand gently touched the side of my jaw. He slowly pulled my face back around to face him. I stared directly into that half smile of his. "You have to know by now that I like you. I'm not going anywhere. I'm a part of whatever this is no matter what."

"You say that now, but wait until it's your mansion that gets blown up." I said as I continued to stare at Philip's smile.

He started to lean towards me. "It's worth the risk."

Just as he was about to kiss me, we heard a knock at the door to the outhouse. We both froze for a moment, until the knock came again.

Philip crept over to the door, and peeped out of a little peephole. He opened the door and stood to the side for Angela to walk in.

"We passed by where the mansion used to be. Police and the fire department are all over the place." Angela said as she stepped into the room. "It's crazy out there."

"Good, we can escape while everyone is busy." I said while catching my breath. I guess it was fitting, I disturbed Angela's happy time, and she returned the favor by disturbing mine. I turned to Philip. "You should go straight home. Maybe even call someone to pick you up."

He smiled at me. "I'll let you keep me in the dark for now MJ." He walked up to me and gently kissed me on my forehead. "Be careful."

"You too," I said before I walked out of the shack with Angela.

TWENTY

I sat in silence as Angela continued to stare at me in the rearview mirror. I knew exactly what went through that mind of hers, the same thing that would've gone through mine. But I didn't have time to daydream about Philip. I almost got him killed. I couldn't put him in danger like that again. I had to stop seeing him until the Mântuitors were taken care of.

Mu-Lan turned down West Pensacola Street heading to Florida State University. I should've known Rachel would have chosen a college to visit on our day as escaped fugitives.

Angela pulled out her cell phone. She made a call. I heard her say 'we're here' in the phone. Then she pointed for Mu-Lan to turn.

A few moments later we were pulling up to Sébastien and Rachel. Both of them didn't look pleased. They looked a little shaken as we pulled beside them.

They got in the Escalade and we pulled off.

Sébastien looked over to me. "Are you okay?"

"Yeah, I'm fine." I said as I glanced towards Mu-Lan.

I didn't know how much she knew. I didn't want to tip her off to our secret, although she had to be suspicious of something, since she knew someone blew up a mansion to try and kill me.

Rachel followed my glance. She understood why I wasn't elaborating on what happened. "We'll talk about it back at the house. I'm just glad you're okay, Haven. I couldn't lose anyone else."

I gave Rachel a slight smile. I'd felt jealous of her and Sébastien. I felt bad about thinking the things I did. She was like family to me, even more so than my own brother. The time for bickering was over. We needed to be tighter to take out the Mântuitors, before they take all of us out.

Sébastien lowered his voice for me to hear him. "Should we do as last night and not head straight back to the mansion?"

I thought about it for a moment. We didn't know if the Mântuitors were tracking us, although I didn't think they stayed around after they blew up the Johnson's mansion. "It might be best to ride around for a little while for safety. I don't think they're tracking us, but we don't want to take that chance and be wrong."

Sébastien and Rachel agreed. The thing we had to do now was convince Mu-Lan to drive us around, without telling her why we didn't want to go home after someone just tried to kill me.

Mu-Lan looked back at me in the rearview mirror. "You guys want me to drive around to make sure none of the Mântuitors are following us?"

Sébastien, Rachel and I had our mouths hanging open for at least two minutes. I was shocked to say the least. How the hell did she know about the Mântuitors?

Angela turned around in her seat. She slowly looked from Sébastien to Rachel to me. "I told her everything. I didn't want to keep what I am a secret from her."

Sébastien looked as if he was about to start cursing in French. Rachel only stared at Angela, while I stared at Mu-Lan. I hoped Angela didn't make a huge mistake by trusting the Asian beauty. Our lives depended on it. If Mu-Lan wasn't who she said she was, then we would all be in more trouble than we could handle.

Mu-Lan made another turn in the car. It was obvious to me someone had to say something. I wasn't prepared to be the one to break the silence in the Escalade. Mu-Lan did it for me. "I've been checking behind us, I don't think we're being followed."

"Okay, let's head home then." I said trying not to freak out in the backseat.

The rest of the ride to the mansion had been filled with awkward silence. Mu-Lan dropped us off where she picked us up. Angela said something to her, before Mu-Lan drove towards the front gates.

Angela stood beside us. "She's going to give us a little

while to sneak back in, and then she's going to ask for me at the gates and come in to talk with you guys."

No one said a word. We exchanged looks before we began our break in.

Rachel used her Blackberry to hack into the backdoor she created in our security system. After she turned everything off, we repeated what we did to escape, to break back in. Once we were over the gates, we quickly made our way to my bedroom window. We were up the side of the mansion walls and through my window within seconds. Rachel turned back on the security system and purged all the data about her backdoor.

Surprisingly, Vincent hadn't disturbed the room. Everything seemed just as we left it. The only thing that was different, had to do with Angela's girlfriend knowing everything about us and waiting at the front gate to enter the mansion.

We sat on the couches in the same places we had earlier that day. We waited for the knock on the bedroom door in silence.

As soon as the knock came, Angela made her way to the door. She opened it to find one of Vincent's human guards standing on the other side. He didn't seem as if he wanted to be knocking on our door. He truly thought we were doing some type of grief ritual. He was being respectful and all. I felt a little bad about the lie we'd told.

"Ma'am, sorry to bother you, but someone is at the gates asking for you. They have a text from your phone number, asking them to come to the mansion." The very large man said.

"Yes, her name is Mu-Lan. Show her to the room. We are finished with the ritual." Angela said with her in charge voice.

She closed the door to my room. Again, we all sat in silence as Angela waited for Mu-Lan by the door. I wished I had that mind reading trick. It would have been nice to know what everyone thought, especially Angela for telling Mu-Lan everything.

A new contemplation entered my mind. If Mu-Lan was truly cool with what we are, then why couldn't things work with Philip and me? Of course I would wait until after the Mântuitors were all defeated. I didn't want to place him in any more danger, but afterwards, I would tell him everything.

Another knock echoed from my door. Angela opened it, and then paused as she stared at whoever stood on the other side of the door, along with Mu-Lan.

Mu-Lan walked in first, and then Philip followed behind her.

My heart almost leapt out of my chest. It was like a nightmare: Philip was at my family's mansion, standing in my room, with my father sleeping beneath us. I would have to rethink that not placing Philip's life in danger thing, since he seemed to do it quite frequently himself.

He stood at the edge of the couch with his half smile. Angela locked the door before she sat back down on the couch. Mu-Lan followed Angela, and sat beside her.

I couldn't take my eyes from Philip. Unfortunately, neither could Sébastien. Philip had no idea what he'd gotten himself into.

"Is it me or is everyone being weird?" Philip asked to break the silence.

"It's not you," I said.

Rachel moved down a little to make room for Philip to sit. He sat down beside her. Leaving Rachel to sit in the middle of my human crush, and my Dayling crush. I felt so glad I wasn't sitting there. No way could I have taken that.

Philip looked around the room. "So this is Mara Jade's lair? I get the retro feel."

"You see, most people don't. They go for the whole pink thing, but I'm old school." I said trying to ease the tension.

"So why are you here?" Sébastien said through clenched teeth to Philip.

"To see a girl." Philip said back to Sébastien.

I could see the macho staring contest beginning to kick off. I wasn't one of those girls that enjoyed watching guys fight it out over them. Especially since one of those guys were less than two weeks from becoming an immortal. "I thought the plan was for you to lay low. You remember your father's friend's mansion being blown up right?"

Philip reluctantly turned from Sébastien. "Yeah. Do you remember me saying whatever was going on with you; I was in it too now? So you might as well fill me in on what's going on, cause' I'm not going anywhere."

Sébastien laughed. It was low, and very creepy. "I want you to say that to her father."

Philip turned back to Sébastien. The macho staring contest was back in full effect. "I will if I have to. I've never been afraid of fathers."

Sébastien laughed again. I on the other hand took in a long gulp. If Philip tried to stand up to my father, nothing on this earth could protect him. I would have to make sure that never happened.

I looked over to Mu-Lan, who watched us with pure curiosity. Having humans on our side could be a good thing. We had human's that worked for us anyway. Even though it would be different for lovers. What would happen if Angela and Mu-Lan broke up? Not to mention, what would Angela's father do if he found out Angela was in love with a human girl?

And yet neither of them seemed to care. Angela looked as peaceful as ever. We were in the middle of a war, our kind was being killed, and one of us worked with the enemy, yet Angela didn't seem to be stressed out about it.

I decided to trust her, by trusting Mu-Lan. I also decided to bring Philip into the fold. Maybe my reasons were selfish. Maybe I wanted the look Angela had on her face, it didn't matter; the decision had been made.

"Okay, Philip, you want to know what's going on?" I said with an even tone. Philip tore his eyes from Sébastien towards me. He slowly shook his head yes. "The guys that blew up the Johnson's mansion were vampire hunters. They are called Mântuitors."

Philip looked around the room at everyone's expressions. Everyone else stared at me. Sébastien looked as if he was about to explode. Rachel, on the other hand gave me a slight smile of approval. It was done with. My idea of living a normal life for my last few weeks in the sun had gone bye-bye.

"Vampire hunters," Philip asked in disbelief.

Mu-Lan spoke for the first time. "Yep, Philip vampires are real, and you and I are the only two humans in this room."

He turned to Mu-Lan. "You believe they are vampires? Real vampires?"

"Not the way you know vampires," Rachel began. "We are called Daylings, because we still live like humans. On our eighteenth birthday, we become Nightlings, something closer to the legends. Just not evil."

Philip turned from Rachel to me. He stared at me with his dark exotic eyes. I gazed into them, looking for the same thing I'd looked for back at the hospital, after I'd saved his life in the alley. Again, I didn't see it. I didn't see the fear I looked for. "Cool."

I shook my head in disbelief. "Cool? You find out you're in a room filled with soon to be blood drinking, day sleeping, mind reading vampires and all you've got to say is cool?!"

Philip had his half smile on his face again. "Dead sexy cool. At least three of you are."

I couldn't help but laugh. A few seconds later, the room filled with really good bouts of laughter from everyone, everyone except Sébastien, of course.

"Now that's over with, what are we going to do next?" Rachel asked as everyone finished.

"Angela gave me the quick version of what was going on. Maybe it would help if Philip and I knew more." Mu-Lan said as she squeezed a little closer to Angela. I still had a hard time dealing with a human, who didn't work for us, knowing about what we were and was in love with one of us. It might have been too much to ask for there being more than one human to fit that description.

I looked over to Sébastien, who pouted on the corner of the couch. I wasn't sure how I felt about him romantically. I was sure we needed him on our side no matter what we decided to do. Also, he really was a good friend to me. "Sébastien, I'm not one to point out the obvious, but you're the closest to Crossing Over than the rest of us. Not to mention you're a shoe-in to be your Father's second in command as soon as you Cross Over, giving you certain privileges the rest of us don't have. We need you to get over whatever is bothering you until this is dealt with."

Rage flashed in Sébastien's eyes for a moment. I could feel the words he wanted to unleash on me building inside of him. I thought all hell was about to break out. Instead, I could see understanding forming in his beautiful blue eyes. "You're right. What is done is done. Nothing is left except to figure out how to save our people from the Mântuitors."

Philip sat up a little on the couch. He again had no sense of fear coming from him. He acted as if talking about vampire hunters was an everyday thing for him. Like talking about a football game to his friends. "So what's up with these guys? They know about you all, and go out of their way to kill you. Even if that means blowing up mansions with innocent sexy high school boys in it."

"Maybe the guys blowing up the mansion were there for you. Messed with any overly religious killer's girlfriend lately?" I joked.

He gazed at me with a grin. "Let me think about that for a little while. I'll get back to you if something comes up."

Angela looked from Sébastien to me. "I think we should tell them everything. Either we trust them or not."

"I'm still not sure we should trust them. So everything isn't on the table. The bare minimal should be enough." Sébastien said as he gazed into Angela's eyes. It wasn't hard to guess Sébastien wasn't going to open up his world to outsiders simply because Angela and I had crushes on the outsiders in question.

Rachel told the story of the Mântuitors. She told as much as we felt they needed to know. Ancient sect of warriors commissioned to hunt down and kill our kind, the fact that they have moved up in the world, and were more powerful than ever before, and oh yeah, we suspect one of our own is helping the Mântuitors hunt us down.

Once Rachel finished talking, the two humans sat in silence contemplating what they were allowing themselves to be dragged into. I wouldn't have blamed them both if they would have stood up, said this wasn't for them, and left without saying another word to either of us.

Surprisingly, or maybe more expectantly, Mu-Lan leaned over and kissed Angela on the side of her face. She whispered in Angela's ear that she would be there for Angela anyway she needed her. Angela's entire face lit up after Mu-Lan pulled away.

Philip winked at me with his half smile on his face. "I guess that means we're in. So what's the plan?"

It was a good question. One I'd been thinking about since the Mântuitors overran the Johnson's mansion. "I'd been thinking. I don't believe the Mântuitors happened to be at the same party we were all at."

Sébastien's eyes seemed to liven up a little. The anger and jealousy had completely left. "I agree. I've been thinking the same thing. Whoever is helping the Mântuitors tipped them off we would be at that party"

"Here's the thing," Philip started. "Whoever you guys' traitor is must be high up on the vampire totem pole. Think about it. How would they know exactly where every family would be? Does everyone have access to this information?"

"No," Rachel began as she followed where Philip headed.

"Do you think it's a family leader?"

Sébastien leaned forward. "Or someone close to a family leader. Maybe a second?"

I sat up in the couch. I leaned forward, causing everyone else to lean forward with me. Okay, we need to come up with a list of all the top players. We need to figure out who has the most to gain from all of this. And we need to think outside the box. I'm betting the Elders are already working on this, but they're not thinking about it from every angle. We need to come at it from places they wouldn't think to go." I looked from Philip to Mu-Lan. "Last chance for you two to get out of this. Remember, they blew up a mansion to kill me, even though they knew an innocent was in there with me."

Philip grinned again. "I've not been called innocent in a long time."

I frowned at him to emphasize the seriousness of what was going on. "You know what I mean."

"Yeah," Philip looked over to Mu-Lan, before he returned his gaze to me. "We understand."

"Good. I think our days of sneaking out are over. We need you guys to be our outside eyes and ears. See if you can get the police report about the explosion. Also, talk to a few people from the party. See if someone thought they saw something they didn't want to share with the police." I said.

Philip stood from the couch. Mu-Lan joined him. Philip looked down at me with his smile. "Got it. We'll get started on the kids from the party."

I stood up in front of him. A part of me couldn't stop thinking about kissing him. I pushed that thought to the side, for now. "Make sure you both are together while you're interrogating the kids from the party. I don't want either of you caught alone."

He continued to smile at me, before turning to Mu-Lan. "You ready?"

Mu-Lan kissed Angela on the side of her face again before joining Philip.

I watched as they made it to my door. I then stopped them. "Oh yeah, don't come back here at night unless it's an emergency. It might not be safe here during the night for you guys."

They bowed their heads in understanding before they walked out of the room.

TWENTY-ONE

We spent all day trying to come up with a list of Elders that would gain from having most of us killed off. It wasn't easy; it wasn't like there was a lot of info about Nightling Elders lying around. I even tried to get a little info from Vincent without allowing him to know exactly why I wanted the info. Instead of learning something useful, I spent most of that time avoiding Vincent's questions about our two guests. I dodged him as best as I could before I returned to my room. We kept the door closed as we tried to figure out who the traitor was.

I kept coming up with one name, but I wasn't comfortable revealing it while his daughter's half-sister sat in the room with me. Myron was at the top of my list. The only reason I wasn't ready to accuse him of being the traitor was because Sophia had been with us at the party. I didn't know how Myron truly viewed Angela, since he was more like a surrogate father and not her real father, but I knew how much he valued Sophia. He would have never put her in that much danger.

By the time night came around, we were still nowhere. Philip had checked in a few times with information about kids they talked with. No one seemed to have seen anything at the party. Also, it would be impossible for him to get the police report on the explosion. Philip said even the Johnsons were finding it hard to get straight answers from the police about what happened. The Mântuitors were well connected, so it wasn't that strange they made sure nothing about their involvement would be leaked out.

We decided to only work on our project while the Night-lings slept. We didn't want any of them listening in on what we were doing, not only with their super hearing, but also with their ability to read minds.

I left the others in my room '*trying to act normal*'. I walked to my favorite place in the entire mansion, the kitchen.

As soon as I walked in the kitchen, I became sorry for it.

Sophia greeted me with her nasty smile. "So you had a visitor today? Your human boyfriend."

I walked by her to the refrigerator. "He's not my boy-friend. He's just a guy I'm cool with."

She laughed. "I thought you weren't cool with anything or anyone." She walked up to me and whispered in my ear. "Face it Haven, you got a thing for the human."

I pulled out an apple and a little juice carton. "Don't you have more important things to do than to bother me? Shouldn't you be helping the others with our Mântuitor prob-lem?"

She took the apple and juice out of my hands. "Your fa-ther wants to see you. He's in the Oriental room."

Sophia flashed her nasty smile at me before she disap-peared from the kitchen. I wondered what my father wanted with me. I didn't think he knew what had been going on with the others and me. There was no way he figured it out, unless I had missed something.

Slowly, I made my way to the sitting room. A million thoughts raced through my head. None of them gave me comfort.

I saw her standing completely still out of the corner of my eyes. Constance wore a white gown that made her look even more like a ghost, since her porcelain skin glistened.

I stopped and turned to her. "Hello Aunt Constance."

The wind around me changed, and then she stood inches away from my face. My heart almost exploded from my chest for the hundredth time.

Constance turned her head to the side as she stared at me. "Tell them Haven."

Damn! Did she know about us looking into Elders? "Tell them what?"

She leaned in closer towards me. I leaned back a little, not sure if she was about to whisper to me or bite me. "Tell them about the dream."

And then she was gone.

Tell them about the dream? Sooner or later, we were going to have to find a white padded room for her to live in.

I opened the door to the Oriental room. Not only my father, but also Axum and Jean-Paul sat in the room.

All three Nightlings focused their powerful eyes on me as I walked into the sitting room. I tried not to think about all the secrets I kept from them. They could rip them out of my head without breaking a sweat. I felt so nervous I almost stumbled as I made my way to the seat they had sat out for me.

It felt as if I had entered an interrogation room. The three of them sat in front of the single chair they had out for me. They watched me as I slowly sat down. I didn't look at any of them in their eyes. I sat quietly waiting for them to start.

My father broke the silence first with a very odd and terrifying question. "So how was your day, mio fiore dolce?"

The way they stared at me clued me in on the fact they knew something. Exactly what they knew, I wasn't sure. I had only one way to find out. "Fine."

"It would be wise to speak truthfully, Haven." Axum said with his thick African accent. He came from a small village on the outskirts of Gao, during Ali the Great's rule.

"Okay, obvious you guys got something you want to know. Ask and I shall answer. You don't play games, and I won't play games." I said trying to sound confident.

Jean-Paul actually laughed. Axum gave me a slight smile, but my father's facial expression didn't change.

My father sat up in his seat. His shimmering dark eyes trapped me into place. My father would never hurt me. I knew he wouldn't, but I couldn't stop feeling the fear building inside of me as he stared at me. "We know you and some of the others left the mansion today. Vincent checked on you while you were supposed to be doing your ritual. He placed a listening device in your room before you returned." He paused, allowing me to understand exactly what he said. They knew about Philip and Mu-Lan. That really wasn't good. "You will invite the human's over tonight. We shall speak with them. Then you shall cut off all communication with them. Is that understood?"

It became time for me to do what I'd never done before. Challenge my father in front of others. "You guys continue trying to keep us in the dark. You have your reasons, but we are in just as much danger, if not more danger, as the rest of you. We're going to find out what's going on, and there is nothing you can do to stop us."

My father was out of his chair and had his hands wrapped around my shoulders before I could blink. Axum and Jean-Paul didn't move as my father held me above him showing his fangs. "You openly defy me?"

I kept thinking over and over again, *my father would never hurt me, my father would never hurt me, my father would never hurt me.* "You and I both know you would never bite me, so you can put away the fangs. You can also put me down. I love you dad, but I'm not afraid of you anymore." I tried to slow my heart as I spoke to him. I felt pretty sure he wouldn't hurt me. Of course there were other things he could do to punish me. I hoped he wouldn't do those either.

He gently placed me on the floor. His eyes flashed with pain. It was the first time I'd seen that in my father's eyes. At least the first time I'd caused it. "You place us all in danger. You place yourself in danger over a human." He slowly sat back in the seat between Axum and Jean-Paul. "You are right. I would never hurt you. But I would send Sophia after the human boy."

My entire body went weak with panic. I could flip out and lose my cool, which would get Philip killed, or I could play whatever game they wanted to play. If my father simply wanted me to stop seeing Philip, he wouldn't have needed the back up to do it. "Okay," I sat down in the seat. "What else do you want?"

"You believe an Elder is helping the Mântuitors? You believe it might be someone close to the Elder, yes?" Jean-Paul asked.

"You've heard our conversations. So you already know the answer to that." I hissed out. I wanted them to know I wasn't pleased with this exchange. Not surprisingly, they didn't seem to care.

"How do you know it isn't a Dayling? What if it is one of you?" Axum said with an even tone.

I finally understood the situation. I understood why they all wanted to talk with me. Actually, I understood a lot at that moment. "You think its Rachel?"

"Can it be?" Axum asked.

I couldn't see Rachel being the traitor. The Elders didn't want to believe it could be one of them. They were trying to find a scapegoat. I wasn't going to allow it to be her. "You guys really don't want to see what's right in front of you. Rachel, or any other Dayling, wouldn't have the power to pull something like this off. She wouldn't know how to contact a Mântuitor, and she definitely wouldn't be able to conspire with them." The Elders didn't speak. Instead, they stared at me as if I was a dumb little girl. I hated the way they looked at me. Okay, so they had centuries on me, it didn't mean they were smarter. Not to mention there was a piece of the puzzle they didn't have. I didn't know if it was important, but I decided to add it just incase. "By the way, I've always heard every Dayling has two Dream Transfers, correct?"

Axum's exotic, shimmering, light brown eyes focused on me. If I were human, I would be beside myself with fear. "Yes. One of your father and one of your mother."

I figured out what my loony aunt was talking about. What she wanted me to tell them. "Well I had a third."

All three of them set up in their seats. But only my father spoke. "Who was this dream about?"

"That's the thing, I don't know. And it was a recent Cross Over." I answered.

"You must tell us everything." My father demanded.

I didn't like the tone in his voice. I didn't like the interrogation at all. I also didn't like the idea of them thinking Rachel was the one betraying us all. I sighed before I told them the story of the recently Crossed Over Nightling running through a park, and feeding on a homeless man. They all listened with extreme interest. They didn't say a word as I completed my story.

My father looked from Jean-Paul to Axum. He then turned back to me. "You may leave now. Do not attempt to leave the estate again Haven. I am tempted to confine you to your room."

I got up to walk out of the room. I headed to the door without my father or the others even glancing at me. They were whispering to each other. I paused at the door and turned towards them. "Philip and Mu-Lan are supposed to come back tomorrow. I will promise not to leave the estate if you allow them to visit us here during the day."

My father's eyes moved from Axum to me. His face became fixed with anger, but I could see him fighting it back down. "You will do what you are told. I am the head of your family. I am your father. I do not have to bargain with you."

He was right with everything he'd said. But I didn't care at the moment. "I love you dad, but I wouldn't be a teenager if I didn't disobey you. I don't believe I'm asking for much. Not to mention I'm starting to get a little tired of how you Elders are handling things. Every effort available should be used in finding out who the traitor is. You guys are so stuck in your old ways you won't allow us Daylings to help you."

The three of them were silent. My father's eyes flashed with fury again, before they flashed with something I wasn't expecting, a hint of delight. "Very well. But what if your human companions are involved with what's going on? Then you will be giving them what they need to kill us all."

"We have no idea who is doing what. You guys think Rachel could be the traitor for goodness sakes. We're all lost with this one. But let us do our thing, while you guys do your thing." I said.

Axum and Jean-Paul both laughed. Jean-Paul shook his head as he looked at me. "Spoken like a leader. Not in the words a leader would use, but a leader in the new world I suppose."

I didn't say anything as I left the room.

So, while we thought it was one of them, they were thinking the traitor was one of us. Again I couldn't see it, but I guess that's how they felt about it being one of them.

Just as I started to head up the stairs, I saw Vincent and Sophia talking in the kitchen. Normally I would do my best to stay away from both of them, but with everything going on, I figured it wouldn't hurt to find out everything they knew.

As soon as I walked into the kitchen, they both looked at me. Sophia gave me her normal annoyed facial expression. She was great at that. Looking at me as if I was the reason it was hot outside, or if it rained, or if there was traffic during rush hour. In her mind, I was the reason for everything wrong in the world.

She'd never cared for me. I'd always believed it had to do with me one day being the head of the family, and if her father had been strong enough to be head now, it would have fallen to her instead of me. But despite my feelings for her, and the way she looked at me, I couldn't deny how she saved me back at the party when the Mântuitors attacked. She'd been there, keeping me alive, and getting me help.

I walked to the kitchen table. Vincent started to leave as soon as I sat down. I wanted to talk with both of them, so I spoke up to keep them both in place. "You guys would tell me if one of you, or even both of you were the traitor right?"

Sophia actually growled at me, but Vincent gave me a slight smile. He understood me asking them both like that, meant I didn't think it was either of them. Sophia wasn't as quick in the understanding department. "You think I would betray my kind to the humans? You're not as smart as I'd thought." She said through clenched teeth.

Vincent didn't explain to Sophia what he'd figured out about how I asked the question. Instead, he went into his own thing. "Have you decided to find out what's happening to your people instead of thinking about your human lover?"

I smiled at him. There was so much about Vincent I didn't like. Most of it had to do with how well he did his job, which was *really* well. There were a few things over the years I could have gotten away with if it wasn't for him. It felt as if he could predict when I was about to break the rules even before I'd decided to break them. I hated him for it. But my feelings for the man had nothing to do with what was going on. He would be a great asset in figuring everything out, but I didn't see him helping me. "You say that as if you're not human. I know you've worked for us a long time, but you're still human, you know that right?" I turned to the fuming Sophia. "I'm sure neither of you are the traitor. And by the way, thanks again for saving me back at the party. No matter how you treat me from this moment on, I'll know deep down inside you care."

She relaxed a little in her chair. She glared at me. "I saved you only because I didn't want to deal with your father's wrath if I'd let you get killed."

I pulled my chair closer to them. Over the years, playing games with them had been fun, but we were in a whole new situation, it was time to get real. "Until we find out who is selling us out to the Mântuitors, I say lets let bygones be bygones. A few of us are working on who is betraying us. Since it is obvious the Elders don't want anyone's help that wasn't

born before the 1800s, I say we should figure this out together."

Sophia and Vincent exchanged glances for a moment. I
so wished I had the ability to read minds, it would have been
helpful to see if they were thinking about helping me and the
others, or laughing me out of the room.

For the first time in my life, I saw Sophia look at me with
something that resembled respect. "Okay pequeña princesa,
I'm in. And I can speak for Nigel too."

Vincent took a sip from the glass of water that sat in
front of him the entire time. "I work for your father, but this
issue is bigger than him or I. So if you think you can figure
this out, then I will help."

"Then follow me," I said before I stood from the chair in
the kitchen.

I started back up the stairs. Sophia and Vincent followed
behind me as I made my way to my room.

When I opened the door, everyone inside stared up at
Sophia and Vincent. For a long uncomfortable moment, the
room became filled with silence. No one in the room trusted
the two I'd brought into our circle without asking them. I
could tell from the way Angela stared from Sophia to me, she
thought I'd lost my mind. And to be truthful, I wasn't sure I
hadn't.

I closed the door behind us. After locking it, I stood between my new guests and my old guests. The only thing I
could think to say was, "guess who's coming for dinner?"

TWENTY-TWO

Sophia and Vincent walked over to everyone else. Sophia sat next to her sister, and then placed her arms around Angela's shoulders. It looked more like a mocking gesture than a comforting one.

Vincent sat where I had sat. I didn't know if he knew he had taken my seat, or if it was destiny that he annoyed me.

I walked over to the couches. The Daylings all stared at me, while Vincent and Sophia smiled at everyone. "I know you guys are wondering what they are doing here." I started. "We need all the help we can get, and no matter how I feel about them, I'm pretty certain they're not the traitor."

Sébastien frowned at me. I didn't know if he was losing faith in my decision-making abilities, or if he still had issues with my relationship with Philip. We didn't have time for petty jealousies. One of our own had sold us out to the enemy, an enemy that was determined to kill us all. Sébastien would have to deal with his alpha male ego some other time. At least that's how I felt, he on the other hand obviously felt differently as he glared at me. "I suppose since you trust them, then that makes them automatically innocent. Since you have the better judgment of us all."

"Exactly," I said ignoring Sébastien's sarcastic tone. Sophia, on the other hand, didn't ignore it. She glanced from Sébastien to me with delight in her eyes. When I saw the gleam building in her eyes as she prepared to say something that would more than likely cause the tension between Sébastien and me to grow even more, I cut her off. "We need to figure out who the traitor is quickly. I think the Elders are preparing to pin it all on Rachel."

Rachel's eyes almost leapt out of her head. Everyone in the room turned from me to her. I had to admit I felt a little relieved all the attention was off of me. I hated it had become focused on Rachel because everyone silently asked themselves, 'could it be her?'

"Why do the Elders think I'm the traitor?" She asked with her eyes still hanging out of her head.

"Almost everyone in your family was killed. You knew where Haven was when she and Philip were attacked." Angela said as she stared at Rachel.

"Yeah, but she wasn't around during the first attack. How could she have known that?" I said in Rachel's defense.

Vincent turned from Rachel to me. His eyes narrowed as he focused on me. For a human, his stare could be intimidating. "When were you and this Philip attacked?"

I explained to Vincent and Sophia about the Mântuitors following Philip and me inside of the Johnsons' mansion and blowing it up.

Sophia actually smiled at me after I finished the story. "So if the Mântuitors wouldn't have shown up, you would have gone skinny dipping with this guy?"

I frowned at her, whether or not if I would have gone skinny dipping with Philip wasn't the point. Also, I didn't want to think about what I would have done if the Mântuitors hadn't shown up. "Like I was saying, Rachel knew about that, but she didn't know about the party we all went to when the Mântuitors attacked the first time."

Vincent leaned back in his seat. His eyes gleamed a little in the halogen light. "You're right Haven, Rachel didn't know about the party, but there was someone who knew about both."

I knew Vincent would imply Philip was setting me up. I figured it would come up sometime during our conversation. I was glad it came up early, so I could get it out of the way. "If Philip wanted me dead, then why did he save me from the Mântuitors?"

"To gain access to us all." Sébastien hissed out. He was getting closer to Crossing Over; the Nightling inside of him was being fueled by his sudden anger. "He used you Haven. He used you to gain entrance inside of the mansion."

Everyone seemed to be pondering Sébastien's suggestion. I didn't want to admit it, but it held a little weight, except every part of me screamed it wasn't true, just like every part of me screamed Rachel wasn't the traitor. "You guys can believe what you want, but Philip isn't involved with this. Anyway, our main goal is to figure out who amongst our kind is betraying us."

Sébastien leapt from the couch and was on me before I could blink. He stood face to face with me, snarling like a wild animal. I could feel the heat from his breath as he glared at me with his exotic blue eyes. I thought about how sexy I'd thought those eyes were. I wasn't feeling the same sensation as he stared at me as if he wanted to tear me apart with his bear hands. "You are so blinded by your mortal lover its sickening. I see why the Elders have issues with making you the head of this family."

Every nerve inside of me wanted to take a swing at him, but I knew better. He was days from Crossing Over, which meant he was stronger than me. Also, there was the little fact that he'd actually had some fighting training, something I hadn't gotten around to.

I started to at least give Sébastien a piece of my mind, since I couldn't give him my fist, when all of a sudden he was snatched from in front of me and slammed back into his spot on my couch. Standing over him, with her fangs extended and dark eyes gleaming was Sophia.

Sophia leaned down towards Sébastien so he could get a better look at her fangs. Everyone in the room had been caught off guard, everyone except for Vincent, who didn't seem interested in what was going on between Sophia and Sébastien. Instead, he seemed to be in deep thought about something else.

I returned my focus to Sophia and Sébastien. Fear built inside of Sébastien's eyes. Sophia didn't retract her fangs as she spoke to him. "Here's the thing pequeño príncipe, no one jumps in my little cousin's face like that except me. I get it, you got the hots for her, but she got the hots for a mortal. It sucks." She leaned even closer to Sébastien. He pulled back a little as she got nose to nose with him. "Get over it. Because if I feel you might be one of those, 'if I can't have her blah blah blah', then I'm going to feast on your entrails. I could care less who your father is." She sat back on the couch. Her fangs had retracted as she turned from Sébastien to me. "So what's next pequeña princesa? The Elders think Rachel is the traitor but you don't. But how can you be sure?"

I found myself still in shock about Sophia's defense of me. I thought she hated me. It felt odd to think of her as being on my side. It felt even odder to think of her as a person I could count on as having my back. It took me a moment to deal with that. I would have taken more time, except everyone had started staring at me again. "Your mind reading ability is one of the best ever. Can't you push inside of her mind?"

Sophia laughed. "She's a Dayling, little cousin. She could have trained her mind to keep me out. Or to only allow me to read what she wants."

"Yeah, but isn't there a way to get around that?" I asked the question even though I already knew the answer. The Elders were going to gather the information from Rachel anyway, so I figured it might be best if we got it the way they were planning on getting it.

Rachel understood what I was suggesting as soon as the smirk crept across Sophia's face. Rachel jumped to her feet and looked from Sophia to me. "Oh no, no way that's going to happen."

"It's the only way to prove your innocence." Vincent said as he returned from his thoughts to our situation. I wondered what he was thinking about, but I had to deal with one issue at a time, like convincing Rachel to allow Sophia to extract the truth from her mind the only sure way a Nightling can, by feeding on her.

Rachel continued to gaze around the room. Everyone watched her. I understood why she didn't want Sophia to feed from her. For one thing, it's gross, and the other thing, Sophia could make it very painful if she chose to. Knowing Sophia the way I did, she would make it as painful as she could.

A flash of surrender covered Rachel's face. She really didn't have a choice. If she didn't allow Sophia to take the truth from her thoughts, then the Elders would in their own way. A way none in the room wanted to experience. "Okay, but take it..."

Before Rachel could finish her sentence, Sophia had latched onto her neck. Everyone in the room froze as Sophia slowly took in large gulps of blood from Rachel. Seeing someone I considered a friend being fed from was a strange experience. It was odd, watching Sophia holding Rachel up, with her mouth attached to Rachel's throat, drinking every drop of blood escaping from the wounds her fangs made.

Rachel didn't scream or struggle in Sophia's arms as I thought she would. Instead, she wrapped her arms around Sophia, pulling her closer to her body. It didn't take a genius to guess that Sophia had decided to make the feeding pleasing to Rachel instead of painful like we all thought she would. The only question left: how much blood would be needed for Sophia to break down Rachel's mental barriers and get the truth.

Sophia quickly released Rachel and took a few steps back. "She's telling the truth. It's not her."

Rachel looked around the room in a daze. Her facial expression was almost something close to disappointment.

Rachel wobbled a little. Sébastien quickly moved beside her before she lost her balance. He helped her to the couch. He gently set her down and tore a piece of his shirt to place over the bite marks on her neck, *typical Sébastien, forever being the gentleman by helping the damsel in distress*.

Vincent stood from the couch and slowly rolled up the sleeve on his shirt, exposing his left arm. "I guess that means I'm next. Remember dear, I'm human, so you don't have to take as much."

I stared at Vincent for a moment in silence. The realization of what he suggested slowly made its way through my mind. Of course he was right. If Rachel had to prove her innocence, then why shouldn't the rest of us? The thought of Sophia feeding from me started to make me sick inside.

Sophia took hold of Vincent's arm. She licked a circle around his wrist. She then slowly bit down into his flesh. Just like Rachel, Vincent's eyes rolled in the back of his head from pleasure. He entangled Sophia's long hair inside of his free hand as she took smaller gulps of his blood.

When she finally raised her head, a low purr escaped her blooded mouth. Her chest moved up and down as she took in deep breaths. She was a Nightling, which meant she didn't need to breathe, but Vincent wasn't the only one enthralled with pleasure.

I'd heard there was nothing like human blood to a Nightling. Nothing on Earth could compare to it. It was better than chocolate.

"It's not him. But he does have a few dirty little thoughts roaming around that head of his." Sophia purred as she smiled at Vincent.

Vincent stumbled back to the couch. He sat down while taking in deep breaths. He looked around the room at the rest of us. "So, whose next?"

Sébastien went next, and then Angela. When Sophia finished drinking from Angela, Sophia stepped back laughing. She gazed at her little sister with malice in her shimmering dark eyes. "You naughty little girl. Does your girlfriend know all the dirty things you want to do to her?"

Angela started to take a step towards Sophia before I stopped her. I glared at Sophia. "You suppose to only be finding out if any of us are traitors, not using something personal inside of us for your amusement."

Sophia eyes seemed to gleam as she stared at me. I could smell the different types of blood lingering on her breath. She looked more human because of all of the blood she'd taken in, but a slight bit of an unnatural porcelain tint still radiated from her as she stood in silence. "Now, pequeña princesa, it's your turn."

Vincent stood from the couch. He had fully recovered from the blood loss. "I think we can safely rule Haven out as the traitor. Since she's been the target of the recent attacks."

"What if that's just to throw us off? Make us seem like we were saving her, but in reality, she was playing us." Sophia said while continuing to stare at me.

"I agree; it's only far if she is tested like the rest of us." Sébastien said without looking at me.

I felt a little shocked by his suggestion. Then again, I'd noticed his changing behavior towards me every since he found out about Philip and me. I guessed he had an alternative reason for wanting to watch Sophia feed from me.

I took a step towards Sophia. "Fine, do what you got to do."

Sophia made sure I could see her bloodied fangs before she quickly latched onto my neck. I felt a slight prick, and then I felt my blood flowing from my body. My mind instantly screamed for me to fight, but then it happened, a wave of pleasure entered me. It felt like nothing I had ever felt before. I could feel my life leaving my body. I could feel myself becoming weaker with every swallow from Sophia, but I didn't care. All I wanted was for the feeling to never stop. I wanted her to drain me completely dry. I didn't care if I died or lived. I didn't care about anything except the pleasure.

Then the pleasure left. I felt myself lose my balance as I wobbled backwards. Sébastien held me up, just as he'd done Rachel. Then, he gently placed me on the couch. The ecstasy continued to roam around my body as I heard Sophia declare my innocence.

Everything in the room felt different. My body felt different. And a slight craving had entered me. I wanted the pleasure back. I wondered if this is what everyone else in the room had felt? I wondered if Sophia might have hit me with a stronger level of pleasure just to screw with me? Nightlings were able to control how much enjoyment, or pain their victims felt. The feeling inside of me felt so intense, I'd become convinced she hit me with an overdose of bliss.

By the time I regained my senses, I figured out the issues Vincent and the others were dealing with. Everyone in the room had been tested, and everyone had passed, everyone except for Sophia.

None of us could feed from her, since we were three Daylings and one human, which meant one thing. We needed another Nightling to join our group.

I slowly stood from the couch. "We need another Nightling to feed from Sophia."

Vincent gave me his all-so-common disappointed look. "That only works on humans and Daylings. It will take more than feeding on a Nightling to crack their defenses. An Elder might be able to."

I turned to him. "Yeah, but we're trying to keep them out of this."

Rachel stood behind Sophia with a frown across her face. "So what does that mean? We have to trust her? That's just great."

Sophia made her way to the couch. She sat down, placing her feet on the table. "You guys will just have to take me for my word it seems."

Everyone in the room stared at Sophia with the same expression. No way in hell would any of us trust her. Never in a million years, but we did need her, so we all sat back on the couches and returned to our conversation about who could be the traitor.

TWENTY-THREE

The next day, I stood at my window looking out at the world around me. Or, at least what I could see from my window. Trees covered most of our estate, but I could see slight glimpses of other houses and how the sun reflected from all the expensive windows of those houses. A few birds flew by, but even they had to be reeling from this never ending heat wave. Pour creatures, hopefully they could find some shade.

Something entered me as I stared out of my window. Something had crept inside of me since I'd awoken in my room alone. The others had staid up most of the night going back and forth on what to do next. We talked about everything from who could be the traitor, to why had I been targeted by the Mântuitors twice. Sébastien had escaped the other day along with me, but the Mântuitors didn't come at him, instead they blew up a mansion, a very creepy tricked out mansion with a high-tech panic room and underground tunnel, to get to me. Didn't know why I was on the top of their must smite list.

But that wasn't what had been on my mind since I'd awoken. Another day had passed. Another day of my last days as a Dayling. For the first time the weight of what I was losing had worked its way inside of my mind. I'd wanted this for so long, not really thinking about everything I would be giving up, like being able to watch the sun reflect from expensive windows, and birds flying through a blue sky. Never knew I even liked that stuff.

A slight knock on my door pulled me out of my thoughts. I turned around and quickly made my way to the door. When

I opened it, my normal snarky remarks towards my quest were replaced with a smile. "Vincent, come on in."

He walked over to one of my couches and gracefully sat. He held a laptop in his hand, which he placed on the table between my couches. "I have something for you."

"A pony," I said before I made my way to the couch across from him and sat down. As always, Vincent ignored my joke. "What's that?"

He turned on the laptop. He placed a flash drive in the side of it. "I've transferred everything we have on the Mântuitors on this flash drive. You know the basics correct?"

I sat back in the couch. "Yep, religious fanatics that used to be apart of the Templars, tasked with killing all of the evil blood drinkers after discovering one centuries ago."

Vincent had the computer facing him, as he scrolled through different files. "As the years passed, they grew more powerful and wealthy. They've spread out through governments across the glob. They even own most of the medical research companies in the world. It seems they not only kill your kind, but they also capture some and use them for experiments."

A sickening feeling came over me. The acts justified for human advancement. These guys really needed to look in the mirror when they throw around words like malevolence towards my kind. "What does all of this mean?"

Vincent leaned back in his seat. He crossed his legs in front of him. "I think whoever is helping the Mântuitors, is also helping them capture some for their experiments. It could be the bargaining chip they used."

"This is just getting better. How many people know about this?"

"That's just it Haven, very few know about this information."

"Which brings us back to an Elder,' I sat up in my seat. My father and the others still didn't want to admit it could be one of them. They had come for Rachel during the night, but Vincent informed them of our test to clear her name. I could have sworn I saw disappointment in their eyes; they really wanted it to be her. "So what's next?"

"You stay locked in the mansion while we keep digging. The fact they came after you twice bothers me." He said while closing the computer.

I couldn't help giving him a sarcastic smile. "Not as much as it bothers me."

He actually smiled back. "You'll be safe, as long as you don't sneak out to meet anymore high school boys. By the way, have you heard from him?"

A quick flash of my spiky haired prince came to me. This boy had gotten way under my skin. I couldn't think about him without getting tingly all over. It wasn't fair at all! "Not yet, but he's suppose to call me later. He and Mu-Lan have a few things they're going to check on when they get out of school."

Vincent locked his eyes on me. "Yes, this Mu-Lan, she is Angela's friend right?"

I folded my arms in front of me. "Not going there. If you want to know something about Angela, then you'll have to ask her."

He gave me a slight smirk. "Is there something about Angela?"

Crap! I kept walking into those. "Is there anything else you got for me about the vampire hunters that are trying to either kill me or capture me to do experiments to better your kind?"

Vincent got the hint, and thankfully changed the subject. "Actually yes," he pushed the computer over to me, before he stood from the couch. "Check out the file about a Mân-tuitor named William Crawford. You might find it interesting."

He walked out of my room after slightly bowing his head to me. I could see my human guards outside of my door as he left. Having them there was taking some time to get used to. But what else could I do while being hunted.

I opened the laptop, scrolled down the list of files until I got to William Crawford, and clicked the file.

It seemed one of our spies had gotten close to Mr. Crawford after finding out he was a high ranking member of the Holy Sect of Mântuitors. William Crawford's family had been apart of the Holy Sect since the beginning. His ancestor had been one of the first Templars to be tasked with hunting down and killing all of the blood drinkers. Another of his ancestors had been the one to discover Daylings. The Crawfords were royalty in the Holy Sect, and young William had been a shinning prince in his day.

He'd hunted down and killed at least five Nightlings during his time. He quickly rose up to the top of Sect, almost being named Prime, which is what they call the head Mân-tuitor. But according to our spy, something very odd happened. No one knew why, but William began changing his views on my kind. Interesting!

I lay on my couch, with the laptop resting on my chest as I continued to read the file.

Our spy had gotten close to William. One day the Mân-tuitor told our spy why he had changed his tune. It seemed when William had reached his late fifties, and was getting ready to be named Prime, he spent a night out with his wife and two daughters. They ate at some fancy restaurant one of his daughters had picked, and was on their way home when a group of hooded car thieves tried to jack them. The five thugs were high on something, and two of them wouldn't allow William's daughters to get out of the car after throwing him and his wife to the ground. William pleaded with the men, but they knocked him around while his family watched. They were about to drive off with his crying daughters, when all of a sudden the men were attacked.

A Nightling had heard the commotion, and rushed to save the innocent family. All that William remembered about her was that she was beautiful beyond words, and had taken the five thugs out with no problem. His wife and daughters didn't know what the woman was, but William did as the Nightling helped him to his feet, and soothed his family. She stayed with them until help arrived, and then left without given her name or asking for anything in return.

After that, William started looking at our world through different eyes. He questioned things the Mântuitors held true for centuries. He began to believe, not all Nightlings were evil. Not long after that, he died of natural causes. But our spy believed members of the Holy Sect killed him to keep him quiet.

My iPhone rang beside me. I closed the computer while still thinking about

William Crawford. They'd killed him because he was seeing the truth, and not the lie they'd passed down for centuries.

I looked over to my phone, to see in big letters, SPIKY HAIRED PRINCE flashing in front of me, with 'Do You Think I'm Sexy' as the designated ring tone. With an uncontrollable smile on my face, I answered the phone. "Unfortunately, yes."

"What," he asked on the other end of the line.

"Nothing. Private joke. So what's new?"

He laughed a little. "Is being strange all apart of your vampire allure?"

I placed the computer back on the small table in-between my couches. "We prefer Dayling or Nightling thank you very much. Vampire is an offensive word to us."

"Whatever you say, MJ. So... anyway... I was wondering... whatcha doing?"

His pauses between words made me cautious for a moment. He sounded nervous. "Laying on my couch reading about a fascinating man. Why?"

He lowered his voice to a whisper. "So, whatcha wearing?"

My body quickly relaxed, for a moment I thought something was wrong, but nope, it was Philip being Philip. "Nothing at all. With this heat wave, I decided to spend the rest of the day in my room completely nude."

"Good thing you and Angela are cousins, or Lan would have something to worry about." He joked.

Lan? Seemed like they were getting closer. "How is Mu-Lan? Are you keeping all the floozies from my cousin's girl while we're locked away?"

"Yeah, except the only way I can do that is by flirting with them myself. It's been hard work, but I'm taking a few for the team." He laughed. "Anyway, I called you for two reasons. The first being Lan and I are going to the police station after school, and talk to a few other people that were at the party that night. I'll call you when we have something." I could hear him fighting back laughter as he continued. "And second, you should have a guest there pretty soon. Lan and I tried to talk her out of coming to see you, but you know how she gets when she has something in her head."

He didn't have to say who *she* was that he talked about. Before I could hang up the phone and call her, I heard a knock at my door. I turned towards it. "Yes?"

One of the guards opened the door. He gave me a frustrated look, which could only mean one thing. "Miss Vigano, you have a guest insisting on seeing you. We've told her you were not in any shape to see anyone, but she insists you would make an exception for her."

I could hear Philip laughing as I hung of my phone. No way would I allow her to come inside, but there was no way they would let me go outside. I needed to think quickly, and there was only one answer I could come up with.

I made my way pass the guard heading towards the library. Angela, Rachel, Sébastien and Vincent were all sitting in the library reading old books. The other Daylings in the mansion were more than likely in the entertainment room. They didn't matter, the Human Liaison sitting in the library did.

Vincent looked up at me when I walked in front of him. "Did you find the story of William Crawford interesting?"

Anxiety worked its way through me. He and I had bonded over the last couple days; he wouldn't mind doing me this one little favor. "Actually I did, but that's not why I came to see you. I need a tiny favor."

He closed the book he had been reading. He gave me his old 'Haven is about to do something stupid' look, which I hated, but ignored. "What tiny favor do you need?"

"Follow me please," I said before turning to walk out of the library. He didn't say anything as he stood from the chair and followed me out of the room. We walked in silence until we came to a window overlooking the front gates. Yep, standing there, looking annoyed and stunning at the same time, was my teenage super model gossiping friend Olivia. "Do you remember her?"

Vincent stared out of the window at Olivia. "Yes, she is your friend from school. Why is she here?"

Time for the favor. "She wants to come inside and see me. I know she can't come inside, and I can't go outside. Getting her to leave without talking to her will be difficult. And if I talk to her, explaining why she can't come inside would take too much energy. So I came up with an easy way of dealing with this."

Vincent narrowed his blue eyes at me. "And what is that?"

I gave him the most innocent look I could conjure. "I think she has a little crush on you. And hey, who can blame her, with your sophisticated good looks and perfect hair and penetrating blue eyes."

He didn't respond to my flattering remarks. "What are

you asking Haven?"

"Go out there, talk to her, maybe offer her a ride home, and she'll forget all about me." I said still smiling.

Vincent looked from me to Olivia, before finally taking his iPhone out of his pocket. He dialed a number, and began speaking after the person on the other end picked up. "I'm on my way out there. Keep the young lady on the other side of the gates. And get my car ready."

He didn't say anything as he turned and walked away.

I sighed, before heading back to the library. When I walked in, Angela was just hanging up her phone, and Rachel looked up at me with a devilish smile. Sébastien wore his Philip frown I've started to distinguish from his other frowns. "What?" I asked as I sat next to Angela.

Sébastien returned to reading his book, while Rachel, and now Angela, smiled at me. Angela spoke up after clearing her throat. "Just got off the phone with Mu-Lan, she told me what she and Philip are doing today."

I continued to look from Rachel to Angela as they continued to smile at me. "Okay, so why are you two creepily smiling at me?"

Angela and Rachel exchanged glances before Rachel cleared her throat this time. "I didn't know you liked to read in the nude."

My entire face turned red before I stood from the chair, and made my way back to my room. He would pay for that, I didn't know how, but he would pay.

TWENTY-FOUR

A week had passed, and we still couldn't figure out who the traitor could be. It was odd, working with Sophia and Vincent. I'd thought of them as my enemies for so long, it was hard to remind myself we had real enemies to deal with, the kind that wanted us all dead.

I found myself sitting in the kitchen alone. I wasn't hungry, so I didn't have anything to eat. I'd talked with Philip during the week. He didn't learn much about the Mântuitors, because they were truly a secret group of very powerful people who lived in the shadows. I advised Philip to watch his back while he investigated them. He told me Lan was watching his back for him. It seemed Philip and Mu-Lan had become close friends as they tried to help us out. I was only jealous for a moment, before my rational mind reminded me Mu-Lan helped because she was in love with Angela, which meant I didn't have to worry about her and Philip.

I looked outside the window in the kitchen. Nighttime approached. Soon the sun would be gone, and another Nightling would be living with us in the mansion. It was Sébastien's birthday, which meant he would no longer be a Dayling like me, but he would awaken as a Nightling like Sophia and the others. I wondered how much of Sébastien would be left after the transformation. I would find out soon enough.

I must have sat in that kitchen without moving for hours. As soon as the sun had set, I could hear the others coming from the lower levels of the mansion. I thought Sébastien would join me in the kitchen, but instead it was Nigel.

Nigel walked up to me with a wide grin on his face.

"Shameful if you ask me." I didn't care about whatever Nigel meant by his words, and he didn't care that I didn't care. He sat beside me on a stool. "When a Dayling used to become a man and Cross Over to a Nightling, the younger Nightlings would take him out for a hunt. It's the only time we're permitted to kill humans, other than self-defense. Anyway, the newly awoken Nightling would spend the entire night feasting on evil human blood. But since the Mântuitors have everyone on edge, poor Sébastien can't even hunt for his first meal tonight."

I tried to ignore Nigel. But I couldn't stop myself from asking. "What do you mean?"

With a smile across his face, Nigel turned towards me. "Since Sébastien couldn't hunt for his first kill, we had to bring one to him. The vilest human we could find is chained up down stairs. I imagine Sébastien is draining the life out of him as we speak." Nigel moved closer towards me. He placed his arm around my shoulder. "Don't worry, Haven, soon you'll know what it feels like to take human life. To take a victim into your arms and drain every ounce of life out of him."

I wanted to shout that would never be me, but I couldn't. I had only a week left before I Crossed Over. A week from becoming the same type of monsters Sophia and Nigel were. I hated them, but I couldn't fight what I would become.

I moved out of Nigel's grasp, deciding not to wait for Sébastien in the kitchen where everyone could have something to say to me about my imminent Crossing Over. Instead, I left the kitchen heading for my room.

Thankfully, it was empty. Angela and Rachel were off reading old manuscripts in the library in hopes of finding something out about the history between our people and the Mântuitors. They thought maybe something in the past could explain what was happening in the present. I didn't think the books would help, but it didn't hurt to try.

I laid on my bed in silence. I tried not to think about what Sébastien did underneath the mansion. I tried not to think about what I would be doing in a week, if I lived that long. It seemed every time I'd left the mansion, Mântuitors were waiting for me. I'd been lucky so far, but eventually my luck would run out.

I must have dozed off for a few moments, because when I awoke, Sébastien stood over me in my room.

At first, I felt a sudden chill run through my body as I instantly noticed the change in him. His skin was different; it had that slight porcelain shade to it that all newly awakened Nightlings had. It also had an unnatural tan to it, the tan of a Nightling who had recently finished feeding. My mind drifted on what Nigel had said. Sébastien had killed a man underneath the mansion. It was a part of him now, and it would be the last time he would have to kill, but a part of me still felt sick at the thought of what Sébastien had just finished doing.

I could see the pain in his shimmering blue eyes, as he understood what raced through my mind. I didn't know if he was reading my face, or my thoughts, either way, I'd hurt him with my disgust.

He gave me a forced smile. "I should go now, and come back another time."

I climbed out of my bed as he made his way towards my door. A part of me wanted him to leave. I wanted to put off the discussion I knew we were about to have, not because I felt disgusted with him, but I would learn what waited for me in less than a week. "Wait, let's talk." I said as I walked towards my couches. I picked the couch closest to my bed, and sat down. Sébastien stopped at the door. He didn't look at me as he faced my front door. Slowly he turned around and made his way over to the couch in front of me.

He sat down and forced another smile towards me. "So how was your day?"

We both laughed. We both enjoyed the moment of levity we shared before we would have the serious talk. "Are you going to start wearing leather and red silk like Nigel?" I asked with a smile.

"Definitely not. I also don't feel the need to torment you like Sophia."

"Good, I was thinking that came with becoming a Nightling." We both laughed again. He seemed to be the same Sébastien. It started to give me hope about myself. Maybe I would Cross Over without losing myself? I'd hoped I could, but after spending time with Sophia and Nigel, and then with Myrene, I thought becoming a fiend was a part of Crossing Over. "So how does it feel?"

He stopped smiling. His beautiful porcelain face became blank. "It's hard to describe. It's something you'll have to experience for yourself."

It was time for me to ask the question I'd wanted to ask, but didn't want to ask. "How did it feel to kill for the first time?"

Sébastien's shimmering light blue eyes focused on me. "Who said tonight was my first time taking human life?" I couldn't tell if he was being serious or not. Sébastien stood from the couch. He reached his left hand out for me to take it. "I want to show you something."

I hesitated for a moment. His words took me off guard. It was Sébastien though; I didn't have anything to worry about.

I took his hand. It felt a little harder than before, and smoother. He felt stronger also, like a powerful force of nature flowed through out his body.

He lifted me to my feet as if I was a feather. His strength had increased ten times more than before. I must admit; it felt a little exhilarating to feel the power in his grasp.

He pulled me over to my bedroom window. He opened the window and stared out into the darkness.

I stood beside him; my heart began to race a little. It had been a while since I'd seen or talked with Philip. I knew he was out in the world trying to find out information that could save my people. This made me feel a little guilty for overly enjoying Sébastien's touch.

He turned his shimmering blue eyes on me. "Are you ready?"

I couldn't take my eyes from his. "Ready for what?"

The next thing I knew, he pulled me closer to his body, and we were out of my room, into the night air. I hated the feeling of flying with Sophia, but with Sébastien, I felt like Lois Lane being flown around Metropolis by Superman.

The heat continued to suffocate the night. Even as Sébastien picked up speed, I could feel the smothering heat covering my body. At the moment, I didn't care. I couldn't think about anything except how good it felt in Sébastien's arms.

I closed my eyes as we floated higher in the air. I could hear Sébastien whisper in my ear, "keep them closed", before I felt a rush of wind, and a jarring feeling of being pulled at the speed of light. "You can open them now", Sébastien whispered again.

I could feel the change in temperature before I opened my eyes. The smothering heat had gone, the suffocating night air that encompassed Tallahassee seemed a million miles away from my body.

When I opened my eyes, I almost let go of Sébastien from the shook of flying over snow-covered mountains. "Where are we?"

"Over the Jotunheim Mountains."

"The Jotu-what-you-said Mountains? Where is that?" I asked.

Sébastien laughed. It sounded different somehow, like wind chimes caught in a slight breeze. It was as if his entire being had changed since he Crossed Over. "The Jotu-un-hiem Mountains are in Norway."

Again, I felt overcome with shock. I knew Nightlings could move pretty fast when they flew, but to go from Tallahassee to Norway in a blink of an eye freaked me out a little.

Also, feeling Sébastien's strong arms wrapped around me began to do something else to my senses. It became hard to think as we soared through the cold air. I breathed heavily into Sébastien's neck. My body became warm despite the chill encompassing the air.

I stifled back a gasp as I spoke. "How did you learn how to do this so fast?"

Sébastien's shimmering light blue eyes were staring directly into mine. His breath didn't freeze in the air as mine did. He resembled a beautiful Greek statue. "All the secrets of the Universe are revealed to you when you Cross Over, Haven. What you feel as a Dayling cannot compare to the sensations of your true self." He paused. His eyes seemed to glow a little as he gazed at me. "You will see how truly beautiful things are."

I stared at his lips, uncontrollably wishing they were over mine. I then felt the chilled air coursing through my hair, and a vision of Philip entered my mind. Sébastien frowned, revealing to me that he did read my thoughts. I'd never had to hide them from him before, I would have to get used to the new Sébastien.

I turned around in his arms so I could face the ground below me. My eyesight wasn't as good as his, but Daylings could see pretty well in the dark. We were flying high above the snow-covered mountains. I was amazed at everything I could see through the darkness blanketing the cold night air. Even though there wasn't much to see, nothing but snow-covered mountains after snow-covered mountains.

"This is unbelievable," I whispered.

"Believe it *ma sucré Lis*." Sébastien whispered back.

We quickly left the snow-covered mountains and found ourselves flying above the half-moon shaped coastal lands of Norway.

We sailed over the beautiful small towns and villages as our bodies warmed in the astonishing weather change caused by the Gulf Stream.

It felt so amazing. I wished Angela and Rachel were with me as Sébastien descended a little so I could have a better view of the beautiful fishing town he told me was called Kristiansand.

As we soared over the rooftops of the Old Norwegian houses, I pictured my closest cousin and my closest friend. I wondered how they would react to being flown over towns in the powerful arms of a gorgeous Nightling.

I cared for Philip. He'd been the first guy I'd looked at in that way in my life. But I had to wonder if I fooled myself by thinking something could grow between us. He was human. I was not. It was that simple. One day soon, in less than a week actually, I'd be able to fly myself around. How would Philip be able to take that?

We flew beside a flock of birds just below the dirty white clouds forming above us.

I turned from the birds to see Sébastien smiling at me. I smiled back, and then turned around just as we started flying over the Atlantic Ocean.

I felt no fear as we swooped towards the darkened water. I felt no fear as I saw sharks and whales and more fish than I could count or name swimming just beneath me. I felt a power and a type of superiority come over me. In a week I'd be the queen of the night. Nothing could harm me. I would be the thing that should be feared.

Sébastien rose high above the clouds. I couldn't help but spread my arms out like an airplane.

For what felt like hours, we soared through the clouds like that, until Sébastien whispered for me to close my eyes again, and then I felt the rush of wind over my body.

When I opened my eyes, we were just about to land on the ground behind a coffee house in Tallahassee. The nice frozen feeling my body had, quickly left as the smothering heat attacked me again. I wanted to go back to Norway until this heat wave was over.

"Did you enjoy yourself?" Sébastien asked as he stood beside me.

Did I enjoy myself? Damn right I did. "It was cool. Nice and cool." I looked around at the coffee house. "Are you sure we're suppose to be out here alone?"

He held his hand out for me to take it. "It's fine. I have permission."

I started to take his hand, and then I stopped myself. I'd wondered if Philip would be able to handle what I would become after I Crossed Over. I wasn't sure if he could, but I wanted to find out. I didn't want to play with Sébastien's feelings by having him think I wanted to be more than friends with him. I mean; I had felt more than friendly while we flew above Norway, but now that I had my feet back on the ground, I had to be honest with Sébastien and myself.

"We need to talk," I said without taking Sébastien's hand.

He stared at me for a long moment. He didn't move his hand from in front of me.

Finally, he pulled his hand down, and placed both his hands inside his pockets. "I know what you are going to say. You are in love with the human."

"I don't know if I'm in love with him, but I feel something for him." I said.

"And you do not feel anything for me?"

I took a step towards Sébastien. "Of course I do. You're one of my oldest and best friends. I want you in my life, Sébastien."

"Just not the way you want him?" Sébastien said as the pain arose in his eyes.

"I'm telling you, you're getting the better part of this deal. You wouldn't want me as anything other than a friend." I joked trying to change the mood.

He stood in silence again. He then glanced at me with a smile. "Let's get something to drink then... friend."

I smiled back. "As long as it's not red. That's your thing, not mine, at least not for another week."

"Did you know that everyone has a different smell to their blood? And most people's blood smells like fruit."

At that moment, I realized I'd been smelling Philip's blood. A part of me was a little freaked out.

We turned to walk towards the coffee house. All of a sudden, Sébastien dropped to his knees holding his hands over his ears.

    As I leaned down to see what was wrong with him, I felt a sharp pain across the back of my head, and then everything went dark.

TWENTY-FIVE

As I slowly opened my eyes, I tried to remember what had happened and where I was. But my mind swirled as if I had drank an entire keg of beer.

The grogginess wasn't the only thing blanketing me, a dull pain raced from my head to the rest of my body – or maybe my head hurt so badly it felt as if my entire body ached from the pain.

I tried to move, but the pain paralyzed me, leaving me lying on my stomach helpless.

Okay Haven, get it together. But even the act of thinking sent spasms of pain through my almost naked body.

I knew I was only in my underwear from the feel of the cold hard cement floor poking at my torn flesh.

My body felt as if someone had dragged me along the floor, scraping off layers of skin and muscle during the process.

I tried to remember what had happened again, and again my body became assaulted with waves of pain and a new sensation of nausea. The next thing I knew, my face was buried in a mound of blood and the remains of a ham and cheese sandwich.

Everything began to come back to me. Flying around Norway with Sébastien. Returning to Tallahassee, only to watch Sébastien bend over in pain, and then... Damn! I began to wish I hadn't remembered.

Someone knocked me out. The Mântuitors, it had to be them.

I heard a door creep open just before I saw a pair of feet

in front of me.

"Are you still sleeping little one? No, you are not. I can hear you thinking. Yes, thinking, thinking, thinking, about the predicament you are in." I heard a woman say as she stood over me... no, not just a woman, but a Nightling. Why the hell did a Nightling stand over me? I felt her strong hands around my mangled hair, then my head felt as if it was about to explode as she snatched me off the ground, bringing my nose against hers. "You have no idea the predicament you are in little one." She slammed me down to the ground, sending me into the blissful world of dreams.

I awoke to find chains around my wrist and ankles. How long I had slept, and why the hell I had chains around my wrist and ankles were lost to me. And the stabbing pain continued to race through my throbbing head. I so wanted to go back to sleep.

A new realization came to me. I could no longer feel the bite of the cement floor against my skin; actually, I felt a pulling sensation from the chains attached to my wrist.

I slowly opened my eyes and waited for the haze in front of me to clear. When it did, a terror like nothing I had felt before engulfed me – *Dear God, I was chained to a wall!*

I tried to put my weight on my legs to ease the pain ripping through my wrist. But I didn't have enough strength to wiggle my toes, so I definitely didn't have enough strength to move my paralyzed legs.

I wanted to cry. But I didn't have the strength for that either. I couldn't do anything except dangle from the smooth wall like one of those dolls with strings attached to them. But there wasn't a puppeteer controlling me, actually, no one was in the room except me.

As soon as the thought enter my mind, a beam of artificial light cut through the darkness. Then, as quickly as it came, the light left as I heard a door closing.

I tried to see what was in the front of the room, and when my eyes focused on where I heard the door close, I longed for the haziness to come back.

I could see three of them, dressed from head to toe in large brown cloaks, with their hoods pulled over their heads hiding their faces and scaring the crap out of me. Three more Nightlings, what the hell had I gotten myself into?

They stood there, at the front of the room, without moving or making a sound. I tried again to build up enough strength to scream, but nothing would come out, nothing in my body seemed to work, except my ability to feel pain.

Suddenly I felt a hand over my mouth. I blinked a couple of times before I noticed only two of the figures where still by the door. Their companion stood in front of me with one of his crusty hands over my mouth, and his dead glowing eyes staring into mine. I almost pissed on myself, and I believe I would've, if I had anything inside of me.

As if examining me, the fiend moved my head from side to side. The movements caused those earth shattering head aches to pulsate through my body.

He sniffed me as if he was an animal savoring the scent of his meal before he devoured it. His porcelain young face twisted from the wicked smile fixed on it. Before I could try and scream again, I felt his mouth around my neck and my blood leaving my body.

My body quivered from pure pleasure. I loved it. For the first time since I found myself in this horrible dark room, I didn't feel the throbbing pain or fear coursing through me. Instead, a type of peace swelled inside me, leaving me wanting the boy to drink every drop of blood from my body. It was almost the same sensation I had felt when Sophia drunk from me.

I felt the boy being violently pulled away from my neck. I cursed in my mind as the feeling of pleasure was replaced with the agonizing pain again.

I rolled my eyes over to my right as I heard a loud thump explode beside me. I saw the boy being pinned to the wall by another figure dressed in a large brown cloak. I glanced to the front of the room. The other two Nightlings were standing there in the shadows. So this was a new guest, *oh great*, how many of them are there?

"Did anyone give you permission to have a drink?" A familiar voice said.

"I only wanted a taste," the boy being pinned to the wall hastily pleaded with a raspy voice.

With one swift, almost invisible move, the boy's head was snatched off.

The other two Nightlings disappeared from the room without closing the door behind them, allowing the artificial light to illuminate some of the room.

I heard the dead Nightling's body hit the ground. My sight was still a little blurry, but there was no way I wouldn't recognize the twisted smile in front of me. "Nigel?"

Nigel leaned in closer to me. The blood from the dead Nightling covered his hands. "Man, it was hard capturing you. I was starting to think you had the luck of the Irish."

"But why?" I forced out.

"Why do you think? To keep your father distracted." Nigel wiped his bloodied hands clean on my flesh. The touch of his cold hands stung my skin. "Your father, Axum and Jean-Paul are the three most powerful Nightlings alive. Going after them would be suicide. So we thought by taking out their kids, they would be weakened."

A new feeling of nausea entered me. "Where is Sébastien?"

Nigel laughed as he kissed me on my forehead. "Don't worry little cousin. He's in another chamber like this one. Something came up, so we've decided to keep you both alive for now." I saw Nigel's fangs before I felt them in my flesh. He began draining my blood quickly. I felt light headed, just before I passed out again. I can't say I wasn't happy for the escape from the pain, into the bliss of oblivion.

I don't know how long I hung in that room. I would wake up to hear people talking in the darkness. I felt so weak I couldn't open my eyes, but I could tell they were there. The voices seemed familiar. But I didn't have the strength to figure out whom the voices belong to.

As for what I dreamed, I didn't remember. Nothing made sense in my head. Everything became jumbled together. And then, all of a sudden I felt nothing. There was no pain, no confusion, and no fear. I felt nothing at all, except for a slight sensation of delight.

I died. I didn't know how I knew, but I knew. I was no longer apart of the living world. It wasn't how I thought it would be, my death that is. I thought it would be, I don't know, different somehow. I didn't see a white light, or hear angels singing. I didn't feel my soul floating away. I felt nothing but the slight sensation of peace.

I still existed. I was aware of myself. It had only been my

body that felt disconnected. My essences continued on as my consciousness gathered in oblivion.

And then it all came back. My eyes shot open as a scream escaped my throat. Pain greater than what I'd felt before I'd died tore through me. I could feel my throat bleeding from the inside. I could feel the blood running down it. And I loved the taste of my own blood.

I had Crossed Over. I was no longer a Dayling. I understood what Sébastien meant when he said the universe had opened up to him. Everything became different to me. The world I knew changed, and all I had once been became foreign. Nothing was left, except... except...

"The Thirst," I heard another familiar voice say. I wasn't shocked when I gazed up at the man standing in front of me. A part of me always felt he was involved. A part of me always knew he was the traitor. "You feel it don't you Haven?" Myron said as he leaned closer to me.

The darkness in the room no longer obscured my vision. I could see every crack in every wall in my prison. I focused my eyes on the twisted porcelain face in front of me. I wanted to spit in it. I wanted to see his expression as my saliva dripped down the smile that was across his twisted delight. Instead, I couldn't do anything except stare at him as I felt the pain inside of me increasing. "Why?"

Myron touched the top of my head. He gently ran his hand through my long mangled hair. I wanted so badly to bite him. "Because of what you feel inside of you. That is what we are, not how your father forces us to live. A little over twenty years ago while I was taking a stroll through New York City, I found myself in a type of trance. A pretty little Punk girl stumbled in front of me. Everything inside of me Haven screamed to take her. I couldn't fight the need for her blood, the need for her life. And then I had an epiphany of sorts. Why should I fight what I am? Why should any of us deny our true nature? We are killers. And humans are our prey. No matter how good or evil, they are our quarry and we are their nightmares."

I could feel my newly developed fangs pressing against my lips. I couldn't retract them. I couldn't do anything but try to push the pain inside of me out of my mind.

When a Dayling Crosses Over to being a Nightling, the newly transformed vampire must feed on blood immediately.

I didn't know how long I could go without having blood. The pain inside of me began to get worse. So I tried to fight back the pain by focusing on something else. "What about the Mântuitors?"

"Yes, going to them was very dangerous. I figured their desire to destroy us would outweigh their desire to destroy just one single Nightling. But I had to set a few things in motion before I involved them." Myron stood in front of me with his eyes glowing in the dark. "After the three most powerful families of our kind are destroyed, I will be the savior of our people. I will unite us under one family. With only one head... me."

I became glad I didn't need to breathe anymore, because I wouldn't have been able to. I couldn't imagine what I looked like. I only knew what I felt like. My ribs felt as if they were caving in on me, my stomach felt as if it had already sunk into my body, while my lips felt like dead skin fell from it. But I still couldn't help but laugh. "You think the Mântuitors are going to allow you to walk away from this? You are insane."

I felt a sudden rush of heat on my face before I even heard the sound of Myron slapping me. My throbbing head exploded. More blood rushed out of my already blood deprived body. I had second thoughts about taunting my captor. "You are but a child. You think like a child. And your father believed that one day I would serve you." Myron pulled my hair back, forcing my head to move upward. "I shall grieve with your father once your body is discovered. I will be by his side the entire time he is stricken with despair. Then, I shall reunite you both." He released my head before he turned around and disappeared out of the room.

I was alone again. I felt glad for it. I couldn't take much more of the pain from listening to him talking.

The door to the room opened again. I didn't understand why they couldn't just let me die in piece.

"Hello again, little cousin." Nigel said as he strolled over towards me. "You really should take better care of yourself, you look horrible."

I wanted to come back at him with something witty and rude, the pain inside of me felt too overwhelming for me to do anything but grunt.

I could feel myself drifting away again. I could feel the

abyss calling to me. I was ready to answer it, but Nigel had other plans. My head exploded again as I felt his hand connect with my face. "Wake up sleepy head. The best part is coming up. But first I want to let you in on a secret. That little dream you had of the newly Crossed Over Nightling. It almost messed everything up." He stood back from me. Even though I couldn't see him, I could feel that twisted smile across his face. "Myron was taking Dayling babies from small families no one cared about, and allowing them to grow up in human homes without knowing what they were. Once they Crossed Over, and killed and killed and killed, it was easier to convince them that they were monsters, easier to recruit them. And then you went and had a Dream Transfer with one of them. I still don't understand how that happened. Thankfully, you waited too late before you told your dad. He might have caught on if he'd known earlier."

Again, as I heard Nigel laughing, I wanted to spit in his face. And again, I wasn't able to. "I can't believe Myron would risk sacrificing Sophia to get to me."

"That's why I was there. The Mântuitors were supposed to get you outside of the party. I was supposed to keep the other Nightlings preoccupied. Myrene was still pissed at you, and was watching you when the Mântuitor chased you out. I had no choice but to follow and protect Sophia."

Haven? I heard a voice call out to me in my head. *Haven can you hear me*?

It took me a minute to recognize the voice. My head still throbbed from the pain, so hearing someone inside of it wasn't helping. But I was still happy once I realized who it was. *Sébastien*? I thought.

Yes, it's me. We can talk telepathically. How are you doing? Sébastien said in my head.

How do you think I'm doing? I need to feed. I thought back. *Wait. Nigel is in the room with me. Can he hear us*?

Damn right I can. I heard Nigel's voice boomed inside my mind. *Don't worry Sébastien; I'll be over there to see you soon.*

If you harm her, I'll kill you. Sébastien's voice said.

Nigel laughed out loud. He didn't speak in my head anymore, which was a relief to me. The two of them were killing me. "He's chained up in another room just like you. Starved just like you, and yet he is threatening me. I'm going to have to teach that boy some manners."

"If you touch him, *I'm* going to kill you." I forced out.

Nigel laughed again. "You two kids are something. And yet, you still chose a human over him. Doesn't make any sense." The door to the room opened again. I heard Nigel slowly laughing. "Showtime."

I could smell them as they entered. They smelled so... good. They smelled like freshly picked fruit. Humans! Two of them walked into the room with a Nightling.

The door closed just as the lights in the room were turned on. My eyes were clenched shut. I didn't want to feel the pain of opening them in the light. I'd been in darkness for at least a week; I didn't want to imagine what it would feel like to open them in a room now filled with light.

I heard one of the human's gasp. I could actually smell the fear coming from him. I could taste the strawberry blood running through both of their bodies. My mind couldn't stop imagining drinking from them. Draining them both dry. I didn't know what they looked like, but my mind made them resemble Brad Pitt and George Clooney. Delicious!

"What is this? What is going on?" I heard one of the human's say. The voice forced me to open my eyes.

It felt exactly how I thought it would feel, pain beyond belief. The thing was, I'd become used to feeling pain, so I could fight my way through it. I focused on the human that had spoken. I knew I had to be wrong about the voice, but as my eyes adjusted, I became able to see him clearly. "Philip?"

Philip's father and Myron stood beside him. My heart almost leapt out of my chest as it shattered inside me, at least until I saw the confusion on Philip's face. *He didn't know*, I thought. He didn't play me.

Philip turned to his father. "Dad, what is going on here?"

Mr. Flowers took a step toward me. His eyes borrowed inside of me. "Look at her Philip. Look at what she is. An abomination!"

"You... Mântuitor?" I forced out at Philip's father.

"As was my father, and his father, and his father's father... and so shall be my son." Mr. Flowers said as he continued to stare at me.

Philip grabbed his father by the shoulder and spun him around so they could be face to face. "Never! I love her dad.

I don't care what she is. And you will let her go."

Myron stepped towards Philip. "As you wish." He then threw the sword he held the entire time on the floor in front of Philip. "You should know that she is a newly changed strigoii. She must feed. It is her nature."

Myron and Nigel disappeared out of the room, leaving Philip, his father and me alone.

Mr. Flowers stared at Philip, as Philip stared at the sword. "I'm sorry son, but this is the only way. Decapitation will kill her." Mr. Flowers took out a dagger, cut Philip across the forearm and made his way out of the room in one swift motion. He moved almost as fast as we did.

The door to my cell closed, leaving nothing except the intoxicating smell of blood. My newly formed fangs ached as the aroma suffocated the room. The thirst pulsated in my head, drowning out every rational thought, becoming the only thing that existed to me.

I could hear him talking, pleading with me in his familiar tone. But all I could concentrate on was my hunger. My throat hurt, my insides burned, my skin felt tight and awkward. I needed to feed. I needed to consume every drop of the strawberry scented blood flooding my imprisonment.

And then, all of a sudden I found myself free from the chains.

TWENTY-SIX

At first, I wasn't able to stand. I fell to my knees, scraping them on the floor. I tried to lift myself up. Instead, I tumbled a little in front of me.

My fangs were biting deeper into my lips. Everything around me swirled. I couldn't think. I couldn't gain control of my limbs. I couldn't do anything except drown in the delight of the delicious smell coming from the front of the room.

A low voice called to me. I didn't care. The thirst needed to be quenched. I needed to sink my aching fangs into the delicate flesh. I needed to feel the life liquid flowing inside of me. I had to have the blood lingering in the air. I needed to devour the sweet strawberry.

I somehow willed myself to my feet. The voice called louder to me, screaming at me, begging for me to do something, but my body moved on autopilot, nothing mattered but feeding.

Two more steps were taken. Each time my legs moved, pain flowed though my body. I thought for a moment I would fall over, but the hunger inside of me wouldn't allow my body to stop moving towards the glorious smell.

The pain I felt inside felt like nothing I could explain. Imagine acid being pushed through your body from an IV, but not killing you. Imagine being buried alive by molted lava, but not dying. Imagine the worst pain you could think of, and then multiply it by a thousand. That's what I felt as I continued to move towards the voice in the front of the room.

Stop! I heard another voice say in my head. *You have to*

fight it, Haven. The voice continued to plea. I didn't care about the voice in my head; nothing mattered to me except the voice in the room, the voice with the wondrous smell coming from it.

A flash flooded my head. I became engulfed with a vision.

A spiky haired guy lay in the grass staring up at me. I lay on top of him laughing. He slowly brushed my hair out of my face. He gazed into my eyes as if he stared at something precious and beautiful. I enchanted him, and I enjoyed every second of it.

He rolled me over. We continued to laugh as he gently kissed me on my cheeks and my forehead, and then my mouth. The kiss was delicious. His mouth over mine, feeling the heat from him consuming me.

He pulled away and just stared at me. I pouted, wanting him to continue to kiss me, but he would only stare.

Night covered us. A gentle breeze moved through the air. We were in some type of forest, or a garden. I didn't know the day or even where we were, I only knew I was with the one person in the world I wanted to be with. And everything was perfect.

The vision ended. I had continued to move while I had visited this imaginary place in my head. The thirst continued to scream inside of me. Everything became more and more confusing.

But I could finally understand the voice in front of me. I could feel him, standing there, staring at me. A new smell lingered in the air. Not only could I smell the sweet strawberry blood filling my nose, but also I could smell tears. One of us cried: either me, or the voice.

"Please Haven, Please," the voice begged as I sniffed in front of him. I still couldn't open my eyes, but I didn't need them to feed.

Another flash crashed inside my head, but instead of a vision, for a split moment, I became able to think clearly, giving me the time I needed to realize who was in the room with me, and what I was about to do.

I fell backwards, away from Philip and his bleeding arm. "Get out!" I screamed through my dried mouth.

I could sense him take a step towards me. I placed my hands up to stop him. He froze in place. "They locked me in

Haven. They want me to kill you. But I can't."

"You do not have a choice, Philip." I fell to my knees. I wanted my father so badly. I didn't want to die like this. "The thirst is too strong. Pick up the sword while you still can."

He took another step towards me. I raised my hands to stop him again, but this time he continued. "You're stronger MJ. You're the strongest girl I've ever met. You can control this." I felt him touch my shoulder. I flinched back from his flesh. It made my body tingle in a way Philip wouldn't like. "Can you take a little? Like they do in movies. You know, drink a little without killing me?"

I wanted to laugh, but I was in too much pain to do so. "Not in the state I am in. If I taste your blood, I'll rip you apart to take every drop inside you."

I could sense Philip kneeling in front of me. "Okay, we don't want that. How long can you go without feeding?"

"I just Crossed Over, I have to feed immediately!"

"That means today is your birthday right? Guess you're legal now." He joked.

Despite the pain, I couldn't help but laugh. The thirst still blazed inside of me. The acid still consumed my body, but I felt a little control coming over me. I mean, the smart part of my brain said for me to rip Philip's throat open and bathe in his blood, but that part of my brain and I never seem to work together.

I slowly balled up on the ground. I tried to focus my thoughts outwards. Finally, I became able to push out, *I won't attack him you bastard. Now what are you going to do?*

Philip tapped me on my shoulder. "What are you doing? Are you okay?"

"No, I'm not okay. Are you paying attention to the situation?" I forced out. "I'm telepathically talking to the bastard that did this to me."

"You can do that? Cool." Philip sat on the floor next to me.

"I know you're trying to be supportive, but I can still smell your blood. Maybe it would be better if you sat somewhere else." Again I forced out.

He stood from the floor. I heard him move away from me. I then heard him lean against the wall. "Far enough?"

"Outside would be better, but I guess that'll have to do."

I don't know how long we stayed like that. I could hear Philip pacing a few times as I continued to ball up in pain on the floor. The crazy thing about it; all I could think about was how I should have allowed him to get his ass kicked in that alley. My life would have been so much easier. I would have killed him and been done with it.

All of a sudden the door to the room opened. I could tell from the way my body reacted that humans had entered the room, three to be exact. My fangs throbbed again.

I heard Philip move from the wall towards the humans. "You bastard! How could you do this?"

Philip stopped in front of the humans. I could smell the anger radiating from him. I could also sense the danger coming from the three humans. "It was a test, my son." I heard Mr. Flowers say.

"And I guess I failed." Philip shot back.

"No, you both passed. I'm going to have your girlfriend restrained. Do not be alarmed. She will be fine." Mr. Flowers said in an even tone.

My body got ready to lunge at them when I felt myself being rolled on my back, and my arms and legs being pinned to the floor.

I growled and hissed at the men pinning me, but I had become too weak to do anything else. I could hear Philip moving towards me just as the men finished pinning me. "What are you doing?" He yelled behind them.

I heard soft footsteps coming towards me. They stopped where I heard Philip stop. "Since the creation of the Mântuit-ors, there has been one rule. Destroy all the moroii and strigoii walking this world, for they are abominations to God, and we shall be his sword. But not all believe this."

Philip laughed. "If you're trying to say you're one of the ones that don't believe this, then you got a funny way of showing it."

"I believed all strigoii are evil, damnations unto God. It was another, a friend, who tried to convince me I was wrong. When I saw your moroii girlfriend in the kitchen. When I found out she was the legendary strigoii Lazzaro Vigano's daughter, I concocted all of this for two reasons." Mr. Flowers walked closer to me. I could feel him staring down at me. "First, was to prove that strigoii are incapable of love. Once she Crossed Over, she would lose all her humanity as a moroii and become the monster we were taught they all are." I could feel Mr. Flowers' eyes leaving me. He looked somewhere else. "My second reason was to initiate you into the Holy Sect of Mântuitors. I would show you what they are, and what we stand for. By killing this monster, you would be reborn into a warrior of God. It seems I am the one who has failed."

I didn't move as they talked. I couldn't believe what I'd heard, and I wanted to correct Mr. Flowers about the old terms, but I decided to try and focus on pushing the pain out of my body.

Then it happened. My senses went into overdrive as they entered the room. It was twelve of them, twelve blood flowing, sweet tasting, heart pumping humans inside the room with us. Six of them were struggling while the other six pushed them in.

"Come," I heard Mr. Flowers say.

"But what about her?" Philip answered.

"She will be fine as soon as you exit this room." Mr. Flowers said. I heard Philip move towards his father. Then I heard Mr. Flowers speaking in my direction. "They are all evil men, murders, and rapist, and child molesters. They feel no remorse for the acts they have committed."

The next thing I knew, I became released from the restraints. I heard the door to the room slam shut again. The lights were turned off, smothering the room with darkness.

I opened my eyes. My heightened vision was taking its time to return to me. But I didn't need to see to find them. I could smell them cowering in the corners. They were bound and gagged, huddled up to the wall like frightened children. I could take my time with them if I wanted, but I didn't want to torment them. I only wanted to feed.

I quickly snatched the first man from the wall. He'd been the largest, which was why I chose him first, with tattoos all over his body, and a baldhead. He struggled in my arms for a moment, and in my weakened state, it took some doing to finally sink my fangs inside of him.

Once I did, the world went away as I drank human blood for the first time in my life. My immortal body convulsed with pleasure. Nothing in the world mattered to me as I drunk, nothing except my victim's blood flowing into my mouth, nothing except quenching the thirst. I was in a type of utopia, until there was no more blood to drink, when my victim had no more pleasure to give me.

Once I finished with the first man, I made my way to the next, and then the next and so forth, until I stood alone in a room filled with six dead bodies.

I looked down at my hands, they were returning to normal, and not the withered up skeletons they were. Well, normal with a porcelain gleam to them. My body felt stronger than it had ever felt before. The pain had gone. Nothing was left except the pleasure, indescribable pleasure.

The door to the room opened again. "Is it safe to enter," I heard Philip say as he peeped around the corner.

I smiled at him. My fangs had retracted. "I'm good." My mind finally became completely clear, which meant, I finally became able to remember I stood in the room in only my underwear. "Wait, wait one second before you come in."

The door began to close. "Are you still hungry, or thirsty, or whatever you guys are?" Philip yelled.

"No, I just need some clothes." I said feeling bashful.

"I mean I've already seen you..." Philip began.

I cut him off. "Can you just find me something to wear?"

He became quiet for a moment, and then he threw one of those brown robes inside of the room. I picked up the robe and then placed it around me. "Okay, I'm ready now."

Philip entered the room first, followed by Sébastien and Mr. Flowers. It was obvious Sébastien had been given the same nourishment I'd been given. I guess it wasn't hard to find scum in the world to feed to Nightlings.

I walked past Philip and Sébastien, heading for Mr. Flowers. Behind him were three other Mântuitors. They all reached for their swords as I stalked towards Mr. Flowers.

I stood face to face with the man. If seeing my glowing green eyes glaring at him caused him any type of fear, I couldn't tell. The man stood in front of me emotionless. "Where is Myron?"

"I do not know. We have been waiting here for him to return. But it seems he knows that things have changed."

"Have they," I asked.

Mr. Flowers looked from me to Philip and then back to me. "Yes. Come, let's leave this room and prepare for our guests."

EPILOGUE

The next night, Mr. Flowers had clothes brought to me. He didn't want me to greet the guests in a robe. I was thankful, because I didn't want to greet them in a robe either.

We were sitting in a large room, with an oversized table in the middle of it. The walls were covered with ancient paintings of men dressed in armor. The floor was covered in a type of red carpet.

I sat beside Philip twitching in my seat. Philip had no idea of the 'extremely' big deal that was about to happen. Sébastien, on the other hand, twitched like me as he sat on the other side.

And then it happened, the thing no one could have ever convinced me would have happened. The doors to the room opened, one off to the right and the other to the left. A group of Nightlings, lead by my father, strolled in from the door to the right, while Mântuitors walked in from the door to the left. Neither group looked at each other as they made their way to the table and sat down.

The group of Mântuitors all seemed to be fairly young; except four of them had white hair.

As for the Nightlings, along with my father, Axum, Jean-Paul, and four other family heads sat in silence around the table.

I glanced around the room, seeing all the tension on each of their faces. Centuries old enemies sat in a room, about to actually talk with each other, instead of draw weapons out and go at it. Both sides looked as if they wanted to be somewhere else, doing anything else.

Finally Mr. Flowers stood from his chair. "My father brought me into this war, bestowing on me the family duty to protect the world from the vampire abominations. I was young, filled with faith, and scared that one day my own son might have to deal with creatures I didn't understand. But I found hope and clarity from a man that not only became one of my closest friends, but also my mentor. His name was William Crawford. He was the best of us all, and was to become the next Mântuitor Prime, until one day he changed his stance on vampires. After years of battling the higher-ups in the Holy Sect, the order came down to assonate William. It was five years ago, when the order came to me." Mr. Flowers paused to gather himself before he continued. "We sat in his office, talking about the politics of the world. I'd laced his drink, and offered it to him in a toast. He knew, somehow he knew I'd been sent to kill him. I could tell it from the look in his eyes, but he drunk the drink anyway. Before he took his last breath, he told me, the only regret he would take with him into paradise, is his blind devotion to a rule he no longer believed was divine. His only wish was that I not follow him into salvation with the same mistake in my heart. Because of this day, I do not believe I shall. I only wish my friend, my mentor, could be here tonight to see this"

Everyone in the room bowed their heads at everyone else.

My father stood from his seat. Mr. Flowers sat down as everyone turned to my father. "When I heard my own brother made peace with the Holy Sect of Mântuitors, only to ensure his own desire for power, I became sickened. But after I received Richard Flowers' invitation to meet in peace for all our kind, I became filled with hope. All Nightlings do not feel as we feel in this room. And all Mântuitors do not feel as you feel. So from this day forth, it shall be our charge to convince them that we, along with William Crawford, are the ones who are right, and they are the ones who are wrong. Nightlings and humans can exist together in peace." My father stared at Mr. Flowers. "As brothers."

Jean-Paul cut his eyes towards Philip and me. "Or in-laws."

Not funny, not funny at all. At least I didn't think so, but everyone else seemed to relax a little more as they laughed at the embarrassment on both Philip and my face.

They all stood from their chairs and cheered. Mr. Flowers bowed his head towards my father. And the world as I knew it got a whole lot stranger.

Philip, Sébastien and I snuck out of the meeting, as the others talked about peace treaties and rules and blah blah blah.

But before we could make it out of the room, my father pulled me over to the side to tell me how much he loved me and how worried he was about me. I decided not to tell him everything Mr. Flowers had done to me. I didn't want to throw a monkey wrench in the whole brotherly love thing, and telling my father how Mr. Flowers helped in torturing me, would definitely do that. Instead, I blamed everything on Myron and Nigel. My father swore to make them both pay, and since he was the great Lazzaro Rota-Vigano, I believed they would pay in the most painful way possible. Good for them!

For the first time in my life, I felt sorry for Sophia. Her father and her best friend were now declared her enemies. There were some in the family that didn't trust her, or Angela for that matter, but I would go to war for Angela, and maybe even Sophia. She did save my life.

After talking with my father, I made my way to the roof of the building with Sébastien and Philip. I found out we were being held in a warehouse a little outside of the city. They were going to destroy the place after we all left. Myron knew where it was, so no one would be safe here anymore.

The night air felt as hot as always. The dryness of the heat almost suffocated me as we walked to the edge of the building and looked down. We were pretty high up, but I didn't feel fear anymore. I was no longer a Dayling. I'd become one of the creatures of the night.

I still had to get used to the slight porcelain tint to my skin. I also had to get used to how the world looked through my new eyes. Even though darkness covered the night, I could see perfectly well for about a mile in each direction. I felt connected to the atmosphere around me. My body felt strong. My muscles felt tight. I felt as if I could leap through the air and not touch the ground for several minutes.

And, the not being able to move during the day thing was a little strange also. I couldn't sleep earlier that day as we waited for night to come. I lay in bed and tried to talk to

Philip, who kept making jokes about all the things he could do to my body since I couldn't move. It had been difficult to talk, so I had to lie there and listen to him without being able to crack one sarcastic joke back. It almost killed me.

I took in a deep breath, even though I didn't need to breathe anymore. I looked over to Sébastien as he stared at the stars above us. *Here is the thing*, I thought to Sébastien. *When I was lost in the thirst, I was given this vision of Philip and me in a forest of some kind. It helped me fight through the haze.*

Yeah, Sébastien thought back to me.

Was that you? I thought.

He turned from the stars. He smiled at me before returning his gaze to the night above us. *You're welcomed, although it pained me to create a vision of you and the human kissing in a forest. You owe me Lis.*

He was right, I owed him more than I could ever repay. If it wasn't for Sébastien, I didn't want to think about what would have happened in that dungeon. From this moment forth, no matter what happens between us, he would always be my friend. *You do know I love you right? Maybe not the way you want, but you will always have a place in my heart.*

A slight laugh traveled inside my head. *Being starved and tortured has left the sarcastic Haven Vigano a bit sentimental. No worries, I have my eye on Rachel now. She doesn't seem to attract trouble like you.*

I shot him a quick smirk.

"Are you two mind talking? Cause' that's not fair." Philip said as he looked from Sébastien to me.

I slowly made my way over to him. I could actually feel the air parting as I walked on the rooftop. I knew I could be standing beside him in a blink of an eye, but I had to learn how to move like a human in front of humans. "Sorry, but you're going to have to get used to it." I stood in front of my spiky haired prince. Nothing in my life would ever be the same. The thing is, I felt happy for it. "Something else you're going to have to get used to."

Sébastien laughed, "have a nice trip." He then turned and walked back into the building.

Philip gave me a confused look. Before he could speak, I had him in my arms and was flying high above the building. His body felt so light in my arms. It also felt so soft and fragile.

Philip wrapped his arms around me for dear life. "What the hell? You can fly?"

"Yep," I gave him a devilish smile. "Have you ever been to Norway?"

ABOUT THE AUTHOR

Gabriel Madison started writing when he was in high school. He attended a private art University in Atlanta Georgia for Media Production where he wrote a few screenplays and made a few short movies, including a twelve-minute vampire movie he adapted from a short story called Midnight Diner. Later, he returned to writing novellas and novel length projects. His first novel, Three Seeds, was released in August. Also, he has a novella called The Green-Eyed Devil coming out as an ebook.

Gabriel was once asked to describe myself; the only answer he could come up with was: storyteller.